Co

In Smoke and Soot I Will Worsl
of Fritz Leiber

The Ghosts of Sauk County   23

Carl Jacobi: Portrait in Moonlight   35

A World of Great Majesty: The Pattern in
Arthur Machen's Carpet   49

A Collision of World-Views: A Look at August Derleth's
The Dweller in Darkness   57

A Torrent of Eldritch Terrors: Fritz Leiber's
'The Death of Princes'   65

A Look at *The Edge of Running Water* by William Sloane   77

A Universe Shot Through with Invisible Forces:
Our Lady of Darkness as a Lovecraftian Novel   83

After the Great Destruction: Günter Eich's
Radio Play *Träume* (*Dreams*)   95

Against the Spirit: A look at Hugh Walpole's
The Killer and the Slain   125

A Work of Love and a Lasting Creation: An Estimation
of Harry Otto Fischer   139

Francis Brett Young and *Cold Harbour*   151

Interpenetrations: Ecstasy and Boundaries in the Works
of Arthur Machen   159

Old England, New England: M.R. James, Mary Wilkins
Freeman, and Sarah Orne Jewett   173

In Lonely Places: The Essential Horror Fiction of
Karl Edward Wagner   187

Somebody Pointed Earth: August Derleth's Science Fiction   203

Story-Telling Wonder-Questing, Mortal Me: The
Transformation of 'The Pale Brown Thing' into   213
Our Lady of Darkness

The Edge of Shadows: A Look at the Shades Series
by Robert Hood   225

The Ninefold Kingdom and Others: Four Fictional Visions
of the Political Future   241

Two Deaths   255

Yours Truly, Daniel Morley: An Examination of Robert
Bloch's Novel *The Scarf*   261

The Secret and the Secrets: A Look at Machen's
Hieroglyphics   281

Touchstones

By the Same Author

Rite of Trebizond and Other Tales
(with Mark Valentine)

The Collected Connoisseur
(with Mark Valentine)

The Silver Voices

The Defeat of Grief

Secret Europe
(with Mark Valentine)

Numbered as Sand or the Stars

Written by Daylight

Cities and Thrones and Powers

The Emperor's Pavement: Pages from a Berlin Daybook

Touchstones

Essays on the Fantastic

John Howard

The Alchemy Press

The Alchemy Press
Cheadle
Staffordshire UK

www.alchemypress.co.uk

Sources and Acknowledgements

Thanks to editors Peter Coleborn, David Longhorn, Rosemary Pardoe, Robert M. Price, James Roberts, Barbara and Christopher Roden, Ray Russell, Benjamin Szumskyj, and Mark Valentine for originally publishing these essays (or other versions of them). Most of these essays have been revised to a lesser or greater extent for this book.

'A Collision of World-Views: A Look at August Derleth's "The Dweller in Darkness"' in *Crypt of Cthulhu* 100, 1998

'A Look at *The Edge of Running Water* by William Sloane' in *All Hallows* 29, 2002

'A Torrent of Eldritch Terrors: Fritz Leiber's "The Death of Princes"' in *Fantasy Commentator* 57-58, 2004

'A Universe Shot Through with Invisible Forces: *Our Lady of Darkness* as a Lovecraftian Novel' in *Ghosts & Scholars* 20, 1995; in *Fantasy Commentator* 57-58, 2004

'A Work of Love and a Lasting Creation: An Estimation of Harry Otto Fischer' in *Studies in Fantasy Literature* 2, 2004

'A World of Great Majesty: The Pattern in Arthur Machen's Carpet' in *Avallaunius* 17, 1997

'After the Great Destruction: Günter Eich's radio play *Träume* (*Dreams*)' (based on 'Sand in the Machine: Günter Eich's radio play *Träume* (*Dreams*)' in *Wormwood* 10, 2008 and 'The Lost Dream: The changes Günter Eich made to his radio play *Träume* (*Dreams*)' in *Wormwood* 12, 2009)

'Against the Spirit: Hugh Walpole's *The Killer and the Slain*' in *Wormwood* 3, 2004

'Carl Jacobi: Portrait in Moonlight' in *Wormwood* 16, 2011 (based on 'Disclosures in Black' in *Supernatural Tales* 4, 2002)

'Francis Brett Young and *Cold Harbour*' as the Introduction to *Cold Harbour* by Francis Brett Young, Ash-Tree Press 2007 (based on 'Francis Brett Young's *Cold Harbour*' in *All Hallows* 36, 2004 and 'The Vision of Francis Brett Young' in *The Lost Club Journal* 2, 2001)

'In Lonely Places: The Essential Horror Fiction of Karl Edward Wagner' in *Dark Horizons* 50, 2007 (published as 'Being Utterly Lost: The Essential Horror Fiction of Karl Edward Wagner' in *Black Prometheus: a Critical Study of Karl Edward Wagner* edited by Benjamin Szumskyj, 2007)

'In Smoke and Soot I Will Worship: The Ghost Stories of Fritz Leiber' as 'The Ghost Stories of Fritz Leiber' in *All Hallows* 4, 1993; in *Fantasy Commentator* 57-58, 2004

'Interpenetrations: Ecstasy and Boundaries in the Works of Arthur Machen' in *Faunus* 26, 2012 (based on 'Interpenetrations: Boundary Imagery in the Works of Arthur Machen' in *Machenalia* Volume 2 edited by R.B. Russell, 1991

'Old England, New England: M.R. James, Mary Wilkins Freeman, and Sarah Orne Jewett' in *Wormwood* 6, 2006 (based on 'M.R. James' New England Reading' in *Ghosts & Scholars* 21, 1995 and 'Lavender and Lilac: Ghosts, Visits, and Old Ladies' in *Dark Horizons* 38, 1999)

'Somebody Pointed Earth: August Derleth's Science Fiction' in *Return to Derleth* Volume 2, edited by James P. Roberts, 1995

'Story-telling wonder-questing, mortal me: The transformation of "The Pale Brown Thing" into *Our Lady of Darkness*' in *Fritz Leiber: Critical Essays* edited by Benjamin Szumskyj, 2007 (based on 'The Addition of Secondary Narratives' in *Fantasy Commentator* 57-58, 2004)

'The Edge of Shadows: A Look at the Shades Series by Robert Hood' in *Studies in Australian Weird Fiction* 2, 2008

'The Ghosts of Sauk County' in *All Hallows* 18, 1998

'The Ninefold Kingdom and Others: Four Fictional Visions of the Political Future' in *Wormwood* 1, 2003

'The Secret and the Secrets: A Look at Machen's *Hieroglyphics*' in *Faunus* 5, 2000

'Two Deaths' in *All Hallows* 12, 1996

'Yours Truly, Daniel Morley: An Examination of Robert Bloch's *The Scarf*' in *The Man Who Collected Psychos: Critical Essays on Robert Bloch* edited by Benjamin Szumskyj, 2009

Dedication

A. Langley Searles (1920-2009)
Scholar of the fantastic, friend across the ocean

In Smoke and Soot I Will Worship: The Ghost Stories of Fritz Leiber

Fritz Leiber (1910-92) was one of the most versatile and highly-regarded writers in the fields of science fiction, fantasy, and horror. He always deserved his high reputation. For example, between 1958 and 1988 he won nearly thirty major awards, including eight Science Fiction Achievement Awards (the Hugos). Several stories that will be discussed below were award winners. Leiber's novel *Our Lady of Darkness* won the World Fantasy Award in 1978; 'The Button Molder' received a British Fantasy Society award for Best Short Story in 1980; and the collection of which 'The Ghost Light' was the title story won a 1985 Locus Award.

Much of Leiber's work achieves classic status due to his unique and personal way of approaching the subject matter of his fiction. Yet by his use of satire, and subtle use of the categories of Jungian-depth psychology, his work resonates with a universal subconscious which makes it possible to feel involved in his fiction, to take the same risks, and to share the moments of white-hot terror that appear throughout his horror fiction.[1]

Leiber is not easily classifiable as a writer. His fiction ranges freely through the genres, and often mixes them. His writings in the field of horror are as likely to contain elements of science fiction, as well as any of the usual trappings of horror fiction.

When it comes to the sub-genre of the ghost story, few, if any, of the traditional ghost story ideas and themes are present in Leiber's output. It could be argued that an article on the 'ghost stories' of Fritz Leiber is a contradiction, unless the definition of what could constitute the ghost is accepted on its own terms, as set out in the fiction in which it makes its appearance.

Assuming this, I intend to survey the few stories that  Leiber wrote during his fifty years as a published writer that I think could be said, however loosely, to fall into the sub-genre of 'ghost story'. Doubtless my selection will be open to debate and comment and it's not exhaustive.[2] As with the best traditional ghost stories, it certainly is a case of the quality of work, not the quantity!

In Fritz Leiber's ghost stories, the actual 'ghost' is usually simply some sort of apparition or entity that rationally should not exist. This is the definition that I shall adopt here. The apparitions and entities do not seem to be ghosts in the traditional sense of a visible disembodied presence that nevertheless has some physical characteristics, and interacts with ordinary human characters. But then, Leiber's work is only traditional in that he often used artistic tradition (for example, the works of Shakespeare) as a starting-point for his own explorations into his own vision of the world – a Leiberian world where warm personal intimate things can encounter the Other, and be changed irreparably in a fraction of a second.

Leiber's most famous ghost story was first published in 1941. 'Smoke Ghost' stands near the beginning of his publishing career, and in it Leiber sets out his agenda of what a modern ghost would be like. The narrator, Mr Wran, muses on what a contemporary ghost might be like:

> I don't mean that [traditional] kind of ghost. I mean a ghost from the world of today, with the soot of the factories on its face and the pounding of machinery in its soul... A real ghost. Not something out of books.[3]

The basic and most important point in this story, and his others, is that modern conditions call for modern ghosts. But modern ghosts still have their traditional requirements, as Mr Wran finds out:

> The thing came slowly towards him... 'The world is yours to do with as you will, save or tear to pieces... I recognise that. I will praise, I will sacrifice. In smoke and soot I will worship you for ever.'[4]

In 'The Hound' (1942) Leiber makes much the same point using the idea of a sort of ghostly wolf, and the man who finds himself pursued and haunted by it.

> Was there any escape from the thing? Answer: No. And yet – there was one bare possibility. Escape from the city. The city had bred the thing; might it not be chained to the city?

Using the title of a story by H.P. Lovecraft that also concerned a haunting by a dog-entity must have been a deliberate tribute by Leiber to his first mentor.[5]

With 'I'm Looking for Jeff' (1952), Leiber combines a *film noir* atmosphere and setting with a revenant that could be a ghost or some sort of zombie. Very much the 'B movie' shocker in the context of Leiber's supernatural horror output, 'I'm Looking for Jeff' is deftly-handled cliché, avoiding his usual subtlety. To further compound the genre-mixing, the story was criticised on publication by James Blish (wearing his William Atheling Jr hat) for being little more than a 'phony realism' crime story.[6]

'A Deskful of Girls' (1958) involves ghostly entities – barely corporeal ectoplasmic skins that have become separated from the people who generated them. The 'ghosts' represent separate emotional aspects of the personalities of the original owners. Here the ghosts are not connected with the dead, but are estranged aspects of the living. And they can be as destructive as the living, if they do not get their way.

A completely alien and non-human apparition or entity is possibly encountered by the characters in 'A Bit of the Dark World' (1962). In what is perhaps Leiber's single most mysterious and frightening story, there is an encounter with

> ...half-dozen or so thin close-placed stalks of what I can only describe as a more gleaming blackness... I followed them up with my eyes as they mounted against the starfields, almost invisible, like black wires, to where they ended – high up – in a bulb of darkness... The black bulb swayed and there was a corresponding rapid joggling in the crowded black stalks – though if they were free to move at the base I ought to call them legs.[7]

Something utterly Other is at work, something that perhaps has connections with the depths of the subconscious, rather than from space or from the dead. The Other, here, is a new sort of supernatural that manifests itself in another, blacker, sort of darkness.

'The Thirteenth Step' (1962) is a short but very powerful story with a hammer-blow ending. It is made all the more effective by what was probably personal experience on Leiber's part. Throughout his career he battled with alcoholism, and 'The Thirteenth Step' takes its title from Alcoholics Anonymous' Twelve Steps. The fact that the actual setting of the story is an AA meeting adds to its ambiguity, and the ambiguous reality (or not) of the terrible entity who could symbolise or personify that Thirteenth Step.

A similar ambiguity characterises the entity that Daloway calls the Black Gondolier in the story of that title, first published in 1964. One of Leiber's best forays into 'urban' horror with thoroughly modern themes, concerns, and setting, 'The Black Gondolier' builds up slowly and relentlessly to a death in a decaying and creepy Venice – Venice, California – and the realisation on the part of the narrator that, ghost or otherwise, Death in a very different guise to the usual one has paid a visit.

> Ghostliness is a matter of atmosphere, not age. I have seen an unsuccessful division in Hollywood that was to me more ghostly than the hoariest building I ever viewed in New England... Good Lord, if there could be such things as ghosts, it would be easy to imagine them in Venice...[8]

In his essay 'Travails of *The Fantasy Novel*: a Project Unborn' Leiber described 'When the Change-Winds Blow' (also 1964) as 'a melancholy short story'.[9] Reading it is a strangely beautiful and warming experience, despite the brooding atmosphere of loss and bewilderment, of barely survivable loneliness and pain.

Can it be, I thought, that not only do the past and future exist forever, but also all the possibilities that were never and will never be realised...[10]

The narrator, while travelling across the Martian desert, sees things in a sandstorm caused by non-existent winds. In a series of possible flashbacks, visions, or waking dreams, he sees or visits places on Earth that had been important to him in his now lost past, and remembers again how his girlfriend met her death.

Leiber also discusses in the same essay another story first published in 1964. Linking 'Midnight in the Mirror World' with 'When the Change-Winds Blow' he describes both as being about lost loves. 'Midnight in the Mirror World' contains what might be Leiber's most traditional ghost. The narrator, the Leiber-like Giles Nefandor, begins to see an apparition in the infinite series of reflections caused by two mirrors facing each other in his house. The woman in black that he sees in the mirror seems to be advancing towards him at the rate of one reflected image each day – and she looks as if she has malevolent intentions. Once Nefandor works out who she must be, he realises that he is actually longing for their meeting, and her deadly embrace. Supernatural terror is accepted and tamed. To Nefandor death becomes preferable to his dull daily life alone.

Leiber uses his background as the son of Shakespearian-actor parents, and his own experiences in the theatre, in 'Four Ghosts in Hamlet' (1965). This is an obvious choice for a ghost story, as Shakespeare's incomparable play contains a part for the ghost of Hamlet's murdered father, who though dead, intervenes in the play and influences the actions of the leading character, Hamlet himself. The same is the case in

Leiber's story. The actors of a touring Shakespearian-theatre company have problems that need to be resolved, and are, after a performance of Hamlet in which no-one can be certain of who played the ghost.

Although several of the stories already mentioned contain apparitions that could be Death himself (or itself), in two other stories, 'Richmond, Late September, 1849' (1969) and 'Horrible Imaginings' (1982), Death makes unambiguous appearances, and is personified as female.

The former story is one of a select sub-genre in which Edgar Allan Poe is the protagonist. He meets a woman in black, who claims to know his writings about the dead women in his life. Finally the now drunken Poe tries to get the woman to agree to an appointment in New York. She refuses, but replies that she will indeed meet him again – except in Baltimore.[11]

'Horrible Imaginings' concerns a lonely widower who begins to see the 'Vanishing Lady' in the corridors of his apartment block. He begins to focus all his now unfulfilled sexual longings onto her, although she still remains elusive. At last they meet and embrace in the lift; and Death claims her latest recruit who desires release from an empty and mundane life.

The female principle as an apparition comes to the fore in another story with a terrifying climax, 'The Button Molder' (1979). Again, whether or not the entity can really be called a ghost is open to question. Told simply by another Leiberian narrator, he uses H.P. Lovecraft's device of stating at the outset of the story what will happen (and has in effect already happened) at its climax. Like Lovecraft, Leiber then proceeds to build up slowly to the shattering finale of the encounter by the means of accumulated personal details and inner thoughts. Leiber's character (never named) comes to consider that the apparition could be 'perhaps an archetype of the unconscious mind somehow made real? The Anima or the Kore or the Hag who lays men out (if those be distinct archetypes)? Possibly, I guess.'[12]

With a similar setting and eventual ending to 'A Bit of the Dark World', 'The Ghost Light' (1984) concerns a small boy's unusual nightlight and the fact that it could be attracting trouble rather than keeping it at bay. Unresolved incidents from the past, and the subconscious, seem to cause consequences in the present, and are manifested when an oil painting is enabled to play a role very different from that for which it was created.

Leiber's novel *Our Lady of Darkness* (1977) harks back to 'Smoke Ghost' in its adaptation of traditional ideas of apparition and entities, but for modern settings and situations. Franz Westen, another Leiber-like narrator, stumbles across the possibility, first raised during the early part of the century, that large modern cities might create and conceal their own kind of ghosts: 'paramental entities' as the novel calls them. In a story that uses and transforms the experience of modern city living in the way that Arthur Machen and H.P. Lovecraft had already done, Leiber has his alter ego slowly encounter a web of old intrigue and barely survivable horror. By the time that Westen discovers his modern place in the old drama, it seems that the Jungian feminine principle is at work again, given power – and animated to destroy him.

Leiber created *Our Lady of Darkness* through the addition of secondary narratives expanding the original magazine novella 'The Pale Brown Thing' (1977) to novel length. These are not mere padding, but do add to the feelings of unease and terror that grow inexorably throughout the book, and allow

Leiber to explore in greater detail his uses of the female 'Anima' principle as symbols, both good and evil, of uncertainty and otherness in life. The feminine and Other can be terrifying. They can also be magical, bewitching, and a giver of strength to endure, and win out with human values against the powers of darkness and chaos.

As discussed at the beginning of this essay, and despite its subtitle, Leiber probably wrote no 'ghost stories' in the traditional meaning of that sub-genre. He did write a baker's dozen or so stories and one novel that use entities and apparitions – however generated – to explore and to come to terms with his own concerns and experiences.

And what is more, unlike so many 'ghost stories' Leiber's are truly frightening, as the reader confronts the truly unknown – not just the dead, but the living: multiple aspects of the self and other people.

Bibliography

First appearance and first publication in a Fritz Leiber collection:

'A Bit of the Dark World' *Fantastic Stories* February 1962; *Night Monsters*, 1975

'The Black Gondolier' *Over the Edge*, ed. August Derleth, 1964; *Night Monsters*, 1969

'The Button Molder' *Whispers* October 1979; *The Leiber Chronicles*, 1990

'A Deskful of Girls' *The Magazine of Fantasy and Science Fiction* April 1958; *Shadows With Eyes*, 1962

'Four Ghosts in Hamlet' *The Magazine of Fantasy and Science Fiction* January 1965; *You're All Alone*, 1972

'The Ghost Light' *The Ghost Light*, 1984

'Horrible Imaginings' *Death*, ed. Stuart David Schiff, 1982; *The Leiber Chronicles*

'The Hound' *Weird Tales*, November 1942; *Night's Black Agents*,

1947
'I'm Looking for Jeff' *Fantastic* Fall 1952; *Night Monsters* 1969)
'Midnight in the Mirror World' *Fantastic Stories* October 1964;
    Night Monsters
Our Lady of Darkness 1978
'The Pale Brown Thing' *The Magazine of Fantasy and Science
    Fiction* January and February 1977
'Richmond, Late September, 1849' *Fantastic Stories* February 1969;
    Heroes and Horrors, 1982
'The Thirteenth Step' *The Fiend in You*, ed. Charles Beaumont,
    1962; *The Black Gondolier and Other Stories*, 2000
'When the Change-Winds Blow' *The Magazine of Fantasy and
    Science Fiction* August 1964; The *Worlds of Fritz Leiber*,
    1976

Notes

1.   I am indebted to the insights given by Bruce Byfield in his
     Witches of the Mind: a critical study of Fritz Leiber,
     Necronomicon Press 1991
2.   The original inspiration to write about Leiber's ghost stories
     came from a correspondence in *The Ghost Story Society
     Newsletter*, March 1991 (p.18). Leiber's bibliographer Phil
     Stephensen-Payne and I contributed lists of what we
     considered to be Leiber's 'urban' ghost stories.
3.   *Night's Black Agents*, Sphere ed., p.11
4.   *Night's Black Agents*, Sphere ed., pp 25-26
5.   *Night's Black Agents*, Sphere ed., p.97. Byfield, op.cit., pp.11-
     13, goes into more detail about Leiber's early 'Lovecraftian'
     fiction
6.   William Atheling Jr (James Blish) *The Issue at Hand*
     (Advent: Publishers 1973), p.22
7.   *Night Monsters*, Panther ed., p.178
8.   *Over the Edge*, Arrow ed., pp.164, 166
9.   *Foundation: the Review of Science Fiction*, No 17, September
     1979, pp.12-26

10.   *The Worlds of Fritz Leiber*, p.119
11.   Poe died in Baltimore. Other classics in this select sub-genre include 'The Man Who Collected Poe' by Robert Bloch, 'Castaway' by Edmond Hamilton, and 'When It Was Moonlight' by Manly Wade Wellman. These stories as well as much other material were collected by Sam Moskowitz in his anthology *The Man Who Called Himself Poe* (1969). Presumably Leiber's story just missed the boat!
12.   *The Leiber Chronicles*, pp.534-535; see also Byfield, pp.66ff

The Ghosts of Sauk County

During the late 1920s and early 1930s, August Derleth (1909-71) was making a name for himself as a writer of competent and enjoyable horror fiction for such magazines as *Weird Tales*.[1] However, by about 1930 he was also setting out on his lifelong career as a writer of 'serious' fiction, most of which came to form his Sac Prairie Saga – a loose series of some fifty books of fiction, poetry, journals, and autobiography set in his native Sauk City and Prairie du Sac region of Wisconsin.

Inevitably, Derleth's parallel careers occasionally came together. His early mentor, H.P. Lovecraft, characteristically recognised this when he wrote:

> As for Derleth – I don't wonder you find his *W.T.* stuff mediocre! He holds all records for leading a literary double life... He despises his pot-boilers utterly & eloquently – but continues to write them because they bring in highly welcome cheques. His real work is of a minor-keyed, delicate quality – brooding memories & impressions woven together as they impinge on a single life-stream, & brief tragic vignettes of hidden lives & strange, lonely people. Some day he will probably go farther in literature than anyone else in the whole *W.T.* crowd.[2]

Derleth always had an eye for the strange and offbeat in the lives of those around him, and his journals, poems, and autobiographical books contain many recollections of 'odd' people and incidents.[3]

Several of Derieth's early historical novels contain

atmospheric portraits of obsessed and disturbed people, encountering madness and dislocation in themselves and others. The late novel *The Shadow in the Glass* (1963) is based on the life of Nelson Dewey, the first Governor of Wisconsin after Statehood was attained in 1848. As an old man, forgotten and near the end of his life, he gets up during the night in order to prepare to travel to a welcome for President Cleveland. As he looks in his mirror, he sees, not his old face, but the face of the vigorous and idealistic young man that he once was:

> It was not really an old man he saw there. His beard, his wrinkles, his bushy brows, his greying hair – all were invisible, only the eyes came through – and his brow, and the shadow in the glass that was the face of a young man... And once again, in the glass, he saw with his mind's eye the face of the young man he had been, and all his being cried out voicelessly – What happened? What happened to us?
>
> He could not bear to look.[4]

The 'ghostly' face in the glass frames Dewey's career, which ends with him being a revenant in what was his own world. That fine artist of the macabre, Frank Utpatel, provided a sensitive cover drawing for *The Shadow in the Glass.*

Derleth's first 'serious' book was a collection of four novellas, *Place of Hawks,* published in 1935. Derleth himself – presumably – later described these stories as 'dark, brooding tales of old families in the Sac Prairie country just after the turn of the century, stories of tragedy and madness, of people caught and helpless in the web of environment and heredity...'[5] The stories are not weird or macabre, in the sense of involving the fantastic or the supernatural, as Derleth's *Weird Tales* work usually did. But they have much in common, even though the quality of the writing was usually higher: evidence of the seriousness with which Derleth took this aspect of his work, and his growing vision of the Sac Prairie Saga.[6]

Throughout his career, Derleth kept returning to the  Wisconsin countryside, and he developed a third type of story – similar in feel to those in *Place of Hawks,* but with a definite horror, or possibly supernatural, content. Such stories are Derleth's dark jewels: brooding and grim, yet with all the exhilaration and joy that idyllic and well-loved settings produce. But, of course, the rural idyll, whether of the Wisconsin landscape itself or of living in it, is far from being the whole story. Sauk County has its rural and small-town life. It also, possibly, has its ghosts.

***

Two stories of this type which I want to examine date from the 1940s, and appeared in Derleth's collection *Sac Prairie People,* published in 1948.[7]

'Where the Worm Dieth Not' shares several characteristics with the *Place of Hawks* stories, and later tales which are similar to them. It is a story told across the years, as the recollections of Jasper Grendon, the Sac Prairie doctor, to his grandson Steve (a recurring character throughout Derleth's work, and very much an alter ego).

Dr Grendon stands apart from the story's events, but he is able to play a decisive part in its resolution. He interprets and comments on the motives and actions of the participants as the passage of the years seems irrelevant as Dr Grendon recalls events, and brings them to Steve (and so to the reader), with freshness and immediacy.

'Where the Worm Dieth Not' opens with Dr Grendon seeing Burdace Nohr and his wife pass the window:

> Little by little, then, the story would come out, the story of Burdace Nohr and Laura – and Anson Nohr: the story Dr Jasper Grendon had pieced out, the story partly told by Burdace himself, and hearing it, you would go back in memory, back over those years past, back twenty years to a February night ... a night of wind and wet snow falling, and the smell of thaw already in the air...[8]

Burdace comes to stay at his uncle Anson's farm, after Anson's wife Emma had died. Burdace finds that his cousin Laura is living there as well – a girl with nowhere else to go, who helped to care for Emma, and now is entirely dependent on Anson. Anson Nohr has plans for her: it soon becomes clear that he wants her married to his repulsive neighbour Kester Bliss, so that their farms can eventually be merged. But nothing is as it seems. Emma Nohr seems to have died under somewhat suspicious circumstances, and Anson seems 'haunted' by whatever it is that lies in their past. He talks out loud to her in the dead of night:

> What was it held his uncle there on the stairs? 'Emma,' the older man said in a low voice, 'Emma, God damn you, answer me!' Burdace watched, at once drawn and repelled by this scene below him: the older man taut on the stairs, all his being emanating a fear so strong that Burdace felt it almost tangibly.[9]

The next morning Burdace is out working on the farm,

when he meets Dr Grendon on his rounds. Grendon makes it clear that Anson Nohr is not at all well-regarded in Sac Prairie. The fact that Nohr's wife died suddenly after much stomach trouble was enough to set people talking; also still having Laura living alone at the farm with him has done nothing to improve his reputation. Burdace says he feels that 'there's something going on' at the farm. Dr Grendon sums up his feelings on the situation: 'There's a biblical passage I'm reminded of – "Where their worm dieth not, and their fire is not quenched." Something burns in Anson Nohr.'[10]

The next day, Burdace meets Kester Bliss, when he comes to the farm to court Laura. While Bliss seems to think that his possession of Laura is a foregone conclusion, Laura's body-language makes it clear that she really wants nothing to do with him or the plans Anson has for them both – and himself.

Inevitably, slowly, against the setting of the winter landscape, Burdace falls in love with Laura, and finds his love returned. They begin to contemplate escaping from the farm, and from Anson's plans. Meanwhile, at night, consumed by his own hell, Anson still speaks to his dead wife; and on one occasion, Burdace sees him trying to open Laura's bedroom door:

'Laura, last night,' he began immediately, 'I saw Anson at your door, I could tell...'

But she shook her head, a frown on her forehead, her mouth turned down in an expression of distaste. There was something fragile about her standing there, some helplessness inherent in her.

'That,' she said. 'I know that. It wouldn't be the first time. I keep my door locked and a chair against it. I always have.'

'But some day he'll go in!' he protested. 'Laura, come away with me, come away now – before something happens.'

She looked past him thoughtfully. 'He'll never come in,' she said. He's been there so often before. Something always keeps him from coming in. It's his conscience.'[11]

In the midst of Anson's nocturnal rages and despair, and among hints of dark designs against Kester Bliss and Laura, as winter gives way to spring, Burdace encounters Dr Grendon on his rounds again. They fall into conversation, and Dr Grendon reveals that he has heard rumours that Burdace is becoming sullen and melancholy. Burdace protests that he has never felt healthier, and the two men come to the conclusion that Anson is spreading rumours about Burdace's state of mind. But the doctor is not deceived:

'Look here, Burdace, keep an eye on your uncle. Just watch him. Don't let him get anything on you.'
  'I don't follow you, Doctor.'
  'A man who stands on the stairs at night to listen to a voice he ought to know comes from a conscience he's half throttled can be expected to listen to other voices.'[12]

As the heady May air blows all around him, Burdace thinks about what Dr Grendon has said to him:

He remembered again Dr Grendon's quotation from the Bible: *Where their worm dieth not, and their fire is not quenched*, and he thought that fire burned unquenchably in all of them in the house. He was aware again of a faint fluttering of fear, a hint of impending disaster.[13]

Matters slowly build up towards their climax. Anson discovers that Burdace and Laura intend to thwart all his plans. Things come to a head when Anson suddenly sends Burdace to the hayloft, to shift some hay. This is unnecessary work, and so Burdace is suspicious. His caution pays off, and he avoids walking straight into a trap set by Anson to fake Burdace's suicide. He is able to escape, and looks back to see how his uncle is reacting:

> But Anson was not following. He had got around the opening in the floor and now stood there motionless, staring into the darkness beyond Burdace, his eyes wide, his mouth open, his face a grotesque caricature of horrible fear. For an eternal moment, it seemed, he stood so, without motion, without sound. Then his voice came hoarsely.
> 'Emma! *Emma!*'
> At the same instant he threw up his arms as if to ward off a blow, quailed and fell backward, crashing through the loft floor to the stanchions below, where he gave back only a long sobbing groan and was still.[14]

Burdace and Laura make good their escape.

The entire story is recalled years later by Dr Grendon, who fulfils his calling: not, this time, by dispensing medical aid, but by defining the possibilities of what is happening in the story, and the lives of those involved, whether living or dead. Grendon articulates the thought already in Burdace's mind, that Anson is living in a private hell of his own making at the farm – living in unquenchable 'fire' in an outwardly beautiful, fertile, and living setting.

The countryside, for Burdace, is a place where he comes to regain his health, and where he also finds love. For Anson, the beauty and the life of the rural setting has become the place against which his obsession with gaining more land is played out. This comes to dominate his entire being, and all his activities and plans. His conscience, where the death of his wife is concerned, is in torment, and he is failing into madness just as Burdace is growing healthier, and expanding his mental horizons with the possibility of marriage.

At the last, the past, with its decayed marriage of Anson and Emma, reasserts itself the last time. As Anson's attempted murder of Burdace goes wrong, and he dies himself, it can be asked: was it supernatural intervention restoring the balance, or had Anson's personal hell finally come to overwhelm and consume him?

**

Although 'One Against the Dead' is also set in the idyllic world of Sac Prairie, the story takes place in the more limited confines of a single house. It is narrated, years after the event, to Steve Grendon by his doctor grandfather. As ever, a small event prompts the old man's memory:

> Grandfather Grendon bent forward.
>
> 'That reminds me,' he said, 'your mother coming down the stairs now from the dark into the light – that reminds me of the night Eleanor died, my sister Eleanor, your great-aunt, Boy, coming down that night, her mind already partly gone. That was a night. Yes, I remember that now... Down she came, like a ghost from the attic of that old red brick house she lived in...'[15]

Years before, Eleanor and Dr Grendon had administered a lethal dose of morphine their sister-in-law, Haidee, who was terminally ill with cancer, and in great pain. Despite the fact that they had carried out an act of euthanasia, asked for by the patient, Eleanor, years later and now very ill herself, becomes convinced that she murdered Haidee, who is coming back to take her revenge:

> 'Eleanor waited until she had gone, and then she turned to me and said, "I talked to her last night. During the night I saw her

and spoke to her." Then she stopped and looked at me slyly, daring me to say it wasn't so, and said, "You think I'm crazy."

'She got angry then, but let her anger cool. "Why don't you pray?" she asked. "You ought to pray. Tonight the woman we murdered comes back, the woman whose blood we've had on our hands these ten years."'[16]

Throughout the windy night, in the old house where Haidee had died, Eleanor slowly loses her mind, and waits for Haidee to return. Grendon sits up with Eleanor, who keeps replaying in her mind the events of the night that Haidee died. At midnight Grendon wakes to find that Eleanor is no longer in bed. Finally convinced that her death is near, Eleanor has got up, and is walking around the gallery of family portraits, talking to each one, saying goodbye to them. Eventually she reaches the last portrait – Haidee's. She stands on a chair to talk to her:

'I'm ready now, Haidee,' she said. 'Ready. And Jasper's upstairs. We're here, both of us, ready. Take these hands and take the blood from them, take the stain away.'[17]

Grendon sees Eleanor's chair tip over, throwing her down the stairs and killing her:

'But what happened?' I asked. 'Did she break her neck?'

'No, no bone was broken,' he said. 'It might have been the hardening of the brain arteries – they're taken that way. It might have been something else. A doctor can't always tell – sometimes never.'[18]

Again, Derleth presents a portrait of a mind apparently sliding into madness, with the accumulated tensions and consequences of past events making themselves present again.

Past and present are connected, and the past is never really dead. Relationships – both those in the present and those that have been put to rest – are penetrated by something intangible: a mind being consumed by an inner fire and aroused conscience – or a ghost, an unquiet revenant.

In the best tradition, Derleth does not give an explicit explanation either way. Events in Derleth's Sauk County, that dark heart of the Midwest, and crucible of actions and desires both past and present, simply unfold and overtake its inhabitants. The small town and rural idyll is not the whole story. There is more to expose and bring to light. Past actions have present consequences. Derleth's universe is nothing if not a moral one.[19]

***

August Derleth's fiction based on H.P. Lovecraft's work has often been criticised for not grasping the world-view lying behind it, thus producing material that, however labelled, does not really work as truly Lovecraftian horror fiction. H.P. Lovecraft's universe was an amoral one. Lovecraft himself called Derleth a 'self-blinded earth-gazer'.[20] As so often in his judgments of Derleth, Lovecraft was right.

But Lovecraft was also right in his estimation of Derleth as a writer when he was on his home ground. Derleth did not limit himself in his horror fiction. He also produced work rooted in his native landscape and with his own natural world-view, and created a kind of horror that was fitting for that world, ideal for a trip to hell and back. A hell on Sauk County earth.

Notes

1.   Derleth published about one hundred stories in *Weird Tales* between 1926 and 1954. See Jaffery and Cook, *The Collector's Index to Weird Tales,* Popular Press, 1995

2. Letter to J. Vernon Shea, *Selected Letters III* pp.396-97
3. For example such published volumes of journal as *Village Year* (1941); the 'Sac Prairie People' poems in *Collected Poems* (1967); *Walden West* (1961); and the novella *The House of Moonlight* (1951)
4. *The Shadow in the Glass* p.5
5. Jacket copy for Derleth's reprinting in the omnibus *Wisconsin Earth* (Stanton & Lee, 1948)
6. In 1938 Derleth was awarded a Guggenheim Fellowship, and was praised by such writers as Sinclair Lewis (a Nobel Prize winner) and Edgar Lee Masters
7. *Sac Prairie People* (Stanton & Lee, 1948). 'Where the Worm Dieth Not' was first published as 'The Sinister Shadow' in *Life Story,* May 1944. 'One Against the Dead' appeared for the first time in *Sac Prairie People.*
8. *Sac Prairie People* pp.115-16
9. *Sac Prairie People,* p.124
10. *Sac Prairie People* p.132. See Mark 9:48
11. *Sac Prairie People* p.147
12. *Sac Prairie People* p.153-54
13. *Sac Prairie People* p.156
14. *Sac Prairie People* p.163
15. *Sac Prairie People* p.288
16. *Sac Prairie People* p.296-97
17. *Sac Prairie People* p.303
18. *Sac Prairie People* p.304
19. This, correctly, forms the basic theme of Evelyn M. Schroth's treatment of Derleth's Sac Prairie Saga in *The Derleth Saga* (Quintain Press 1979)
20. Letter to Frank Belknap Long, *Selected Letters III* p.295

Carl Jacobi:
Portrait in Moonlight

During the last few years of the twentieth century, and even into the twenty-first, a few members of a very special group of writers were still alive, and in some cases, publishing new stories. They were a pulp fiction Brat Pack in their day: writers who wrote for the legendary *Weird Tales* – the 'Unique Magazine' – during its first incarnation between 1923 and 1954. One of the longest-lived survivors from that select group from a long-vanished era was Carl Jacobi.

Carl Richard Jacobi was born in Minneapolis on 10 July 1908. In common with much of the population of the American Midwest, Jacobi was descended from immigrants of German stock. He began to write while still in his teens, and contributed several stories to his high school magazine. Going on to attend the University of Minnesota in his home city, Jacobi studied English Literature and Composition. He worked on campus publications, and soon began to submit fiction to the numerous small literary magazines being published at the time.

Jacobi achieved his first success with the story 'Mive', which appeared in the Fall 1928 issue of *Minnesota Quarterly*. 'Mive' was also Jacobi's first appearance in *Weird Tales*; when it was reprinted in the January 1932 issue it was highly praised. The enigmatic and memorable title was a deceptively simple way of leading or enticing the reader into a highly effective piece of mood writing. The narrator simply goes out for a long walk through a landscape that may or may not be terrestrial; he wanders towards an ill-regarded swampy area. Soon he decides to leave the road and strike off into the swamp: the Mive. There he encounters an abnormally huge butterfly. Then he comes across something else even larger... He escapes from the Mive back to the 'normal' world outside. But the thought of what he saw and what it meant haunts him: 'I looked back. There it lay, far below me, vague and indistinct in the deepening gloom, the black outlines of the cypress trees writhing in the night wind, silent, brooding, mysterious – the Mive.'[1]

H.P. Lovecraft was always willing to extol the work of new writers when he felt it was deserved. Writing to Jacobi, Lovecraft told him: '"Mive" pleased me immensely, & I told Wright [Farnsworth Wright, the editor of *Weird Tales*] that I was glad to see at least one story whose weirdness of incident was made convincing by adequate emotional preparation & suitably developed atmosphere.'[2] With what was effectively his first story Carl Jacobi had made an auspicious start.

The use of distinctive and evocative titles was a Jacobi trait from the beginning. The title is an integral part of the story that follows it; Jacobi was aware of the value of making a title stand out and becoming a sort of recognisable trademark. This was another feature which often distinguished Jacobi's best fiction from that of his fellow writers, and added to the overall sense of the strange and bizarre that he aimed to create.

After graduation Jacobi found a job as a reporter and reviewer on the *Minneapolis Star* newspaper. But he wanted the uncertain freedom of making his living as a fiction writer, so he took the plunge and went freelance. At that time pulp fiction was booming in the United States; hundreds of magazines were being published, catering for a huge readership with a wide range of tastes. Although some magazines specialised in a particular sort of fiction, all tried to give their readers what they wanted: entertainment through well-told stories. An author who could sit at his typewriter and produce saleable first-draft copy all day and every day could make a reasonable living even during the Depression. However, despite maintaining an often high rate of production, with a good number of sales, Jacobi was not always able to make a living by writing full time. He spent much time in revising and perfecting his stories before submitting them; and although better quality stories were the result, this was not a sensible attitude to have when trying to survive in the pulp jungle. More seriously, Jacobi had become the sole provider for his family, and his parents depended on the money he brought home. Eventually Jacobi was forced to seek full-time employment, and for a while edited a radio trade journal. Because of his parents' reliance on him, Jacobi was not called up for active service during World War II; in 1942 he went to work for Honeywell as an inspector, and remained there until his mother's death in 1965.

Because Jacobi was limited to only writing in his spare time, the quantity of work that he published was considerably reduced. But this did not usually apply to its quality: if anything, the stories he published from the mid 1940s onwards showed an improvement on what he had written before. Jacobi continued to demonstrate that he had the skill to create stories with a sense of place and an atmosphere of doom and weirdness – a talent that had always distinguished him from the outset, and which showed to advantage in his best work. Over the years Jacobi carefully created a consistent world, setting many stories in his own slightly skewed-from-reality version of Carver County, Minnesota and other parts of the American Midwest.

The last pulp fiction magazines disappeared during the 1950s; *Weird Tales* had folded with its September 1954 issue.

However, a number of science fiction magazines continued to be published; and Jacobi, who had sometimes written science fiction, was able to carry on writing and selling science fiction throughout his career. He used his skill at creating alien and bizarre settings, transferring them to other planets. Like the science fiction written by his friends and fellow pulp writers Clark Ashton Smith and August Derleth, Jacobi's stories in the genre tended to concentrate on mood and atmosphere, with attendant strange and often horrible happenings, rather than make any serious attempt at utilising scientifically accurate technology or possible rationales. Nevertheless, Jacobi's science fiction has remained engaging and enjoyable.

In Minneapolis Jacobi found himself amongst a number of like-minded friends: people who liked to read, and sometimes write, supernatural stories and science fiction. He helped create the Minneapolis Fantasy Society, which included in its membership the authors Donald Wandrei, Clifford Simak, Gordon R. Dickson, and Poul Anderson. Their meetings and discussions were high-points in an often stressful life.

The immediate post-war years saw the appearance of

Jacobi's first book *Revelations in Black* in 1947. Published by August Derleth and Donald Wandrei's specialist company Arkham House, *Revelations in Black* collected twenty-one tales published during the previous fifteen years or so, including 'Mive' and the noteworthy title story.

'Revelations in Black' was only Jacobi's second story to appear in *Weird Tales*, in the April 1933 issue. On a cheerless September afternoon in an unnamed city the narrator wanders into an antique shop owned by an Italian, who proceeds to try to sell him various items. He shows no interest until he is shown a beautifully-bound book. The book turns out not to be for sale, as it was one of three volumes handwritten by the proprietor's brother, who died insane shortly after completing them. The book's title, *Five Unicorns and a Pearl*, further intrigues that narrator, but the Italian refuses to sell. Finally he agrees to a loan of the book for one night only. Later that evening, the narrator starts to read the book. The opening passage perplexes and unsettles him:

> The roar of the present was in the distance when I came to twenty-six bluejays silently contemplating the ruins. Passing in the midst of them I wandered by the skeleton trees and seated myself where I could watch the leering fish. A child worshipped. Glass threw the moon at me. Grass sang a litany at my feet. And the pointed shadow moved slowly to the left.[3]

There is more in the same vein; the narrator finds himself seized by deep feelings of uneasiness. Suddenly he decides to go out, and walks as though attracted to a part of the city he didn't know. Eventually he discovers a deserted garden hidden from the road by a high wall. Then he realises that the enigmatic place described in the book corresponds with the garden. And then a veiled woman wearing black joins him.

While the ending of 'Revelations in Black' is hardly a great surprise to the reader, Jacobi created a sustained piece of the uncanny which, although rooted firmly in a contemporary setting, also diverged rapidly into a world existing alongside it, and connected with it, but which otherwise existed as if in another dimension or plane of experience.

'The Face in the Wind' (*Weird Tales*, April 1936) is set on the decaying estate of Royalton Manor, where the house and estate are separated from an ill-regarded marsh by the dilapidated 'frog wall'. The new owner of the estate is warned not to move anything during his reconstruction of the wall, but of course the inevitable occurs. A local young man sees a vision of beauty and horror, and the owner becomes aware of a huge birdlike creature that may or may not be connected with Classilda Haven, a woman in her eighties who has established herself in one of the estate cottages. The young man paints a picture in which the narrator sees a beautiful and yet terrible face. A copy of *Restitution of Decayed Intelligence* by Richard Verstegen supplies the narrator with the connection between Classilda Haven and all the strange happenings on the estate. Verstegen's *Restitution of Decayed Intelligence*, a genuine book published in 1605, became a consistent feature of Jacobi's work, turning up in stories over the years in the same way as the fictional *Necronomicon* did in H.P. Lovecraft's fiction. A 'forbidden' and usually fictional book was often used as a resource to provide relevant and useful quotations, insights, and incantations as and when required. Many of the *Weird Tales* writers made use of such a book, and Jacobi was no exception.

'The Digging at Pistol Key' (*Weird Tales*, July 1947) has a more exotic setting. The protagonist, Jason Cunard, is an expatriate Englishman living on the British-run West Indian

island of Trinidad. His property on Pistol Key happens to be
the place where local legend says a hoard of treasure was once
buried by pirates, so Cunard is constantly bothered by treasure
-seekers digging holes on his land. In a fit of rage Cunard kills
his houseboy after accusing him of a crime that he later finds
he hadn't committed. Cunard buries the body secretly and puts
out the story that the boy ran away. Soon Cunard feels that he
is being haunted by an old black woman. This is the
houseboy's mother, who had a reputation as a practitioner of
obeah (sorcery) and who committed suicide. Eventually
Cunard becomes obsessed with finding the buried treasure
himself, and goes out one night to follow the pirates'
instructions. The next day Cunard is found dead in the hole
that he dug. But it wasn't buried gold that he had found...

Arkham House published Jacobi's second collection
Portraits in Moonlight in 1964. It collected fourteen stories
and featured an eerie and effective dustjacket by Frank
Utpatel, who drew the jackets for many Arkham House titles
and whose skill at depicting the uncanny and bizarre, but
without spoiling it by reducing it to banality, made him
Jacobi's equivalent in graphic art. *Portraits in Moonlight*
included stories first published in *Weird Tales* between 1946
and 1950. There were also a few stories dating from the later
1950s, mainly examples of Jacobi's particular brand of exotic
science fiction. The horror fiction represented in *Portraits in
Moonlight* is vintage Jacobi, and if a single book must be
ranked as his best, this is it.

In the title story 'Portrait in Moonlight' (*Weird Tales*,
November 1947) Jacobi again used one of his favourite
settings, the Caribbean island of Trinidad. Clarkson buys a
painting from a local artist. On the back is an odd inscription:
'Put me in the moonlight'. But instead of hanging the picture

in the moonlight, Clarkson hangs it in the sunlight. One morning, he notices that he looks and feels younger. He goes on a trip to Martinique, and feels even younger and healthier. Old acquaintances compliment him on his appearance. Soon Clarkson puts two and two together, and rushes back to Trinidad. But he never gets off the boat back in Port-of-Spain. And as for what the picture was found to be showing...

'Witches in the Cornfield' (*Imagination*, August 1954) was first published under the rather trite and revealing title 'The Dangerous Scarecrow'. Mr. Maudsley and Mr. Trask are scarecrows, named by the children Jimmy and Stella after two farmers in the district who have disappeared. The original Trask simply vanished, while Maudsley left in a hurry soon afterwards, and was rumoured to have moved to New Orleans. No-one except the children seem to notice that the scarecrows are very gradually moving closer together. Jimmy finds an old voodoo knife while playing in Maudsley's former barn, and decides to give it to the Maudsley scarecrow. Stella gets the idea of giving the knife to Mr. Trask. Meanwhile Mr. Trask continues to move towards Mr. Maudsley. One day the scarecrows are found next to each other, and Mr. Maudsley's head has been sliced off. The next day Jimmy and Stella's father reads out a macabre item from the local paper: 'One thing here, though – they found a fellow with his head cut off right in the middle of a city street.'[4] No guesses which city.

'The Corbie Door' is an entry from the silver age of *Weird Tales*, having first been published there in the May 1947 issue. Robert and Debora Fielding move to Corbie House, which Fielding's Uncle Charles has left to him. The house and environs are as odd as any conjured up by Jacobi during his career. Exploring the grounds, Fielding comes across a double row of columns, each surmounted by a corbie. And in the side wall of the arcade he finds a door with corbies carved into the panels. Before exploring further, Fielding discovers the house's library, with its copy of *Restitution of Decayed Intelligence* and the journals of various ancestors. Corbie House has a terrible past, rather like that of Exham Priory in H.P. Lovecraft's magnificent 'The Rats in the Walls' (1923). Fielding explores beyond the corbie door and enters a borderland world where he sees a rite performed, and a woman who resembles Debora. Eventually both Fieldings are found dead, but by different means...

'Matthew South and Company' (*Weird Tales*, May 1949) is a jewel of a story. Henry Walters is a rich owner of a sugar mill living in Port-of-Spain, Trinidad. He fervently dislikes his name, and avoids using it as much as possible by using a string of pseudonyms. When Walters is dreaming about a new name, he suddenly writes down 'Matthew South'. Later he stops off at his club for a game of cards. In a room which was supposed to be closed for repairs he falls in with three strangers, and Walters enjoys a friendly game. But when he checks the club register for their names, all he can find written there are the words 'Matthew South and Company'. Soon 'South' is exerting a malign influence over Walters, and forces him to kill the other two members of the first card game – two men who also had names that Walters had also thought of. Finally Walters meets South alone and shoots him. The verdict is suicide, but there was no motive for the murder of three friends with whom Walters used to play cards before he met Matthew South and Company.

These four stories also have the common thread running through them of the influence of sorcery. This was an abiding interest, along with the tropical settings that went with it. Jacobi, a man who rarely left his native Minnesota, either made good use of his native Midwest landscape in his stories, or got away from it entirely. The stories in *Portraits in Moonlight* are more developed and assured than the earlier ones reprinted in *Revelations in Black*, and do not reflect the natural variations in the quality of Jacobi's output. This would become noticeable when other stories first published at the same time as those in the first two collections were reprinted in the later collections *Disclosures in Scarlet* and *Smoke of the Snake*.

Arkham House was the natural choice to take on Jacobi's third collection, publishing *Disclosures in Scarlet* in 1972. *Disclosures in Scarlet* brought together seventeen tales and once again featured a superbly atmospheric cover by Frank Utpatel. The original publication dates of its contents ranged from the late 1940s up to 1971, and the stories themselves were a varied mix of science fiction and horror. *Weird Tales* had folded in 1954, and science fiction magazines had experienced boom and bust during that decade. The market for short stories had been augmented by the rise of paperback anthologies that featured new stories rather than reprints from magazines. Nearly half of the stories in *Disclosures in Scarlet* were first published in original anthologies, as well as in magazines generally regarded as specialising in science fiction, such as *Fantastic Universe*, *If*, and *Galaxy Science Fiction*. Carl Jacobi was always able to sell to a wide variety of markets, especially when editors were liberal in their definitions of the various subgenres of fantastic literature.

'The White Pinnacle' first appeared in August Derleth's original anthology *Time to Come* (1954). The story was ably, if briefly, summed up by reviewer Damon Knight as 'a preposterous farrago of unexplained and unconnected creepy doings on a mysterious planetoid.'[5] Prospectors discover an asteroid that has an atmosphere and plant life. (Knight was right to ridicule Jacobi's science, and Derleth should have known better.) The prospectors land and it very soon becomes apparent just how odd the life-forms they encounter are. And there is also the mysterious white pinnacle itself: an outcrop of rock carved with strange hieroglyphics. These are quickly translated, and Jacobi winds up a confusing story by having the narrative found later by the crew of another ship. 'The White Pinnacle' was not quite the best example of Jacobi's science fiction. In contrast, however, Jacobi published an excellent example of it in the prestigious *Galaxy Science Fiction* (June 1970). The evocatively titled 'The Player at Yellow Silence' concerns a mysterious contestant and a game of golf played for a far more important outcome than a mere trophy changing hands. It was hardly an original idea, but one that Jacobi handled with ease in a well-executed story. 'The Singleton Barrier' first appeared in the original anthology *Dark Things*, edited by August Derleth (1971). It is a terse and vivid story about an oddly-designed wall in the middle of the woods deep in Jacobi's home territory, the American Midwest. Vance Singleton comes upon the wall by accident during a rainstorm, and is immediately taken with its 'gypsy' design, and the fact that he thinks that he can hear sobbing sounds coming from the other side. In the local town he finds out that the house behind the wall was the site of a tragic death, and that the man involved in the affair lives over the road opposite where the wall now stands. Singleton visits the man, and notices a copy of Verstegen's *Restitution of Decayed Intelligence*. Also he has found out the meaning of the odd designs on the wall. Later Singleton returns to the wall, and enters the enclosure. There he discovers what actually happened, and the real reason for the wall's existence.

Jacobi's final collection of weird fiction was *Smoke of the Snake*, published in 1994. It contained fifteen stories, including one in collaboration with Jacobi's friend and noted science fiction writer Clifford Simak. There was a sprinkling

of stories from the 1930s and 40s, with more from the 1950s onwards. Also collected were some of the contributions that Jacobi made to the high-quality small press magazines *Whispers* and *Midnight Sun* during the 1970s and 80s – by which time he had become regarded as an 'elder statesman' of the field.

'The Elcar Special' was a piece of black humour that contains Jacobi's recurring devices of a wall and references to obeah practices. A somewhat shiftless character takes a job helping the owner of a car collection to look after his prize possessions. Among these is the Elcar Special – a special vehicle with a mysterious past. The narrator is out driving the Elcar Special when his personality seems to change. He finds a package hidden in the car, and somehow under a strange influence, makes a journey that uncovers the car's past, and the murder of a woman connected with it. The humour lies in the stolid character of the dodgy and feckless narrator being confronted, in the

American Midwest, with a classic car, West Indian obeah, and old murder. A weird mixture well handled.

'The Tunnel' was one of Jacobi's last stories, and first appeared in the Winter 1988-89 issue of the recently revived *Weird Tales*. Jacobi had lost none of his skills at creating a menacing atmosphere in an exotic setting, this time in Central America. A tunnel engineer is hired to supervise the construction of a railway tunnel rather too close to an Indian shrine and site of an ancient temple. Jacobi's consistently used 'forbidden' book, *Restitution of Decayed Intelligence,* makes its final appearance, and the warnings given about the fates of previous explorers are, of course, ignored.

During the later 1980s Jacobi's health began to deteriorate seriously. Years before he had been diagnosed with Parkinson's Disease; as he grew older, its effects made themselves felt. Still living in Minneapolis, his last years were spent in a nursing home. Carl Jacobi died in his native city on 25 August 1997.

Because he never published any novels or magazine serials, Jacobi's reputation rests entirely on the short stories he originally published in scattered and ephemeral fiction magazines. He was a born storyteller, and a distinctive one, from first to last. He brought his own off-beat and slant vision to bear on his native American Midwest, as well as on the glamorous Far East and Caribbean settings that he loved. Jacobi's best fiction exemplified the bizarre, the fantastic, and the downright strange and odd. His use of landscape, (both terrestrial and alien) and such artificial intruding constructions as isolated walls, lakes, roads, and houses, helped to build and sustain the vague sense of unease and looming doom that characterises his best work and passes to the reader. Carl Jacobi was nearly always a smooth and polished writer, who

took great pains over his work. He was a pro. And most
writers would consider that to be a suitable epitaph.

Notes

1. *Revelations in Black* p.233
2. Letter of 27 February 1932, *Selected Letters IV* p. 24
3. *Revelations in Black* p.7
4. *Portraits in Moonlight* p.25
5. Damon Knight, *In Search of Wonder* (3rd edition, 1996)
    p.152

A World of Great Majesty:
The Pattern in Arthur Machen's Carpet

In *The London Adventure* (1924) – which is, possibly, one of the longest shaggy-dog stories ever told – Arthur Machen mentions a short story by Henry James entitled 'The Pattern in the Carpet'. Machen summarises this story, in which a great author tantalisingly points out to an admirer that there is a single unifying theme or pattern to all his large and varied output, which can be discerned by those able to see it.[1]

In this essay I wish to show that the same can be said of Machen's own work. The majority of his varied output over some fifty years points to one central insight, explores one theme, displays in differing ways a single overall pattern in the carpet:

> Here, then, is the pattern in my carpet, the sense of the eternal mysteries, the eternal beauty hidden beneath the crust of common and commonplace things; hidden and yet burning and glowing continually if you care to look with purged eyes.[2]

In his fiction, his essays, his more overtly autobiographical work, Machen remains true to this belief. He was, effectively, engaged in nothing less than the creation of an alternative religion.[3]

Perhaps 'alternative' is not the right word to use. Machen would never have contemplated setting up anything as a replacement for, or a competitor with, Christianity (at least, the Christian tradition that he preferred and adhered to). But he was aware and concerned that the truths and insights, as he saw them, of Christianity were slipping into irrelevance and disdain for most people. Machen was highly critical of those he held to be largely responsible for this state of affairs: the churches themselves, including his own Church of England:

> Well, I have long maintained that on the whole the average church, considered as a house of preaching, is a much more poisonous place than the average tavern... And the main responsibility for this dismal state of affairs undoubtedly lies on the shoulders of the majority of the clergy of the Church of England... They pass their time in preaching, not the eternal mysteries, but a twopenny morality, in changing the Wine of Angels and the Bread of Heaven into gingerbeer and mixed biscuits: a sorry tran-substantiation, a sad alchemy, as it seems to me.[4]

Machen was not quite such an orthodox Christian as he might sometimes have liked his readers to think. For a time at the turn of the century he was a member of the Order of the Golden Dawn.[5] But this sort of affiliation can be seen as a part of Machen's need to augment Christianity as he – and most people – encountered it. The 'Holy Things' and the eternal mysteries were not on offer in most English churches. The 'numinous' was scarcely to be found. Machen wished to change that, and to raise people's consciousness of them, to do the job that the Christian churches seemed unable or unwilling to.[6]

The pattern in the carpet of Machen's work, then, was to provide what he felt to be lacking in contemporary Christianity, and in his modern world.

In his essay on Machen in *The Weird Tale* (1990) S.T. Joshi sums up Machen's concept in one sentence: 'the awesome and utterly unfathomable mystery of the universe.'[7] Machen sought to build a body of work that tried to put over this most central aspect of religion as it should be – now as then – by a variety of means in work as diverse as articles in popular newspapers, 'yellow' stories and novels that scandalised certain parts of literary society, to the volumes of autobiography and theory of literature that attracted a small but dedicated following.

For those of a conventionally religious mind, Machen's work can provide, if desired, a welcome extra dimension to their thought and practice. For both the initiated, and those for whom organised religion holds little or no appeal, Machen's work can resonate with the instinctive need for, and awe of, the numinous that most people have.

Arthur Machen was an early doubter of the notion that humanity's progression is to be largely an unstoppable upward and onward one. He rejected a faith in what he saw as mechanistic science and an eventual utopian future as was characterised by many of the works of such contemporary writers as H.G. Wells.

Machen was convinced that the religious insight of humanity being in need of redemption and the need for the restoration of a true and God-intended nature was a valid one. The myth of the Fall and the doctrine of Original Sin symbolised these truths, which needed to be remembered as an antidote of realism. As far as Machen was concerned, as mentioned above, the organised religion of the churches tended simply to moralise rather than restate this central truth. An awesome and mysterious universe, with its eternal truths that gave a place, a reason, and a destiny for humanity, needed to be recalled for our own-mental and spiritual benefit, let alone out of any more conventional religious motive.

He felt that the churches were failing in their mission to put this over to people. The traditional methods, practices, and language of Christianity were not reaching (if they ever really had) the majority of people who needed to receive the message. It is not far-fetched to imagine that Machen felt that he had to assume some responsibility to help promote his values through use of his talents.

In his career as a writer for over half a century, Machen pursued a mission that had as its basis the idea that art – literature – can aid the restoration of humanity, and point it towards eternal values so easily overlooked in everyday life, and not touched upon by organised religion in its system of expression and activity.

This is the theme of *Hieroglyphics* (1902). The test that separates literature from writing that is not literature is simply that

> ...literature is the expression, through the aesthetic medium of words, of the dogmas of the Catholic Church... No literal compliance with Christianity is needed, no, nor even an acquaintance with the doctrines of Christianity. ... unless you have assimilated the final dogmas – the eternal truths upon which these things rest, consciously if you please, but subconsciously of necessity, you can never write literature, however clever and amusing you may be.[8]

The point is that the 'final dogmas' need to be assimilated, by any means, even secular ones. The churches were basically exclusive institutions, despite the best efforts of the Victorians to bring religion, through the churches, to the people. Machen had a unique opportunity, as an author and popular journalist, to reach people that the churches never could, or failed to hold.

If the churches were regarded as places to attend once a

week, or to use for occasional rites of passage, then Machen made it clear that the eternal values as he wrote about and promoted them, were to be found anywhere and at any time. Awe could be found in the most 'unreverend' places and in situations and language distinctively different to that offered by the churches.[9]

Machen understood that, especially in a fast-changing and increasingly materialistic world, there was still a need and desire for the numinous, for Mystery. If the utterly awesome nature and mystery of the universe was the main connecting theme of Machen's work, then London and Gwent were the physical settings in which he played out his and his characters' understandings of Machen's mission.[10]

London becomes 'the concrete image of the eternal' – a place for the sort of encounters that would otherwise only occur in the privileged lives of official saints and other holy people.[11] Machen is emphatic that 'miracles need to be taken out of Judaea' so they can as well occur in Bethnal Green as Bethlehem, and to Dyson as well as God's Son.[12]

Enraptured by his own experiences and understanding of the universe, Machen set himself up as a spokesman for Miracle and Mystery. Increasingly suspicious and dismissive of science, and exasperated at the churches' moralising tendency, Machen wanted to show that humanity's real existence was not to be lost, cut off from its roots, in the great cities, with nothing but the dullness and grimness surrounding it.

It is a pity that Machen so consistently distrusted science, and only ever wrote about it with ferocity and disdain – and massive ignorance. It was as if science and religion had to be in conflict, and contradictory, for Machen's assertions about the awesomeness of the universe, and humanity's place in it, to be views worth holding and propagating. This certainly need not be the case. The world as we know it – and humanity itself – is literally star-dust. Everything that now is, animate or not, is comprised of elements created from the material of stars now dead. This is a discovery of modern science that can only begin to bolster Machen's point of view, and not diminish it.[13]

Machen wished to remind people that they held a special place on earth – and if traditional Christian doctrines cannot make clear the consequences and responsibilities that come with that, then he would do so through fiction. *The Terror* (1917) is an example of the consequences of humanity's unfeeling rejection of its spiritual birthright.

If people were dust, and would return to dust, then at least that dust was the dust of stars, to which while alive, if they but knew it and wished it, all the mystery and glory of God's creation was there for them. Machen did not use a building or a pulpit, but a city and the countryside, and the resources of his art, to put his message across. It is a message that, like that of traditional religion, seems to only ever speak to a few.

Man from the beginning has been profoundly irrational; that is, he has sought for God, and truth, and beauty, by the ways of religion, philosophy, and art. What is the convinced rationalist to say to this? There is only one thing that I can say ... There was a creature which, by its mere existence, reduced all the arguments of rationalism to rubbish. That creature is man: the eternally irrational ... It is by this madness that man is differentiated from other animals, and it is the business of rationalism to bring back man to sanity; that is, to bestiality.[14]

By embracing and promoting the 'irrational' Machen's outlook, which, like conventional religion, will not go away, can bring esteem and an illusion-free conviction of its status to humanity. Both are needed as much now as they were in Machen's lifetime.

Notes

1. *The London Adventure* pp.73-74
2. *The London Adventure* p.75
3. Religion can be defined as a system of faith or worship. I intend the word to have something to do with transcendence and the Transcendent.
4. Introduction to 'The Bowmen' reprinted in *The Collected Arthur Machen* pp.296ff
5. Aidan Reynolds and William Charlton, *Arthur Machen*
6. See Ninian Smart, *The Religious Experience of Mankind* p.49f for a discussion of 'numinous'. Smart defines it as 'an experience of unseen presences that can range from the uncanny to the sublime and holy'.
7. *The Weird Tale* p.l3
8. *Hieroglyphics* pp.l60ff
9. See *The London Adventure* p.l3; *The Collected Arthur Machen* p.323
10. As in, for example, *The Three Impostors*, 'The Great Return' etc
11. 'The Joy of London' in *The Secret of the Sangraal* (2007 edition) p.79
12. *The Collected Arthur Machen* p.298
13. For a concise view of Machen's negativity towards science, see S.T. Joshi, *The Weird Tale*, pp.15-16. For a consistently Christian and rigorously scientific account of science and theology, see John Polkinghorne, *Science and Christian Belief* (1994). Chapter 4 on 'Creation' is especially worth reading in the context of Machen and science.
14. 'Tom o' Bedlam and His Song' in *The Secret of the Sangraal* (2007 edition) pp.278-279

A Collision of World-Views:
A Look at August Derleth's
The Dweller in Darkness

August Derleth's novelette 'The Dweller in Darkness' (1944) is a curious story. It is one of a group of stories that Derleth wrote which, in effect, show the collision of two world-views, both of which have become regarded, until fairly recently, as 'Lovecraftian'.[1]

The first world-view is that of H.P. Lovecraft himself, as shown in such stories as 'The Call of Cthulhu' and his other late work. In this world-view, the universe is a blind and mechanical place, in which the human race and its world and aspirations have no special significance. There is no God; there is no special right of humanity to exist unmolested. Any existence of human civilisation owes its survival not to benign forces or the lack of malign ones, but simply to the fact of chance. Derleth included these stories, as well as unrelated stories by other writers, in a grouping he called the 'Cthulhu Mythos'. (He also included several Lovecraft stories that bore no real connection with this theme, except for their common fictional New England setting.)

The second world-view is that of Derleth himself. And because he included his own work, and the 'posthumous collaborations' with Lovecraft, under the general Cthulhu Mythos heading, the existence of two world-views rather than one is not at first sight obvious. Derleth's world-view is much more conventional, and has the universe as a setting for a conflict between good and evil, in which humanity sometimes becomes involved. But whereas Lovecraft had his 'gods' simply going about their business, with humanity getting in the way by accident, and so discovering that the universe is simply amoral, with Derleth it became the case that the 'gods' were divided into good and evil camps, with humanity being able to avoid getting caught in the crossfire by the use of what amounted to magic. In recent years this second world-view has become known as the 'Derleth Mythos' – and usually in a pejorative sense.

I do not want to go into detail here about the ramifications of the Cthulhu Mythos and Derleth Mythos. That can be followed up elsewhere.[2] Instead I do want to examine 'The Dweller in Darkness' as a story which shows the ambiguities of both world-views coming together in a single story. We get many Lovecraftian trappings, such as mentions of Arkham and Miskatonic University, Cthulhu, Nyarlathotep, and so on – but they are set within Derleth's good versus evil framework, a setting which Lovecraft would not have shared. On the plus side, instead of a story set in New England we get one set in northern Wisconsin, a regional setting that Derleth knew and used to good effect. The story also contains plenty of dialogue and much humour.

After a quote from Lovecraft's 'The Picture in the House' –

setting the scene for awful goings-on in remote places – the story begins with a pastiche of the opening of 'The Dunwich Horror':

> Until recently, if a traveller in north central Wisconsin took the left fork at the junction of the Brule River highway and the Chequamegon pike on the way to Pashepaho, he would find himself in country so primitive that it would seem remote from all human contact.[3]

The scene is Rick's Lake, the area around which 'had a history that gave pause to even the most intrepid adventurer.'[4] Over the years people have vanished, and folktales have become rife. With several nods in the direction of 'The Whisperer in Darkness', Laird Dorgan and the narrator decide to go to Rick's Lake in order to investigate the disappearance of Professor Upton Gardner, the latest folklore collector and intrepid adventurer to go missing in the area. In true Lovecraftian spirit, the men find a collection of letters and notes left behind by the professor. The usual forbidden books are there – the *Necronomicon* and *Pnakotic Manuscripts* – made available by the modern technology of photocopying, and thus avoiding the fate that Wilbur Whateley suffered in the library of Miskatonic University in 'The Dunwich Horror'.

Derleth also expands the canon. One of the professor's letters made enquiries about 'whether it is possible to purchase through one of the local bookstores a copy of *The Outsider and Others,* by H.P. Lovecraft, published by Arkham House last year'![5] (Derleth always encouraged direct sales, his business acumen ably tying in with the desire to cut out the distributor and get the vital facts out to where they're needed – and fast!)

Lovecraft's own creation has engulfed our world. Derleth

draws HPL into the exalted company of people like Abdul Alhazred and Dr Henry Armitage, who knew what was *really* going on. In another modern touch, and another nod to 'The Whisperer in Darkness', Dorgan and the narrator resolve to buy a Dictaphone, since Gardner had written about strange noises coming from the forest. Then they could record the sounds for themselves, and have definite evidence that Something Is Going On.

Some locals appear on the scene, and speak in the usual Lovecraftian phoneticese, hinting of strange things in store. Old Peter, the Zadok Allen character this time around, tells of a great slab with a drawing of 'jest things' on it.[6] Resolving to get information out of Old Peter by the time-honoured method of getting him drunk, the two go back to consult Professor Gardner's notes.

These notes serve to make the connection between Rick's Lake and Lovecraft's aquatic beings. Even the American Midwest isn't safe, any more than the Eastern Seaboard was. Derleth then also sketches out his notion of making Lovecraft's 'gods' and creatures into elementals, as well as supplying some that were lacking from this scheme that HPL never dreamed of. Before our very eyes the Cthulhu Mythos becomes the Derleth Mythos. The universe is now the backdrop for a struggle between beings of Earth and Air, and Fire and Water:

> Cthulhu or Kthulhut. In Rick's Lake? Subterrene passage to
> Superior and the sea via the St. Lawrence?
> Hastur. But manifestations do not seem to have been of air
> beings either.
> Yog-Sothoth. Of earth certainly – but he is not the Dweller in
> Darkness...
> What of fire? There must be a deity here, too. But no mention...[7]

The narrator sits down to read his way through *The Outsider and Others.* (Derleth always tried to fill orders by return.) He decides that Lovecraft was On To Something in his fiction, and Gardner had got on to it as well, independently. And this time it is going on in Wisconsin... The two men go to visit the discredited Professor Partier, who also knows the full facts about the Mythos, and who explains the full pantheon of the Derleth Mythos, and how it has constantly been hidden from most of the human race for aeons. Partier advises them to forget about the whole business:

> Lovecraft knew! Gardner and many another have sought to discover those secrets, to link the incredible happenings which have taken place here and there on the face of the planet – but it is not desired by the Old Ones that mere man shall know too much. Be warned![8]

But there is a story to be told, and one to sell. Dorgan and the narrator go straight back to Rick's Lake, and begin the process of getting Old Peter drunk. He soon reveals that the slab in the depths of the forest is a thing that is connected with apparitions of Things.

By now the two decide to check out their Dictaphone recordings. After the usual night-sounds of the forest, they hear *a weird voice.* Then Upton's voice addresses Dorgan, and tells him that he has been with Nyarlathotep, but is now getting second thoughts. He wants him to summon Derleth's fire elemental Cthugha:

> Listen to me! Leave this place. Forget. But before you go, summon Cthugha... When Fomalhaut has topped the trees, call forth to Cthugha... When He has come, go swiftly, lest you too be destroyed. For it is fitting that this accursed spot be blasted so

that Nyarlathotep comes no more out of interstellar space...[9]

They pay a nocturnal visit to the slab. Then 'what we saw there sent us screaming voicelessly from that hellish spot.' For half a page of italics the Dweller in Darkness, with his hideous flute-players, has conveniently dropped by to visit a little. But: 'Incredible as it may seem, the ultimate horror awaited us.'[10]

Dorgan and friend run back to their hut, but are pursued by odd footsteps. They get back safely, and flake out. Then Professor Upton appears at the door, cool as Kadath in the Cold Waste. With a profound bow to 'The Whisperer in Darkness' he dismisses all their worries, and rationalises all that has happened. And he accidentally destroys the incriminating Dictaphone cylinder with his voice and the other voice and noises on it. And so all go bed, tired out.

An hour later, they find that Gardner has never slept in his room, and all his letters and notes have disappeared. Now at last they realise their mortal danger. They must get away, as originally instructed, but first they must summon Cthugha. As soon as his home star Fomalhaut rises above the trees, Dorgan chants the formula and they run for it.

Destruction. But the men have time to see the footprints made by whatever had pursued them earlier, and to connect them with Gardner's 'reappearance' and the apparition of the Dweller in Darkness...

Although it is enjoyable fun, I find myself unable to admire this story (or others like it). Perhaps this is because it isn't really a Derleth story any more than it is really a Lovecraftian one. To be sure, all the right names are there, and all the right moves are made. But there is too much explanation and too much is revealed and systematised in a way that Lovecraft never did.

Lovecraft did not believe in his creations, although the amoral and neutral universe, and the puny value of humanity within it, was a world-view deeply held by him. Derleth, in writing his 'Mythos' fiction, is also playing to these rules, although it is clear that he doesn't subscribe to them, and so effectively changes them. In Derleth's Mythos fiction there is still too much of his Roman Catholic Christian cultural background and seemingly genuine belief, to make his use of Lovecraft's world-view palatable or credible. Instead, ever the pro, Derleth adds to the rules and changes them. The Derleth Mythos takes over from Lovecraft's vision. We get a whole new game, not an updated version of the original one.

It would be unfair to criticise Derleth for not writing Lovecraft stories. Only Lovecraft could do that. Derleth's weird and macabre fiction was always pure entertainment for him, let alone the reader. The underlying morality – or lack of it – of the universe doesn't enter into it. Derleth knew how to enjoy himself, entertain his readers, sell his wares, and – more than Lovecraft ever did – get paid for it!

Notes

'The Dweller in Darkness' was first published in Weird Tales, November 1944. It was reprinted in Derleth's collection *Something Near* (Arkham House 1945) and in his anthology *Tales of the Cthulhu Mythos* (Arkham House 1969). Page numbers refer to this edition.

1.   The classic 'revisionist' exposition is Richard L. Tierney's 'The Derleth Mythos' in Darrell Schweitzer, ed., *Essays Lovecraftian* (T-K Graphics 1976). Derleth's Lovecraftian stories can be found in such collections as *Something Near, The Mask of Cthulhu* and *The Trail of Cthulhu.*

2. See 'The Derleth Mythos,' as well as the discussion in the final chapter of S.T. Joshi, *H.P. Lovecraft: A Life* (1996).
3. 'The Dweller in Darkness' p.111
4. The Dweller in Darkness' p.112
5. The Dweller in Darkness' p.117
6. 'The Dweller in Darkness' p.119. Zadok Allen appears in Lovecraft's 'The Shadow over Innsmouth'. The teetotal HPL showed considerable verve in handling this aspect of his narrative!
7. 'The Dweller in Darkness' p.121f
8. 'The Dweller in Darkness' p.128f
9. 'The Dweller in Darkness' p.133f
10. 'The Dweller in Darkness' p.138

A Torrent of Eldritch Terrors:
Fritz Leiber's 'The Death of Princes'

The American science fiction magazine *Amazing Stories* (also known for a time as *Amazing Science Fiction*) was possibly *the* science fiction magazine to read throughout most of the 1970s. This was due to its editor, Ted White, who against all the odds – a tiny budget, and almost nonexistent distribution – produced one of the liveliest, readable, and controversial magazines that the science fiction field has known.[1]

The fiftieth anniversary of the first issue of *Amazing Stories* occurred during Ted White's tenure and was marked by the issue dated June 1976. (The first issue had been dated April 1926, but by 1976 the magazine was being published on a quarterly schedule, hence the difference in dating.) The anniversary issue was an excellent one, containing stories by Isaac Asimov, Harlan Ellison, Robert F. Young, Barry Malzberg, and, among still others, Fritz Leiber.

Fritz Leiber was a frequent contributor to *Amazing*'s companion magazine, *Fantastic Stories*, and had been since the 1950s. By 1976 he was regularly reviewing books, and had published much fine fiction, including several of the popular Fafhrd and Grey Mouser stories. Thus Leiber's name was well -known to the readers of Ted White's magazines, and his name on the cover of an issue of *Amazing* would be an additional incentive to buy that particular issue. It was good news for both White and Leiber – to say nothing of the reader – that 'The Death of Princes' turned out to be one of the best and most characteristic stories that Leiber ever wrote.[2]

'The Death of Princes' is a haunting, personal piece, an apparently rambling narrative that evokes a deep chill of terror and the unknown, and yet is grounded in the known world, sexuality, and enduring human relationships. The immediate reason for discussing this story are these thematic links with much of Leiber's other work, in particular the contemporary novel *Our Lady of Darkness* (which first appeared as a magazine serial titled The *Pale Brown Thing* in 1977 before being expanded and retitled in 1978 for book publication) and the novelette 'The Button Molder' (1979).

The story is told in the first person by Fred, who, like Leiber, was very tall and born in 1910. This turns out to be a most significant year. Fred is one of a group of friends, all born around that time. The 'leader' of this group is the charismatic, talented, and mysterious Francois Broussard, who seems to have a 'cosmic' element in his character and being. Leiber uses Lovecraft's device of stating at the beginning of the story what the end result will be – the possible explanation of a problem, anomaly, terror, and so on:

> Ever since the discovery Hal and I made last night, or rather the amazing explanation we worked out for an accumulated multitude of curious facts, covering them all (the tentative solution to a riddle that's been a lifetime growing, you might say) I have been very much concerned and, well, yes, frightened...[3]

Leiber then spends the rest of the story showing and explaining his working: how Fred and Hal came to their frightening conclusions, what their consequences could be, and explaining more of the situations between the members of the group of friends that allows the story to be written in the first place.

In 'The Death of Princes', then, Fred and Hal have pieced

together an explanation for all the strangeness and cosmic consciousness that they have experienced with Broussard over the previous fifty years or so. As the story's title makes clear, the explanation is linked to a comet, and, in this case, Halley's Comet:

> Sometimes at that point Francois would quote those lines of Calpurnia to Caesar in Shakespeare's play 'When beggars die, there are no comets seen; The heavens themselves blaze forth the death of princes.' (Shakespeare was a very comet-conscious man; they had a flood of bright ones in his time.)[4]

Halley's Comet last passed close to the Earth in 1910; in 1976 it was due to return ten years later, in 1986.

That return may well be momentous for the entire human race, let alone Fred, Broussard, and their friends. It becomes clear that the fact that all of the group were born around the time of the comet's last close passage to the Earth was no coincidence. They had always thought of themselves as being slightly apart from everyone else, and Broussard in particular exemplified that.

> Anyhow, there we were with our dreams and our ideals, our feeling of being somehow different, and so you can imagine how we ate up the stuff that Francois fed us about being some sort of lost or secret aristocrats, almost if we were members of some submerged superculture... I remember the exact words Francois used once. 'Every mythology says that upon occasion gods come down out of the skies and lie with chosen daughters of men. Their seed drifts down from the heavens. Well, we were all born about the same time, weren't we?'[5]

Throughout the story, Fred recalls previous occasions on which it seems that Broussard's cosmic side has been in some sort of rapport with the comet. He seems not to be quite at home living under conditions of gravity. He is aware of the positions of stars on the other side of the world, as if from an all-space perspective. He dreams of a group of shapes far out in space – things shaped like the five Platonic solids.[6] The freezing chill of outer space and ancient time comes to twentieth-century Earth. Broussard feels that the shapes could be alien computers, or a space mausoleum, complete with ghosts as deadly as being suffocated in the dust of the cometary head that surrounds them. And when the comet comes close to Earth again, in ten years' time...[7]

'The Death of Princes' is Leiber on top form. The preoccupations of his later life and work are all there: astronomy, San Francisco, architecture, sex, drugs, and so on. Even Fred's wife, Daffodil, is given a flower name, like Leiber's wife Jonquil, and Franz Westen's Daisy in *Our Lady of Darkness*.

As in much of Leiber's work, especially in such stories as *Our Lady of Darkness* and 'The Button Molder', fiction is used to examine and meditate upon humanity's place in the universe, usually as shown to an elderly, often lonely, man who can be compared to Leiber himself. As Leiber was moving steadily towards his seventies at this time, it isn't too fanciful to imagine that this was Leiber's own concern as well.

And we were going downhill into the last decade or two of our lives. In that sense we had certainly become the Doomed. And yet our mood was not so much despair as melancholy – at least I'm sure it was in my case. That's a much misunderstood word, melancholy – it doesn't just mean sadness. It is a temperament or outlook and has its happinesses as well as its griefs – and especially it is associated with *the consciousness of distance*.[8]

This is the cosmic perspective, experienced or encountered second-hand by Fred and his friends as they grow older. Leiber, as a writer of science fiction, fantasy, and horror, knew how a cosmic perspective can make the most ordinary surroundings and events to be no protection against terror, fright, and awe. Leiber shows his Lovecraftian heritage in this.

The conclusion of the story, the confirmation of the revelation, brings it back full circle. Fred and Hal piece all the parts of the mystery together: the changing position of Halley's Comet, and Broussard's activities and pronouncements in the light of this knowledge:

> 'You know how it used to take Francois twelve hours to get his answers back in 1950?' I said, trembling a little. 'Well, Halley's comet was in aphelion in 1948 and twelve hours is about the time it would take to get a radio answer back from the vicinity of Pluto, or of Pluto's orbit – six hours out, six hours back, at the speed of light. The ten-hour times for his answers in 1930 and 1970 would fit too.'[9]

Leiber uses modern ideas – radio communication, computers, space probes – as vehicles for his brand of cosmic horror and wonder. Yet when it comes down to it, in 'The Death of Princes' it is a human being who has lived his whole life in the shadow of the cosmic, and is only just realising it as he nears the end of his life, who experiences and mediates the horror. Once the vista has been opened, it cannot be shut away again.

Annotations to 'The Death of Princes'

p.479

1.18ff   Compare with the worldview of H.P. Lovecraft, in such stories as 'The Call of Cthulhu' and 'Nyarlathotep'. Also note use of the word 'eldritch'!

1.24   Leiber was born on 24 December 1910.
1.28   Robert Heinlein (1907-88) U.S. science fiction writer,
          noted for the libertarian content of much of his work, and
          the concept of the 'competent man'. His controversial
          novel *Farnham's Freehold* (1964) involved 'survivalist'
          elements in the story.
1.34   In Greek mythology Pandora was the first woman,
          created by Zeus. She was given a sealed jar or box,
          containing all the evils of the world, which were released
          when she opened the box.
p.480
1.27   Mark Twain (1835-1910) US writer, pseudonym of
          Samuel Langhorne Clemens.
1.31   Fritz Leiber was 6'5' tall.
1.36   Jacques-Yves Cousteau (1910-97) French diver and
          underwater naturalist, author of a book entitled *The Silent
          World*. 1.41. Carl Gustav Jung (1876-1961) Swiss
          psychologist. Leiber was heavily influenced by Jung's
          concept of the Anima/female and Animus/male principles
          co-existing in everyone. See Bruce Byfield's study of
          Leiber *Witches of the Mind*, pp.40ff. Jung's 'Flying
          Saucers: a Modern Myth' (1958) was collected in
          Civilization in Transition (1964).
1.42   Colonel Estobani [not traced]
1.46   Leiber was an avid field astronomer in his later years. See
          the autobiographical *Our Lady of Darkness* and 'The
          Button Molder'.

p.481
1.2   The Southern Cross: the constellation Crux Australis, not
          visible in northern latitudes.
1.13   Cavendish's differential engine – probably a mistake for
          Charles Babbage (1792-1871) inventor of the differential
          engine, a mechanical computer. The 'Cavendish' would
          refer to Henry Cavendish (1731-1810).

1.27f   George Bernard Shaw (1856-1950) Irish playwright and
          critic. *Back to Methuselah* was published in 1921.
          Heinlein's *Methuselah's Children* (not *Children of
          Methuselah*, as in the text) appeared in *Astounding
          Science Fiction* Jul-Sep 1941; book version 1958.
1.35f   Aldous Huxley (1894-1963) UK writer, long resident in
          the USA. *After Many a Summer Dies the Swan* was
          published in 1939.
1.42   Erich von Daniken (b. 1935) Swiss writer, whose theories
          that aliens have been involved with past civilisations has
          brought him much attention since the late 1960s.

p.482
1.7   Pisces, the Fishes, and Aquarius, the Water Carrier:
          Zodiacal constellations best visible from northern
          latitudes in autumn.
1.11   Hydra, the Water Snake or Sea Serpent: constellation best
          visible from northern latitudes in spring.
1.12   Leo, the Lion: Zodiacal constellation, best visible from
          northern latitudes in spring.
1.21   Heinlein's Martians appear in his novel *Stranger in a
          Strange Land* (1961).
1.25   Mike is a computer in Heinlein's novel *The Moon Is a
          Harsh Mistress*, published in 1966.
1.47   The Platonic solids were used by the astronomer
          Johannes Kepler in an attempt to account for the values of
          the radii of planetary orbits. He visualised the planetary
          orbits as a series of spheres, each having one of the
          Platonic solids inscribed within it.

p.483
1.3f   Johannes Kepler (1571-1630) German astronomer.
          Mysterium Cosmographicum was published in 1596, and
          advocated an underlying mathematical harmony
          underlying the universe (see above).

1.12   Cheops' pyramid is the largest of the pyramids at Giza,
            and is generally dated to around 2600 BCE. Leiber would
            have been interested in the theories of Robert Bauval and
            Adrian Gilbert, in their book *The Orion Mystery* (1994),
            in which they claim the resemblances between the
            constellation Orion and the positions of several pyramids
            on the ground point to an advanced star religion in
            ancient times.

1.20   The quotation is from *Julius Caesar*, Act 2 Scene 2.

1.30   Sheldon Lee Glashow (b.1932) US physicist.

1.41   The *Bremen*, German ocean liner.

1.42.   Andre Gide (1869-1951) French writer. Gertrude Stein
            (1874-1946) US writer, long resident in Paris.

p.484

1.23   Thomas Stearns Eliot (1888-1965) US writer, long
            resident in the UK.

1.24   Ernest Hemingway (1898-1961) US writer. James Joyce
            (1882-1941) Irish writer. Albert Einstein (1879-1955)
            German/US physicist. Sigmund Freud (1856-1939)
            Austrian psychiatrist. Alfred Adler (1870-1937) German
            psychiatrist. Norman Thomas (1884-1968) US socialist
            and pacifist. Robert Maynard Hutchins (1899-1977) US
            academic and educational reformer.

1.26   Charles Lindberg (1902-70) US aviator. Amelia Earhart
            (1898-1937) US aviator. Greta Garbo (1905-90) Swedish/
            US actress.

1.35   A.E. van Vogt (1912-2000) Canadian science fiction
            writer. *Slan* (*Astounding Science Fiction* Sep-Dec 1940;
            book version 1946) is an early example of a 'superman'
            novel: slans are telepaths, mutated due to exposure to
            atomic radiation.

1.37   The first issue of *Amazing Stories* was dated April 1926
            and featured as a serial Jules Verne's *Off on a Comet* (!).
            The cover, by Frank R. Paul, illustrated the story.

p.485

1.27	Joseph McCarthy (1909-57) US politician, noted for his persecution of alleged communists in US public and artistic life.
1.40	A reflecting telescope reflects the image from the lens onto a mirror, and up into the eyepiece. Thus the observer looks down into the telescope, rather than up through it.
1.49	Crater, the Cup: faint constellation, visible from northern latitudes in spring.

p.486

1.1	Virgo, the Virgin: Zodiacal constellation, best visible from northern latitudes in spring. Canis Minor, the Little Dog. Procyon is the brightest star in this tiny winter constellation.
1.2	Cancer, the Crab: Zodiacal constellation, best visible in spring.
1.15	'Colossus of the North' – a frequent Latin American perception of the United States.
1.19	Jack London (1876-1916) US writer, also referred to in *Our Lady of Darkness*. Francis Drake (1540-96) English explorer and adventurer, an early discoverer of San Francisco Bay. [I believe there is physical evidence of this.]
1.21	Daffodil – compare with Leiber's wife, Jonquil. (The narrator's wife in *Our Lady of Darkness* is called Daisy, and Tansy in *Conjure Wife*.)
1.29f	Robert Graves (1895-1985) UK writer, long resident in Spain. Graves' utopian novel (UK title *Seven Days in New Crete*) was published in 1949.
1.43	Albrecht Durer (1471-1528) German artist. 'Melancholia' dates from 1514.

p.487

1.6   John Glenn (b. 1921) US astronaut.

1.7   Willet windows [?]

1.30   The following are all US actresses: Linda Blair (b. 1959),
           appeared in *The Exorcist*. Mackenzie Phillips (b.1960)
           appeared in *American Graffiti*. Melanie Griffith (b. 1957).
           Tatum O'Neal (b. 1962) appeared in *Paper Moon*.

1.31   Nell Potts, Maire Rapp, Catherine Harrison, [not traced].
           Roberta Wallach, daughter of Eli Wallach.

1.37   US President Richard Nixon resigned in 1974 after an
           often controversial political career.

1.43   A nova is a 'new star' – a previously faint or invisible star
           which has exploded, thus suddenly increasing in
           brightness. Nova Cygni appeared in the constellation of
           Cygnus, the Swan, a northern circumpolar constellation.
           (Coordinates RA 21.09, Dec +07.56. See the mention in
           'The Button Molder', *Chronicles* p.527.)

p.488

1.1   A space probe, Giotto, was launched to intercept Halley's
           Comet during 1985-86.

1.17   Willy Ley (1906-69) German/US science writer, a regular
           contributor to science fiction magazines, as Leiber was.
           The book on comets is *Visitors from Afar: the Comets*.

1.22   The Ecliptic is an imaginary line drawn on the sky, the
           plane of which passes through the centres of the Earth and
           Sun. The Moon and planets lie approximately in this
           plane.

p.489

1.24f   *The Mysterious Stranger*, published in 1916, concerns the
           visit to an Austrian village by a man who turns out to be
           Satan. *Captain Stormfield's Visit to Heaven* was published
           in 1909, although written in the 1870s. 'My Platonic
           Sweetheart' [not traced].

Notes

1. See Mike Ashley, 'The Amazing Story, Part 6' in *Amazing Stories* June 1992
2. 'The Death of Princes' was reprinted in *The Leiber Chronicles* (1990). Pagination refers to this appearance.
3. 'The Death of Princes' p.479
4. 'The Death of Princes' p.483
5. 'The Death of Princes' p.484
6. 'The Death of Princes' pp.482f; see also *Our Lady of Darkness* p.186
7. 'The Death of Princes' pp.483, 479
8. 'The Death of Princes' p.486
9. 'The Death of Princes' p.488

A Look at *The Edge of Running Water* by William Sloane

William Sloane (1906-74) wrote only two novels. Both of them can be considered to be science fiction with strong elements of the occult and supernatural. The first was *To Walk the Night* (1937). In this essay I intend to discuss Sloane's second, and unfortunately last, novel *The Edge of Running Water* (1939).

The opening of the novel is very much in the H.P. Lovecraft mould:

> The man for whom this story is told may or may not be alive. If he is, I do not know his name, where he lives, or anything at all about him, except that there is something which it is vital for me to tell him. It is a strange, clumsy method of communication, this expedient of writing an entire book without even the certainty that it will come into his hands, and yet I can see no other way of warning him.[1]

Not only is the first paragraph of *The Edge of Running Water* notable for its Lovecraftian feel; Sloane sets his entire story in a small New England coastal community (Barsham Harbor, Maine) which could, in its vividness and isolation, and taciturn inward-looking inhabitants, easily be HPL's Kingsport or, stretching it, Innsmouth. Sloane catches the feel of rural New England just as Lovecraft did, and shows every sign of having known at first-hand the locations he wrote about.

Reading the novel's first couple of pages, it soon becomes

clear that there is Something Going On that it is Better Not To Know About. The narrator, Richard Sayles, is invited by his old friend Julian Blair to visit him at his huge old house on Setauket Point. Blair's beloved wife has died, and Blair has retreated to isolated Maine in order to pursue his research.

Blair's work is simple enough: to provide the answer to one question: What lies beyond the grave? Sayles states his view soon enough:

> That question must never be answered. A year ago it would have seemed to me ridiculous to assume that there are some facts it is better not to know, and even today I do not believe in the bliss of ignorance or the folly of knowledge. But this one thing is best left untouched. It rips the fabric of human existence from throat to hem and leaves us naked to a wind as cold as the space between the stars. The fringe of that cold touched me once. I know what I am talking about.[2]

Sayles has discovered that we do, indeed, live on islands amidst black seas of infinity, and something of that darkness and chill will break through into our apparently safe world if we let it do so. We were not meant to voyage far in that direction, and even the motive of love will be no protection.

Julian Blair has become obsessed with the notion of reaching out beyond death, beyond the end of physical life, to where the mind goes after death. Blair wishes to find out about the afterlife, to communicate with his wife there. At any cost.

This constant pushing out at the rim of the known world into the unknown and dangerous one beyond is contrasted with the parallel story of the growth of love between Sayles and Blair's sister-in-law, his dead wife's much younger sister Anne. The two people find interest and affirmation in each other in this world – and that is all they desire. This is at total variance with Blair's obsession with the next world – an obsession shared by his assistant Mrs Walters. That sought-for

THE EDGE OF
RUNNING WATER

WILLIAM
SLOANE

A chilling mystery that hurdles
the boundaries between the natural and the supernatural

next world, the world of the dead Helen Blair, intrudes gradually, bit by bit, becoming more and more real for the experimenters, even as Sayles and Anne Blair fall more in love against the background of its approaching chill. Both worlds grow slowly reachable.

The novel's setting – the Talcott Place – is a rambling, somewhat dilapidated New England mansion in the best Lovecraft tradition. It is remote, and ill-regarded, along with its outsider inhabitants, by the suspicious neighbours and townspeople. Again the mundanity, the comparative normality of the house and locality, is contrasted with what is going on behind its seldom-opened doors.

Slowly, as Richard and Anne's love blossoms, Blair and Walters' experiment moves towards its climax. Blair invites Sayles to the room in which he has been experimenting. What Sayles sees is like a séance:

> My impression was of seated figures, human and yet horribly not
> human, ranged round a black table with a sort of lectern at one
> end... They were, I saw, all alike, all polished till the copper of

their wires glowed... From head to foot they were made of wire
and there was something terrible in the fact that I could look
clean through them...[3]

The experiment begins. A 'blackness' starts to become
apparent over the centre of the table, and the air in the room
begins to rush into the dimensionless 'hole' forming there in
mid-air. Sayles is revolted by the combination of 'séance and
black mass' that he witnesses: 'This ... thing ... you just
showed me, that cannot be the other world you meant. That
black thing was no world. It was opposite to any world at all.'[4]

Blair is not to be put off from switching his machine on
again. He is by now half-mad with obsession, and the longing
for new knowledge, even if there is great risk in getting it. A
group of men from the town arrive at the house as the final
phase of Blair's experiment begins. Blair has locked himself in
the room with the figures. A glow begins to show in the space
between the door and frame. A great rush of air is being
sucked into the room. Then – an explosion.

The house began to burn within a few minutes... It burned high
and yellow against the dark sky... Of Julian we speak scarcely at
all these days, but neither of us believes, I think, that he was in
the house when it burned. We know that he was neither there nor
in any part of this substantial earth.[5]

The Edge of Running Water is told after the event, as the
opening makes clear, and certainly there is a 'happily ever
after' for the narrator and his love, if not possibly, too, for
Julian Blair. Unless someone else tries to gain the knowledge
that Blair sought, and which led to death and destruction, and
threatened to open up a black and icy void into this placid
world, and drag everything through it into another place, a non

-world where perhaps even the dead do not belong. Let alone the living.

Notes

Page numbers refer to the World Books edition of 1945, which is not hard to obtain. Paperback editions have been published in the UK by Panther Books (1965) and in the USA by Del Rey Books (1980).

1.   *The Edge of Running Water* p.11
2.   *The Edge of Running Water* p.12
3.   *The Edge of Running Water* p.218
4.   *The Edge of Running Water* p.225 (lacunae are in the text)
5.   *The Edge of Running Water* p.254

A Universe Shot Through with Invisible Forces: *Our Lady of Darkness* as a Lovecraftian Novel

Fritz Leiber's novel *Our Lady of Darkness* operates on several levels and different meanings can be read into it. During successive readings, and enhanced with a knowledge of the author's background, influences, and other circumstances, *Our Lady of Darkness* can accumulate a depth and impact which go beyond that experienced on a first or more superficial examination. Fritz Leiber encountered the work of H.P. Lovecraft in the year before Lovecraft's death. The two men – one coming towards the end of his career while the other had barely begun his – maintained a brief but intense correspondence. Leiber began his literary career with a voice very much his own; yet he always readily acknowledged Lovecraft's part in nurturing his writing and testified to his (non-stylistic) influence on his work.

This essay seeks to explore some ways in which *Our Lady of Darkness* may be referred to as being 'Lovecraftian'. In his review of *Our Lady of Darkness* the author and critic John Clute bases his assessment on the fact that the novel works on at least two levels.[1] For Clute, the surface meaning of the story – Franz Westen's haunting by an external paramental entity – is an 'inversion' of its true content and meaning. This is, in reality, Leiber working through his 'haunting' of grief and guilt caused by his wife's death (Jonquil Leiber died in the summer of 1969). The fictional Franz Westen's experiences, his continuing guilt and grief over his dead wife Daisy, make this reading legitimate. It can be seen as thinly disguised autobiography on Leiber's part, or as a reasonable explanation for character motivation within the world of *Our Lady of Darkness.*

Of course one reading of a story should not necessarily exclude another. The 'inversion' of meaning from the external to the internal does not make the novel any less frightening or harrowing: perhaps the opposite. But it does call into question definitions of the supernatural and how it interacts with humanity, and the place of both in the universe. It has been argued, not least by Leiber himself in his essay 'A Literary Copernicus', that Lovecraft's works contain similar tensions:

> Howard Phillips Lovecraft was the Copernicus of the horror story. He shifted the focus of supernatural dread from man and his little world and gods, to the stars and the black and unplumbed gulfs of intergalactic space... When he completed the body of his writings, he had firmly attached the emotion of spectral dread to such concepts as outer space, the rim of the cosmos, alien beings, unsuspected dimensions, and the conceivable universes lying outside our own space-time continuum.[2]

On the surface, much of Lovecraft's fiction deals with the breaking-in of the supernatural, or Other, into the lives and ordinary worlds of identifiably ordinary people. But the stories may also be read as the experiences of people being forced to come to terms with their true place in the universe. Instead of being the 'privileged' victim of something special and unusual, essentially a subjective experience, a character's world-view is inverted to make him the passive and often accidental victim of objectivity. He encounters the cosmos

Outside, and the natural transactions of some of its inhabitants, who happen to be far more powerful than humanity.

Lovecraft found no meaning, or possible meaning, in the universe around him: 'My objectivity, always marked, is now paramount and unopposed... I can at last concede willingly that the wishes, hopes, and values of humanity are matters of total indifference to the blind cosmic mechanism.'[3]

Such meaning as was perceived was imposed – a product of human traditions and imagination. As noted above, according to Leiber, Lovecraft was a Copernicus of literature. Like the medieval astronomer who removed the Earth from the centre of the Solar System and put the Sun there, Lovecraft inverted the traditional human-centred universe of horror fiction. Instead, he con-fronted a puny humanity with its rightful place in the cosmos: the reality that people are of no special importance or position. They are marginal, and if they get in the way of the designs of larger entities, then they suffer the consequences, for no other reason. The universe is indifferent, not hostile. Hostility is an anthropomorphic meaning imposed on it.

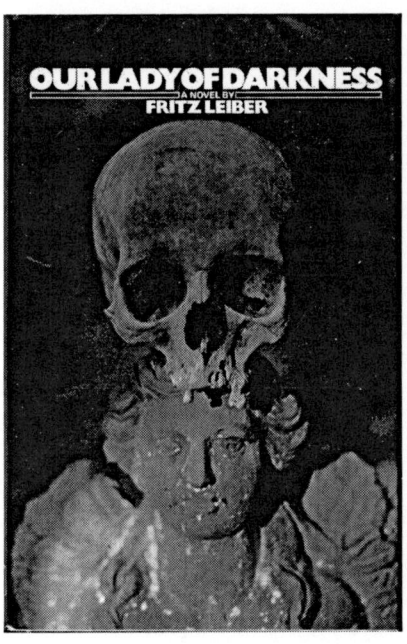

***

Lovecraft's fiction can thus work as a set of 'meditations' on humanity's wider and unrealised status. *Our Lady of Darkness* can be discussed on this level as well. Franz Westen comes slowly to realise that something lies under his apparently quiet world. While visiting Corona Heights, a hill visible from his home in San Francisco, he experiences this shift or inversion of his world: 'Corona Heights had lost its magic for him, he just wanted to get off it as soon as possible... Really, he couldn't get home too soon.'[4]

Our Lady of Darkness bears other kinships with Lovecraft's works. Leiber put himself and his situation, and his heritage from past experiences, into his work, as Lovecraft did. The parallels between Leiber and Westen are numerous. Like one of Lovecraft's New England scholars and antiquarians, Westen embodies Leiber's own interests and reactions to his world. Leiber testified that Lovecraft was 'the chiefest influence on my literary development after Shakespeare'[5] although this influence was not stylistic (unlike so many other Lovecraftian writers).[6] Rather, it was Lovecraft's attitudes to weird fiction which were important to Leiber:

> My reason for writing stories is to give myself the satisfaction of visualising more clearly and detailedly and stably the vague, elusive, fragmentary impressions of wonder, beauty, and adventurous expectancy which are conveyed to me by certain sights... These stories frequently emphasise the element of horror because fear is our deepest and strongest emotion, and the one which best lends itself to the creation of Nature-defying illusions. Horror and the unknown or the strange are always closely connected...[7]

These views are discernible in much of Leiber's work, and particularly his later fiction including *Our Lady of Darkness*. Both authors focus on the weird phenomenon, the unknown and strange, and the dislocations that are caused by it. In *Our Lady of Darkness*, this takes the form of a 'paramental' entity. It is always somehow there, always lurking and threatening, like a spider at the centre of its urban web. Both writers are concerned with the effects of the interaction between the weird phenomenon and human characters, but the characters are usually put in second place to the phenomenon itself. The human beings have to have their existence justified by their experiences of and reactions to it.

Both authors made use of modern, contemporary settings. Lovecraft used his native city of Providence, as well as wider New England and New York settings (and in 'At the Mountains of Madness' he achieved a fine sense of place with Antarctica). Leiber used Chicago, New York, San Francisco and the West Coast. They each refer to places where they have lived, and streets and buildings that they knew, giving their stories a sense of place and immediacy of action.

Leiber and Lovecraft often made their own interests those of their characters. Particularly relevant here was their mutual interest in astronomy. Astronomical and cosmic references reinforce the smallness of their characters' lives under the vast sky of stars, and the exhilarating fear that is the result.

***

Our Lady of Darkness is permeated with literary references, including many connected with Lovecraft and his work. Corona Heights forms one of the main settings of the novel. It is a 'high place', where the entity first begins to filter into Westen's world:

> The solitary, steep hill called Corona Heights was black as pitch and very silent, like the heart of the unknown. It looked steadily downwards and north-east away at the nervous, bright lights of downtown San Francisco as if it were a great predatory beast of

night surveying its territory in patient search of prey... Yet the impression lingered that the hill had grown restless, having at last decided on its victim.[8]

Similar 'rock crowned hills' play parallel roles in Lovecraft's stories 'The Dunwich Horror', 'The Whisperer in Darkness' and 'At the Mountains of Madness'.[9] Westen brings these stories to mind as he considers Corona Heights.[10]

On glimpsing the TV tower on Mount Sutro, Westen recalls a line from Lovecraft's 'The Haunter of the Dark':

...the watcher of another ill-omened hill (Federal in Providence) sees 'the red Industrial Trust beacon had blazed up to make the night grotesque'. [9] When he'd first seen the tower he'd thought it worse than grotesque, but now – how strange! – it had become almost as reassuring to him as starry Orion.[11]

Lovecraft's Arkham House collection *The Outsider and Others* (published posthumously in 1939) forms a part of Westen's 'Scholar's Mistress' – a vaguely woman-shaped accretion of books and magazines on his bed.[12]

Many of Lovecraft's stories involve Abdul Alhazred's *Necronomicon*, a fictional volume of source texts of which Lovecraft and his imitators made much use. He evolved a consistent history of the *Necronomicon*, and the book almost became a character in its own right. In *Our Lady of Darkness*, Leiber invented the much more recent book *Megapolisomancy*, by Thibaut de Castries. De Castries hurls invective against modern (turn of the 20th century) cities in a way very similar to Lovecraft at his most negative, as in his story 'He':

At any particular time of history there have always been one or two cities of the monstrous sort ... but we live in the Metropolitan (or Necropolitan) Age, when such disastrous blights are manifold and threaten to conjoin and enshroud the world... Since we modern city-men already dwell in tombs, inured after a fashion to mortality, the possibility arises of the indefinite prolongation of this life-in-death...[13]

It becomes clear that de Castries' book is to play an active part in *Our Lady of Darkness*, as Alhazred's does in Lovecraft's work. The book is a source, and gives clues to what is really going on. De Castries has also hidden a curse, an invocation of the power of the modem 'necropolitan' city. Lovecraft occasionally uses the language and imagery of curse and invocation to summon and banish the godlike entities that threaten his fictional world. The bringing of apparently dead and hidden things to life, to disturb their contemporary worlds, is a theme which runs through both Lovecraft's and Leiber's work. In *Our Lady of Darkness* the hidden curse adds to the suspense and expectation of Westen's eventual meeting with the paramental entity itself.

The curse is written out and hidden in the fictional journal of the real writer – and close friend of Lovecraft – Clark Ashton Smith (1893-1961). This came into Westen's possession at the same time he had bought his copy of *Megapolisomancy*. Leiber has the journal make reference to Lovecraft; another touch of realism, since Smith was a correspondent of Lovecraft's: 'I should write Howard about it, he'd be astounded and – yes! – transfigured, it so agrees with and illuminates the decadent and putrescent horror he finds in New York City and Boston and even Providence...'[14]

Westen also notices the similarity in name between de Castries and Lovecraft's real revision client Adolphe de Castro.[15] When Westen consults his friend Jaime Donaldus Byers, Byers mentions Lovecraft's prose-poem

'Nyarlathotep', and goes on to tell him that de Castries and de Castro could not have been the same person.[16]

Much later in *Our Lady of Darkness*, as the novel nears its climax, the significance of *The Outsider and Others* being part of the Scholar's Mistress becomes apparent. It is open at the story 'The Thing on the Doorstep', which was a departure for Lovecraft in that it has a strong female lead character, Asenath Waite. Her body dies in a particularly repulsive way. In a reverie Westen begins to think about death, and moves on to consider Lovecraft's 'The Colour Out of Space', in which a New England family succumbs to a wasting illness due to the cosmic 'pollution' of their water supply. (Leiber recalled how much this story depressed him when he first read it in *Amazing Stories*.)[17] Westen seems to be falling under a malign spell of listlessness – his will to act to save himself sapped away, in the same way that Asenath Waite grew to dominate her husband's will.[18] Westen tries to hear the music that his friend Cal would be playing at the concert he was due to be attending. Music has the power to save and deliver from chaos, but silence is all that Westen can experience: 'A small sob formed and faded in his throat. He snuggled close to his Scholar's Mistress, his fingers touching her Lovecraftian shoulder. He thought of how she was the only real person that he had. Darkness and sleep closed on him without a sound.'[19]

Westen has been gazing at the portrait of Daisy, and she begins to resemble the entity that has en stalking him throughout the story. He hears a scuffing sound in the wall (like that in Lovecraft's 'The Rats in the Walls'). Eventually he dreams Daisy is alive again, but that cannot possibly be right. All the horrors of cancer and runaway bodily growths (as in 'The Colour Out of Space') burst out briefly in a nightmarish scene in which it becomes clear that Daisy's life is the false life of growing malignant tumours.[20] Westen wakes up, and de Castries' curse is activated, as the entity confronts Westen face to face at last.

A Lovecraftian story might end at that point, with a scribbled manuscript, handwriting scrawled until the very last possible moment by the doomed protagonist. In contrast, *Our Lady of Darkness* ends happily and gently, after the destruction of the entity by a counter-invasion against the forces of chaos and darkness. Or is all as it seems? The final words of the novel – 'Everything's very chancy' – sums it up, and Leiber's world-view within it, as well as Lovecraft's attitude in his work. The mystery and danger *are* still there, after all.

***

In many ways both Lovecraft and Leiber were 'outsiders'. Bruce Byfield makes the point that writers tend to be individualists, and somewhat in tension with the people and places around them.[21] Lovecraft and Leiber were heavily influenced by their families: Lovecraft had his mother, aunts, and wife, as well as the memory of a father he hardly knew, due to his premature death; Leiber had his parents, women relatives and friends, and in particular his wife. As he recounts in his autobiography, the numerous women in his life served him as anima figures.[22] Women played an ambiguous role in both writers' creative lives, and it is not too fanciful to see reflections of this in their writing. Lovecraft's work flourished after the break-up of his marriage, and return to Providence in 1926; his mother's death in 1921 had liberated him enough to allow the possibility of marriage in the first place.[23] Leiber's writing was interrupted by grief and the resurgence of his alcoholism after Jonquil's death in 1969; his greatest stories date from the 1970s. Women in all of his tales have an ambiguous role as both supporters and stiflers of individuality and creativity. Lovecraft and Leiber used their experiences of women in their work, whether reacting against them, or harnessing their influences. Or, as is more likely, a combination of the two.

***

Both writers often used the device of 'confirmation rather than revelation' in their fiction. The ending is stated, or strongly implied, at the outset, so it comes as no surprise; suspense mounts throughout, to arrive at the known conclusions.[24] Lovecraft utilised this technique in such stories as 'The Whisperer in Darkness' and 'The Thing on the Doorstep'. In *Our Lady of Darkness* the eruption of the entity comes as no real surprise at all. The reader is expecting it. But as the evidence and expectation mounts, so does the tension. It hardly flags throughout the length of the novel, although the shorter magazine version – 'The Pale Brown Thing' – may gain further in this respect. As with Lovecraft's late and greatest work from around 1928 onwards, increased length allows the author to plunge the reader into his world, in greater depth, hoping (against hope, perhaps) that what is to be confirmed may still yet not happen. But to no avail.

Lovecraft and Leiber were both 'literary Copernicuses', taking horror fiction beyond traditional notions of supernatural dread, and so effectively ensuring that the genre has a future. The field developed with them, and continues to do so after their deaths.

Lovecraft's work confirms that it is chaos that really rules in the universe, although most people are for most of the time mercifully ignorant of the fact. He left it at that. Lovecraft's fiction concerns those who find out this truth and have to live the rest of their lives with it, or who die because of the revelation. In *Our Lady of Darkness* it is only probable that chaos is dispelled by order. But it is still acknowledged at the very end, and may not be dead but only waiting, to be returned to activity again. *Our Lady of Darkness* is Lovecraftian on this level at least. People find themselves living on a knife-edge of illusory sanity in an everyday world of chance and cosmic indifference. Only reacting in the right way to this information, plus luck, can enable them to survive. The two writers use the products of their lives and experiences in order to communicate this. H P Lovecraft would have approved of *Our Lady of Darkness*, and would have agreed that his early estimate of Leiber's talents in 1937. Lovecraft's comment that '[Leiber's]...tales and poems, while not without marks of the beginner, shew infinite insight and promise...'[25] has been borne out.

Our Lady of Darkness can be called a Lovecraftian novel – but it is still all the more a Leiberian one.

Notes
The title of this article comes from Leiber's essay 'A Literary Copernicus' (1944) in S.T. Joshi, *H P Lovecraft: Four Decades of Criticism* (Ohio University Press 1980). Page references for *Our Lady of Darkness* are to the UK Millington/Fontana editions.

1.   *Foundation* 14 (September 1978) p.64
2.   'A Literary Copernicus' (1944) in S.T. Joshi, *H P Lovecraft: Four Decades of Criticism* (Ohio University Press 1980) pp.50-51
3.   'A Confession of Unfaith' (1922) in H.P. Lovecraft, *Miscellaneous Writings* (Arkham House 1995) p.537
4.   *Our Lady of Darkness* p.38
5.   Quoted in Bruce Byfield, *Witches of the Mind: A Critical*

Study of Fritz Leiber (Necronomicon Press 1991) p.11

6.   In 1976 Leiber published an excellent Lovecraft pastiche 'The Terror from the Depths' (first collected in *Heroes and Horrors* (Whispers Press 1978) utilising characters from Lovecraft's work in a Leiberian California setting.

7.   'Notes on Writing Weird Fiction' (1932/33) in *Miscellaneous Writings* p.113

8.   *Our Lady of Darkness* pp.7-8

9.   For example 'The Dunwich Horror' (p.161) and 'The Whisperer in Darkness' (p.245) in *The Dunwich Horror and Others* (Arkham House 1985), and 'At the Mountains of Madness' (pp.103-104) in *At the Mountains of Madness* (Arkham House 1985)

10. *Our Lady of Darkness* p.87

11. 'The Haunter of the Dark' (p.95) in *The Dunwich Horror*

12. *Our Lady of Darkness* p.68

13. *Our Lady of Darkness* p.69;'He' (p.266) in *Dagon and Other Macabre Tales* (Arkham House 1986)

14. *Our Lady of Darkness* p.71

15. *Our Lady of Darkness* p.72

16. *Our Lady of Darkness* pp.104-105

17. Byfield, p.11

18. 'The Thing on the Doorstep' (pp.288ff) in *The Dunwich Horror*

19. *Our Lady of Darkness* p.176

20. Lovecraft himself died of cancer on 15 March 1937.

21. Byfield p.8

22. 'Not Much Disorder and Not So Early Sex' in *The Ghost Light* (Berkley 1984)

23. See L. Sprague de Camp, *Lovecraft: A Biography* (1975), especially chapter 10

24. 'A Literary Copernicus' p.56 – Leiber has always attributed the phrase to fellow writer Henry Kuttner (1914-58)

25. H.P. Lovecraft, *Selected Letters V* (Arkham House 1976) pp.432-433

After the Great Destruction:
Günter Eich's Radio Play *Träume* (*Dreams*)

The writer who doesn't want to distract, but be effective, must summon up the courage to also write against the reader.

Günter Eich: 'Sleeping Powder or Explosive?'

Poets who frighten no-one are worth nothing at all, only merely chattering about.

Günter Eich: *The Surf at Setúbal*

1 Backgrounds and Contexts

As it enters its second century, the medium of radio is generally considered to be a respectable one. Radio productions do not, as a rule, give rise to the sort of controversies that productions on television and in film can. However, this has not always been the case. Nearly sixty years ago radio was the medium for a highly original and remarkable work, one that generated considerable controversy at the time. This was the radio play *Träume* (*Dreams*) by the German poet and playwright Günter Eich, first broadcast in 1951. A deeply unsettling and enigmatic play, *Träume* makes use of many fantastic and bizarre elements, from the gruesome to the darkly comic. And throughout, the play is touched with the fleeting and vivid realities and intensities of dream.

Günter Eich was born on 1 February 1907 in the small Prussian town of Lebus an der Oder. He attended the Frederick William University (now the Humboldt University) in Berlin where he studied Chinese language and literature.

Eich transferred to Leipzig University in 1927, where he
studied economics in addition to his other subjects. During
1929-30 he attended the Sorbonne in Paris where he continued
with his Far Eastern studies. Another two years of economics
followed, but Eich never completed his courses. Instead, he
decided to become a full-time freelance writer.

During his time in Berlin Eich had started to write poetry
and other short pieces. He contributed to *Anthologie jüngster
Lyrik* (*Anthology of Recent Lyric Poetry*) edited by Willi Fehse
and Klaus Mann and published in 1927. In 1929 he wrote a
radio play in collaboration with Martin Raschke. A collection
of poetry, *Gedichte* (*Poems*) appeared in 1930. For the next
decade Eich wrote poems, short stories and other prose pieces,
and worked on material for Berlin Radio.

When Adolf Hitler and his National Socialists came to
power in 1933, Eich sought to keep his distance from their
pervasive and arid cultural policies. Although the number of
suitable outlets for his work diminished, Eich was able to
survive as an active writer. It is therefore quite likely that he
must have made some sort of compromise, if only outwardly,
with the new regime. Like the vast majority of men of his
generation, Eich served in the armed forces during the Second
World War. He served for at least a part of the war in the
Luftwaffe in a ground-based capacity, and attained Non-
Commissioned Officer rank. Subsequently he always refused
to discuss his experiences. In 1945 he was captured by
American forces near Remagen, and whilst being held in a
camp for prisoners of war resumed writing poetry. After his
release in 1946, he settled in Geisenhausen, Bavaria.

At the time of Eich's birth, Lebus an der Oder was well
within the heartland of eastern Germany, in the ancient
province of Brandenburg. During the closing months of the

Second World War, the Soviet advance into Germany itself was marked by the flight westwards of millions of refugees who had lost their homes and most of what they possessed. Many thousands lost their lives. In 1945 Lebus an der Oder became a border town, located squarely on the new frontier with Poland formed by the Rivers Oder and Western Neisse. Although Eich himself was not directly affected by the changes, it is not hard to believe that the themes of dislocation, loss, and destruction that appear in *Träume* had at least a part of their origin in those catastrophic events. The complete and permanent reversal of the long-established expansionist concept of the 'Push to the East' (*Drang nach Osten*) resonated for many years in German politics, literature, and film, as it still does to a lesser extent today.

After 1945 Germany was again home to a lively literary culture. Eich became involved with the new literary magazine *Der Ruf* (*The Call*) in Munich. Shortly after it was formed he joined the group of writers who called themselves *Gruppe 47* (Group 47). In 1950 he won their Prize for his radio play *Geh nicht nach El Kuwehd!* (*Don't Go to Al-Kuwaid!*). More prizes followed over the next twenty years or so: the Bavarian Academy of Fine Arts Prize for Literature (1952), the Prize of the War Blind for Radio Drama (1952), the Georg Büchner Prize (1958), the Friedrich Schiller Memorial Prize (1968), and others.

Eich's work was rooted firmly in the chaotic conditions of the immediate post-war period and the 'Economic Miracle' (*Wirtschaftswunder*) years of the 1950s, and tried to articulate the concerns and experiences of a generation. The generation to which Eich belonged had seen the end of empire and the gradual erosion and final destruction from within of the fragile Weimar Republic whose democracy had succeeded it. In consequence all political ideologies had become discredited. Although it was the National Socialists who had actually executed the Republic's death warrant, the Communists had equally proclaimed their contempt for it, and their desire to overthrow it. Most other parties and institutions had been unwilling to stop them, at least until it was too late. Eich's generation had seen the resulting Second World War and the subsequent defeat of Germany, together with its ambiguous resurrection as two very different states as part of one nation.

Eich intended his writing to be one of the 'spanners in the works' that a society needed in order for it to confront genuine reality. The society he knew had allowed democracy to wither away and had been complicit in unholy alliances and unbelievable atrocities. By the early 1950s it was becoming prosperous again and increasingly self-satisfied. It needed to be reminded of the true reality which included all the uncomfortable and half-forgotten truths, all of the compromises and misuses of power, all of the horrors that had unfolded and flowered so hideously only a few years before.

Eich published several more collections of poetry, and a total of approximately thirty radio plays. He developed his theories of how literature and the writer interrelate with all aspects of the world, and how they understand each other. Günter Eich died in Salzburg, Austria, on 20 December 1972.

2 The Radio Play

The radio play is a work of art in its own right, and is extremely well-suited to adaptations of fantastic fiction, or for original work of a fantastic or speculative cast. A radio play is more than a work of literature. Unlike a film or work of graphic art, a radio play can truly allow the imagination its full rein. Writer and listener, together with those who actually produce the play and enable the author's concepts to be realised in sound, are effectively able to collaborate and thus co-create a work that can make a unique impact each time it is broadcast.

Reading the text of a radio play is never quite as effective as listening to it, at least in its immediacy, although the economy that the medium demands can mean that a radio play's text has the concentrated force of shorter-length fiction – the medium that fantastic fiction has always excelled at, and to which it is best suited. Eich constantly used such themes as sleep, death, and the unclear dividing line between reality and unreality, or different realities. These, enhanced by the accompanying effects as an integral part of the experience, are perfect subjects for presentation in a radio play. A sound, an effect, can paint a thousand words, and launch a thousand thoughts.

3 The Dreams That Are More Than Dreams

Träume (*Dreams*) is one of Günter Eich's best known radio plays. Although it is presented as a single play, and works as one, *Träume* is actually a set of five short self-contained plays for a small but varying number of voices. Each play is the dream of the person introduced in the brief prose foreword that accompanies each dream. The dreams are linked by connecting passages in verse form, printed in italics in the text, with opening and closing sections that amount to a prologue and epilogue. Two different narrative voices each speak the forewords and the connecting passages.

The dreams are dreamt by different characters in a wide variety of everyday settings and situations. Each takes place on a different continent. Whilst the dreams do have a basis in reality – the locations and the people in them – the dreams are not true in any literal sense. As in the case of real dreams, this isn't to say that the sort of events in them have not happened or could not happen. Eich's dream plays, like any dreams, shift randomly between reality and unreality. They mix the absurd, bizarre, humorous, and terrifying, from wherever they come. No doubt this often includes experiences, philosophies, desires, and fears: everything that can spring from the conscious and subconscious mind of the dreamer.

There are no explicitly stated connections between what the listener is told about the dreamers in the forewords and what they dream. Nevertheless a range of connections can be implied. In the same way, the exact dates given for the dreams bear no clear-cut significance. However, various national and international events and concerns occurring at approximately the same times are undoubtedly relevant. These include such issues as the consequences of the nuclear destruction of Hiroshima and Nagasaki, the developing Cold War, and the effects of developing and testing atom and hydrogen bombs.

I intend this to be a basic commentary on *Träume*, working through the play and summarising and examining each of the five dreams, as well as the verse linking passages. I will also consider the changes that Günter Eich made to *Träume* after its first performance, and some of the reasons why he might have made them. This will include the short-lived 'Sixth Dream'. All passages and other texts quoted have been translated by me. The text of *Träume* I have used is that reproduced in the study edition edited by Klaus Klöckner (Berlin: Cornelsen Verlag, 2nd edition 2007). This also contains Eich's revisions and the text of the deleted 'Sixth Dream', as well as much other background material, including listeners' reactions.

[Opening Passage and the First Dream]
There is an immediate sense of foreboding as the play begins:

> *I envy all those who can forget,*
> *who lay themselves down to soothing sleep and have no dreams.*

The narrative voice goes on to say that he is convinced that not even sleep, let alone the sleep of someone with a clean conscience, is any good when put against the reality of the world:

> *There is no more pure happiness (– was there ever? –),*
> *and I'd like to be able to wake up one or another sleeper*
> *and say to him that's as it should be.*

> *See what there is: imprisonment and torture,*
> *blindness and paralysis, death in many forms,*
> *the bodiless pain and fear that life means.*

The terrors of the world should be inescapable even through sleep:

> *Everything that happens concerns you.*

First Dream
During the night of 1-2 August 1948 the master locksmith Wilhelm Schulz from Rügenwalde in Eastern Pomerania, now of Gütersloh in Westphalia, had a not particularly pleasant dream. In this respect one doesn't have to take it too seriously, as it was traceable to the since-deceased Schulz's stomach trouble. Bad dreams come from the stomach which is either too full or too empty.

In an undefined country, but probably in Europe, a train is

travelling slowly across the landscape. A family, consisting of an old man and woman, their adult grandson, his wife and two children, are inside a closed goods wagon. The grandfather is reminiscing, not for the first time, about how they came to be in their situation. They were forced to leave their home by four identically-dressed men with inscrutable (*undurchdringlich*) faces. They don't know how long they have been on the move, but the children have no idea at all about many of the commonplace objects that the grandparents talk about. When a shaft of light enters through a hole in the wall, they have the chance to finally catch a glimpse of the world outside the wagon. What the grandson sees is incomprehensible and terrifying. He doesn't have the words to accurately describe what he can see. The old man looks, and sees the sort of landscape that he had been reminiscing about. Then he sees that things are 'different' (*etwas ist anders*). Soon after they decide to block the hole, preferring the unreality of what they know to the new reality of what they cannot yet understand. Meanwhile, they realise that the train is now accelerating. It continues to go faster.

There are echoes of the recent mass deportations perpetrated by the Nazis and their allies, as well as those that took place on Stalin's orders. The dreamer Wilhelm Schulz was probably a refugee himself: Eastern Pomerania (*Hinterpommern*) was placed under Polish administration in 1945, and has remained part of Poland ever since. (This and the other territorial losses suffered at the time were accepted; even so, the status of the eastern frontier had to wait for a definitive resolution until 1990 when a treaty was signed between Poland and the newly reunited Germany.)

Schulz was a locksmith, and the people in his dream are locked into their world of the railway wagon. Schulz has died

– presumably so have the people in his dream.

[Passage Between the First and Second Dreams]
The narrative voice tells the listener to think about mankind being its own enemy (*der Mensch des Menschen Feind ist*) who ponders on destruction. The narrative voice orders the listener to 'think about it' (*denke daran*) several more times in a variety of places and situations, such as while tasting wine in Randersacker, picking oranges in Alicante, or working on an assembly line in Detroit. The listener is to think about it even when lying in the embrace of his wife and when his children are laughing. A time will come when everyone will try to evade responsibility for the terrible things happening in the world:

> *Think about it, that after the great destructions [die Zerstörungen] everyone will prove that he was innocent.*

But nevertheless everyone is involved, and shares the blame.

Second Dream
On 5 November 1949 in Tientsin the fifty year-old daughter of the rice merchant Li Wen-Tschu dreamt a dream, which without doubt could throw a bad light on the old girl. Yet her parents and siblings are reassured that she is a good-natured and benign person. Presumably the pleasant dreams of this world will be dreamt by the villains.

In China, a man and a woman take their little son to a strange house, in answer to an advert. They hesitate outside, making him presentable, as if visiting an old relative they wished to impress. Once inside, they negotiate to sell the child to the old couple who had placed the advert. Pretending that they will shortly return for him, the parents pocket a cheque and leave their son behind. The boy is calmed by being told that there is a model railway for him to play with in the kitchen. But he is to be murdered, so that the old man can drink the boy's blood and prolong his own life.

The dream seems to be a particularly nasty one for someone from such a respectable and fortunate background. Even so, the position of a rice merchant and his family in the new People's Republic of China of 1949 may well have been precarious. Rice was a staple food, a necessity for life, and people would do desperate things in order to obtain it and survive. The powerful had a better chance than the weak. It is as if the system needed to feed off its weakest and most helpless members in order to ensure its own survival and continuation of power.

The Second Dream is the most concrete and believable one in *Träume*. It is also highly distressing. Although the child is lied to by his parents and other adults, he continues to trust them. His parents betray him and are effectively his murderers. Perhaps this is why this dream in particular generated so much controversy. It goes against everything that a society which considers itself civilised stands for – but all too often can allow to happen.

[Passage Between the Second and Third Dreams]
The narrative voice tells the listener that even at the X Hour (*Stunde X*) – the time when an awaited and feared event finally occurs – he will still remember that the earth was beautiful. He will think about such things as friends, kindness (*die Güte*), and love. He will remember a variety of people, places, and occurrences from his childhood, all of which were pleasant.

Third Dream

As is known, there can be many different kinds of X Hour. On 27 April 1950 the car mechanic Lewis Stone, in Freetown, Queensland, Australia, had a dream of one. It may be reassuring to mention that Stone himself at present delights in the best of health and has long forgotten his dream.

In Australia, the members of a family – a father and mother, their young children Bob and Elsie – are enjoying a happy evening together when their neighbour comes round and tells them that 'the enemy' (*der Feind*) is coming. The family cowers in their darkened house as a hulking form (*ein unförmiges Wesen*) approaches. When there are heavy knocks on the door, they make their escape, taking nothing with them. In the town nobody will give them refuge, and nobody wants to know them anymore. The mayor tells them that they no longer have a home in the town and that they are thieves, because Elsie was able to keep hold of her beloved doll. The family reach the outskirts of the town. They have left their erstwhile neighbours' fear (*die Angst*) behind them. But they have nothing, except their children, and nowhere to go.

The secure setting of small-town Australia seems an odd place for a dreamer to have such a vivid and yet ambiguous nightmare. It contrasts with Stone's day-job as a car mechanic, which is about as down to earth and mundane as it's possible to get. Perhaps Stone's dream was influenced by recent events in Europe, and altered to his own Australian setting. Even so, he forgets it, further strengthening the sense of not being involved. Eich is hinting ironically that robust good health, security, and the ability to forget uncomfortable dreams can breed complacency.

As with the First Dream, there are echoes of the forced deportations of people from their homes, in particular of Jews in Germany, France, and elsewhere who had been completely assimilated and otherwise indistinguishable from their neighbours and friends. At the X Hour, the moment of truth when events reach their climax, the family is able to realise what it has in order to stay together and survive in a suddenly totally uncertain world. The family's 'enemy' is vague but menacing and apparently inescapable. It could be symbolising everything in the modern world that disrupts family life and breaks the ties that hold together families, and so communities, countries, and the human race.

[Passage Between the Third and Fourth Dreams]
The narrative voice tells the listener that it is easy to find your way around: there are signposts on roads and rivers can be easily identified. Maps show seas in blue and forests in green. But the narrative voice also says that in contrast, the landscape of his companion's heart is what is hidden to him (*wie verborgen / ist mir die Landschaft deines Herzens!*) The secrets of the mind are not to be explored (*durchwandre*). The narrative voice reflects that every century gives us new things to hide, and is a new territory (*das Gelände*) that is overgrown from love's prying eyes by isolation like thick foliage.

Fourth Dream
> On 29 December 1947 the cartographer Ivan Ivanovich Boleslavski lay ill in his apartment in Moscow. He had feverish influenza and slept for two days with short interruptions. He dreamt a lot, mostly of countries that he had never seen. It is of course still possible that during the remaining years of his life he will get to see them.

In the uncharted African jungle (*der Urwald*) two explorers, Vassily and Anton, have just been given a superb meal by their native cook. Suddenly distant drumming starts, and Vassily realises that he no longer knows why they are in the jungle. Anton scoffs at this, and starts to think of reasons for the expedition. Soon the explorers find that all their porters, luggage, and equipment have disappeared. Only their cook remains, but not for long. With the vanishing of their links with the outside world, the explorers find that the things they knew begin not to make sense. Words start to become meaningless. The only escape is sleep. As the sound of the drumming grows stronger again, their memories fade away.

A map maker would of necessity have access to information about all manner of distant and exotic places, unlike the majority of the population of the Soviet Union. Maps can be taken for granted, and not having them can mean not only getting lost, but forgetting the existence of the real world outside that they represent, and remaining trapped in narrow and inaccurate points of view.

The explorers, in eating a meal of vegetables and fungi produced by the jungle, become absorbed by it. The explorers' consequent loss of memory, purpose, and identity, and their connections with where they came from could be a comment on totalitarian regimes' readiness to write and rewrite history and to distort reality to suit their purposes as they see fit, notwithstanding what is real. People who collaborate in this are often artists, the explorers of the mind and explainers of the world. They eat the regime's food and are taken in by it, erasing the memory of what it was like before until nothing genuine remains.

Maps are supposed to show the world as it is: to impose a clarity and certainty on it, and enable people to get their bearings and find their way around. The explorers' maps are stolen, adding to their forgetting and losing their way, both physically and mentally. Many frontiers had been changing recently.

[Passage Between the Fourth and Fifth Dreams]
This is presented as prose, rather than the verse of all the other connecting passages. The listener is told that the ancient Greeks believed that as the Sun made its way across the heavens, its friction generated a continuous and never-changing sound (*einen Ton, der unaufhörlich und ewig gleichbleibend*) that the human ear cannot detect. The narrative voice goes on to ask how many such inaudible sounds are there around us. One day they will make themselves heard and our ears will fill with horror... (*Eines Tages werden sie zu vernehmen sein und unser Ohr mit Entsetzen erfüllen...*). We cannot always perceive the world as it really is, the world behind the scenes that has always continues on its amoral way and always will. The sounds are those of the mechanism of the world, its system, in operation.

Fifth Dream
...Mrs Lucy Harrison, Richmond Avenue, New York, heard them on 31 August 1950, in the afternoon when she was dozing off over the torn hem of a skirt she was repairing.

In New York City, Lucy's mother has come for a visit. Lucy lives with her husband Bill in a beautiful modern flat high in an apartment block on Staten Island. The mother complains of a strange noise, which Lucy explains away as being the lift. They switch on the radio, where the mother's favourite song 'Where is my rose of Waikiki' is being broadcast. Then they begin to listen to a lecture on termites, and how they destroy everything, gnawing away from the inside, until there is nothing left, and the structure collapses into dust. As a thunderstorm approaches, the weather becomes oppressive and the mother drowses on the sofa. The tension in the air increases. The strange noise is still there. Both women wait anxiously for Bill to return from work. He is late. When Bill arrives at last, he refuses to kiss Lucy, or even to let her touch him. Everyone has become hollow, dead. Things are coming to an end. The strange noise won't go away. The thunderstorm gets closer. Not even their love can save them.

The beautiful and prosperous setting of Lucy's apartment contrasts with the imagery and destructive power of the termite colony. Yet both are hive-like places, the home for millions of creatures all scurrying around. The human city in the dream soon becomes a nightmarish place. There is a destructive power at work there as well. The gnawing away of human values from within has become unstoppable. The urbane city has become the urban colony. Love hasn't been enough to keep the encroaching hollowness at bay. In contrast to the Third Dream, here the enemy destroys an entire world, none of whose institutions and traditions turned out to be strong enough to withstand it.

[Conclusion After the Fifth Dream]
The narrative voice gives the listener an unpleasant (but by now hardly surprising) message:

> *Wake up, for your dreams are bad!*
> *Stay awake, because the Hideous [das Entsetzliche] is coming*
>   *closer.*

> *That which long dwelt in distant places, where blood was shed, is*
>   *also coming*
> *to you, to you and your afternoon sleep,*
> *in which you are reluctantly troubled.*

But if it doesn't come today, it'll come tomorrow,
be certain of that!

The narrative voice says that if an untroubled sleep is a luxury, it is also an abdication of responsibility and a flight from reality. If the listener thinks that unpleasant present day happenings are not his concern, and that they can be sorted out later, then he is asleep and needs to be woken up for his own good. The listener is in danger of being imprisoned if he allows himself to sleep, and to take little or no notice of what is going on in the world:

> *'Ah, so you're already asleep? Have a good awakening, my*
> *friend!*
> *The fence-posts are set up and electricity is already running*
> *through the wires [die Umzäunungen].'*

> *No, don't sleep while the stewards [die Ordner] of the world get*
> *busy!*
> *Be suspicious of their power, which they pretend to acquire for*
> *you!*

At the end, the narrative voice gives the listener a little hope, a way of survival:

> *Watch out that your hearts are not empty, in case they are*
> *counted [gerechnet]*
> *with the gaping void [die Leere]!*
> *Do what's pointless [das Unnütze], sing the songs that no-one*
> *expects you to!*
> *Be uncomfortable: be sand, not the oil, in the machinery [das*
> *Getriebe] of the world!*

4 The Listeners' Nightmares

Träume was first broadcast by NWDR (North-West German Broadcasting) of Hamburg on 19 April 1951. It proved to be highly controversial from the start. The radio station received numerous telephone calls from listeners both during and after the broadcast. Many listeners also followed up with letters. The reactions were generally hostile both to *Träume* and its author:

> Tell me, what crap you served up again in the broadcast this evening! It makes you sick. You know, you can give up all radio plays. It's totally disgusting!

> That really borders on lunacy that does! In today's difficult time, where everything's a struggle, what you broadcast just makes one throw up. It's really revolting.

> Can't that man be locked up? It's all so hopeless. The times are such that people are nervous enough as it is. And such rubbish is provided! I can say to you that we will take the appropriate steps with the newspapers, so that such stuff will be censored. It is unbelievable, what you offer to the public!

> It really is the height of nerve, that in the evening such things should be put out on the radio. Tomorrow I will get in touch with the press and try to find out whether the broadcaster could not have been able to provide something else, to please one in the evening, when one sits by the radio after the burden and heat of the day. We certainly do not pay our last penny for that.

In the last listener's comments quoted, it is intriguing to note the use of the phrase 'burden and heat of the day'. This is a quotation from the Bible (Matthew 20:12). The phrase may have sounded as mannered in German as it would in English, but the listener probably said it for a reason, and expected it to be recognised. The full verse is: 'Saying, These last have wrought but one hour, and thou hast made them equal unto us, which have borne the burden and heat of the day' (translation in the King James Version). This is from the parable Jesus told, in which labourers were hired at different times of the day to work in a vineyard, thus working longer or shorter hours depending on when they were taken on. But when the vineyard's owner came to pay the workers at the end of the day, he gave them all the same wages, much to the annoyance of the people who had been hired first.

Martin Luther's 1545 translation of the Bible renders 'the burden and heat of the day' as *des Tages Last und Hitze* – exactly the same phrase the listener used. (Luther's translation is regarded as having played much the same part in the development of the German language as the King James Version of the Bible and Shakespeare did in the English language.) Perhaps it is not too fanciful to imagine the listener, livid with indignation, saying that those who have borne the great burden of living through the Third Reich and its aftermath deserve not to have to be haunted by the nightmare implications of *Träume*. And he used well-known Biblical phrase to express himself.

When the listeners' responses started to arrive, it must have seemed to the Eich that *Träume* had lived up to his most hopeful expectations. Günter Eich had proclaimed that he wanted to challenge the emerging post-war society in West Germany. This meant its institutions and its often dubious perceptions of its own recent past, and what seemed to be its willingness to sleepwalk into the future, wilfully forgetting what had happened and what was taking place in the contemporary world.

It wasn't only some of the first listeners on NWDR who found hearing *Träume* an uncomfortable experience. A few months later, *Träume* was considered by the League of the War Blind (*Bund des Kriegesblinden*) for its Radio Play Prize (*Hörspielpreis der Kriegesblinden*). The jury's rejection in July 1951 was stated in no uncertain terms:

> *Träume*, a radio play by Günter Eich, one so brilliant, disdains formal expression just as it spurns having any encouraging message. Fear, and how it shadows the people of today, is portrayed in harrowing visions – without Eich speaking a word of comfort or of a way out. This radio play thus went against the whole objective of the Radio Play Prize, and so did not find the necessary approval of the Prize's judges.

Possibly the criticism levelled at *Träume* by the League of the War Blind Radio Play Prize jury touched Eich particularly deeply. It was one thing to want to wake up and annoy the general population, but those who lost their sight because of the war could perhaps be considered to have already received their own rude awakening – and more so than many. Nevertheless, despite having lost out in 1951, Eich won the Prize in 1953 for *Die Andere und ich* (*The Other Woman and I*).

The many reactions to *Träume* showed without doubt that the play had the sort of effect that Eich had been striving for. He had achieved his own definition of what it was to be a worthwhile writer: someone that was worth more than merely 'chattering' about. Nevertheless, the controversy over *Träume* led Eich to consider the future of his play, and to make revisions that would have the effect of addressing the criticisms, but not at the cost of sacrificing the message. If anything, the message would be strengthened.

5 Transition and a Lost Dream

After its first broadcast, *Träume* did not merely fade away, out into the air. Although a radio play is primarily a listening experience – and a fleeting one in the sense that a word, a phrase, or a sound, vanishes the moment it is produced, broadcast, and heard – the experience may remain in the listener's mind afterwards. Remembering can also be a form of periodic recreation. Yet there would effectively be no evidence to show that a play has ever existed and been broadcast. Nevertheless, even if for no other reason, the strength of the reactions that *Träume* generated were enough to ensure that did not happen.

Apart from such minor alterations as the insertion or deletion of a word or line, Eich made three significant changes to the text of *Träume*. These were:

1. The deletion of the original opening and its replacement by a new one.
2. The deletion of the Second Dream and its replacement (in the same position in the play) by a new 'Sixth' Dream.
3. The deletion of the penultimate line of the closing section and its replacement by a new and expanded conclusion.

As is often the case with stage plays and film screenplays, the scripts of radio plays can eventually achieve publication. *Träume* was no exception, but transition from voice to print did not occur without any further changes being made. Eich chose not to reinstate the original opening of *Träume*, and the new ending also remained in place. However, the substitution of the new Sixth Dream proved to be temporary, and Eich duly restored the original Second Dream. The text of *Träume* was first published in *Vier Spiele* (*Four Plays*) in 1953, and the published version has always incorporated these modifications.

The most notable of Eich's revisions after the first broadcast of *Träume* had been the removal of one entire dream section and its replacement by a new one. Although its subsequent complete vanishing in turn from the standard text could be seen as being rather appropriate for a work based on the ambiguous reality of dreams, it is nevertheless a pity. The Sixth Dream stands as an uncanny and nightmarish episode in its own right, and is of the same high quality as the other dream plays that make up *Träume*. Therefore I will also take this opportunity to call attention to an unfairly 'lost' dream.

6 A Beginning About Endings

Instead of an introductory poem spoken by a single narrative voice, the opening as first broadcast consisted of two voices reflecting and speculating on recent and future events:

[Original opening before the First Dream]
1st SPEAKER: On 1 July 1949 in Dortmund a child was born with two heads and three arms. This caused the claim to be advanced that the increase in births of deformed people and animals could have been due to fallout from the atomic bombs dropped on Hiroshima and Nagasaki, and the atomic bomb tests at Bikini. Meanwhile, though, the registrar responsible had to decide the difficult question of whether one or two births were to be registered.

2nd SPEAKER: The atomic bomb test at Bikini took place on 1 July 1946. The explosion of the atomic bomb was carried out under water. At the beginning of the trials it was not known how much of a chain-reaction there could be. It will be the future task of science to ascertain, by experiment, under what circumstances any life on Earth would become impossible, and, with that, science rendered superfluous.

1st SPEAKER: The atom bomb compares to the hydrogen bomb as a catapult compares to a modern anti-aircraft gun. Therefore outlaw the atom bomb!

2nd SPEAKER: In the *Handbook for Staff Officers*, 1980 edition, there will be the following sentences: The spreading of germs over enemy territory is an obsolete measure in warfare. It is not an ineffective one, but cannot be seen as decisive.

There is a different sense of doom and foreboding from that of the revised opening. The voices express and reflect on one of the main concerns of the time. There is the testing of atomic bombs, the development of the hydrogen bomb, the possibility of a chain-reaction destroying the planet, and the effects of fallout from the tests leading to illness, deformity, and mutation. As well as being of major importance for Eich, these issues were of course the concerns of millions of people throughout the world. They also appeared, to a lesser or greater extent, as the themes of many works of literature and film being produced at the time. In particular, much science fiction dealt with these issues, sometimes to the point of seeming to be almost obsessed by them.

In the section connecting the first two dreams, the narrative voice tells the listener to consider (*denke daran*) that humanity is its own worst enemy, and is pondering on destruction. Korea and Bikini Atoll aren't located on a map, but in people's hearts. The Korean War began in June 1950 when the forces of Communist North Korea invaded the Western-backed (and undemocratic) South Korea. The testing of atom bombs at Bikini Atoll started in June 1946. The listener is again told to think about it:

Think about it:
Korea and Bikini lie nowhere at all on the map, but in your heart.
Think about it: you are to blame for all the horrors
that play themselves out far away from you—

7 New Dreams for Old

It was the Second Dream that listeners felt to be particularly reprehensible. As has been described, it was the most concrete and believable of the dreams in *Träume*, as well as being the most upsetting.

The new Sixth Dream was as bizarre and outlandish as any of the other dreams, and fitted in seamlessly with the overall existing design of *Träume*. However, the shock value as compared with the original Second Dream is not so obvious, and the situation is not handled in such a clearly personalized way. The Sixth Dream also contains a clear element of black humour, as is the case with most of *Träume* except for the original Second Dream, in which it is entirely absent. Death is kept at a greater distance, and its impact is muffled, despite the large number of deaths occurring in the dream. There are no screams to be heard: appropriately, only the results of the depersonalized process are heard, and even those are at one remove from the main characters, and so the listener.

Sixth Dream

On 3 November 1950 the tax officer Ahmed Bayar should have made a journey from Smyrna to the capital on official business. During the night before, he slept very badly. His dream proved this, as we portray in what follows. In reality the journey to Ankara passed without incident, and to the full satisfaction of the traveller and his superior.

Bayar and his wife have arrived unexpectedly at a hotel in the

small Turkish town of Balat, and have taken a room for the
night. Balat is on the site of the ancient city of Miletus, and
lies to the south of Izmir (also known as Smyrna). The Bayars
had been travelling by train to Ankara, the capital, and had
been asleep when their train stopped. Thinking they had
arrived in Ankara, they panicked and left the train in a hurry.
But the fast train is not scheduled ever to make a stop in
Balat...

In their hotel room the Bayars are bothered by music and
the noise of dancing and celebrating coming from the room
directly above them. They decide to complain, and to ring for
the chambermaid. When Bayar presses the button, they hear
the noise of something falling to the floor (*ein Geräusch, als
fiele etwas zu Boden*) in the room next to theirs. Bayar rings
again. They hear the same noise again. The chambermaid still
doesn't appear.

Leaving his wife in their room, Bayar goes upstairs to
complain in person about the noise. A gentleman (*der Herr*)
and lady (*die Dame*) let him into the room, and the noise stops
at the same time. The two call Bayar by name: they know who
he is, and tell him that they have been waiting for him. They
tell Bayar that the 'Committee' is also waiting for him. The
Committee's job is to ensure welfare (*die Wohlfahrt*). They
invite Bayar to sit down and have a drink, while his wife
remains asleep downstairs. Told to ring the bell to order
champagne, Bayar does so and hears the noise of something
falling again. The gentleman and lady, on behalf of the
Committee, offer Bayar a job: he will be paid one pound for
each time he presses the button. This is piecework – there will
be no basic fixed salary. Bayar is told to try it out, and presses
the button several times in quick succession. He hears the
noises as before.

Bayar asks what happens when he presses the button. The gentleman casually tells Bayar that the button operates a guillotine. Bayar says that it's certainly quite a joke to play on him: no-one would really want a job operating a guillotine. The gentleman responds that there is always someone willing to do it. Mr Bayar has been working as an executioner, for one pound a time. He says that he doesn't want the money any more. But the party's over, and tomorrow will be a hard day for Bayar. The gentleman bids good night to the new executioner (*Herr Scharfrichter*).

Officials and bureaucrats are always needed to administer the machinery that allows judicial or state-sanctioned executioners to operate. The machinery needs credulous people who are willing to do anything when they are told to do it, no matter how daft (at best) it sounds. The power of authority includes not having to tell the whole story when wanting to get people to carry out its designs. Of course, officials can be frightened of the powers of their superiors, and the consequences for not co-operating. Not everyone is a hero.

However, the Nuremberg trials of 1945-46 established the principle that such a response as 'I was just following orders' or 'I did not know' cannot be accepted as the whole story, and thus be an unchallengeable defence. The 'Committee' has echoes of all the Central Committees, Politburos, Grand Councils, and other cabals that are the powers dictators hide behind in order to run their repressive and totalitarian states. In this case although Mr Bayar's wife is asleep, she isn't uninvolved. She had been the first to suggest that her husband complains about the noise. As Eich has made clear in the passage connecting the first two dreams, everyone is really involved. He later reinforced this in the final line of the revised opening:

Everything that happened concerns you.

Work that pays a pound each time does not seem to be much of a wage. Life is not the only thing that is sold cheaply. Presumably there will be a constant supply of 'clients' for the new executioner...

8 An Ending About Beginnings

As described above, *Träume* originally concluded with a message whose measured tones left the listener in no doubt of its unpleasant but hardly surprising significance. The version as spoken in the first broadcast continued as follows:

'Oh pleasant sleep
on the pillow with the red flowers,
a Christmas gift from Anita, which she embroidered for three weeks,
oh, pleasant sleep,
after the juicy roast joint and tender vegetables.
While dozing off one thinks about last night's cinema newsreel:
Easter lambs, awakening nature, the opening of the casino in
*   Baden-Baden,*
Cambridge's victory over Oxford by two-and-a-half lengths, –
that suffices to occupy the brain.
Oh, this soft pillow filled with the choicest down!
On it one forgets the aggravations of the world, for example that
*   news story:*
The accused, an abortionist, said in her defence,
'The woman, mother of seven children, came to me with a
*   suckling baby,*
for which she had no nappies and which
was wrapped-up in newsprint.'
Now, these are the court's concerns, not ours.
One can do nothing about it, if one has a somewhat harder time of it
than the other,

And with the hydrogen bomb, that will also last some time.'

'Ah, you're already asleep? Have a good awakening, my friend!'

With this conclusion Eich intended the essential message of *Träume* to be that the listener should not take refuge in sleep, but wake up and face reality – unpleasant as that often was. The play's conclusion is totally uncompromising. Eich's revision removed the penultimate line referring specifically to the hydrogen bomb, thus also removing it as a framing device. (With the replacement of the opening there was no longer a frame any more.) He added to the epilogue the stirring ending already discussed, in which a way out (or way forward) was given to the listener. Günter Eich had listened to his critics and refined what he wanted to say.

9 Origins, Realities, and Meanings

Träume is permeated throughout by moods of anxiety and fear. These arise from the text, which when broadcast is enhanced by the appropriate music and sound effects. There is love and tenderness in the play, but they are sharply contrasted with the realities of the situations the characters find themselves in – and which they can scarcely expect to survive.

Günter Eich was determined to present a world with no illusions. As there are no pleasant dreams in the play, presumably the listener is not to regard any of the dreamers as being 'villains' (Second Dream) as they get on with their lives. The true villains are elsewhere, doing other much more dangerous things. The dreams are all bad: from the physically nightmarish (Second Dream) to a great science fictional destruction (Fifth Dream). The other dreams are at best odd and strange, mixing up concerns of a worldwide significance with highly personal and apparently trivial episodes. An example is the Third Dream with the 'enemy' being both a vague and amorphous threat (its journey from Sydney and approach to the house) and yet highly concrete (its actual arrival at the family's house and the effect that has). The daughter's doll is seemingly insignificant. But significance can lie in details. In the Fifth Dream there is the song on the radio, representing what is already known and cherished, which contrasts with the radio lecture on termites and how they can destroy everything they encounter. Eich doesn't give the listener the pleasant dreams of the villains and the 'stewards of the world': their dreams are pleasant because they are busy taking away our freedoms.

The overarching theme of *Träume* can be summarised as the necessity for removing illusions, that the consequences of rejecting a horrible reality are themselves more horrible. In each dream the participating characters are confronted with reality – a different and terrible one – which is not what they wanted or expected to be the case. Their only way of coping with the new reality is to accept it. That leads to more horror and dread, but at least it is not illusion. Any rejection of the new reality is illusion, and a good illusion is not preferable to a bad reality, no matter how terrible the revelation is for those who are confronted by it. Young children appear in the First, Second, and Third Dreams. The suffering of children is even more undeserved than that of any adults who suffer. Children don't have the chance to really accept or deny true reality. They simply have to go along with it, even more so than the adults, and often because of them. This is the true reality of the world that Eich doesn't flinch from depicting.

At the moment of Germany's final defeat, and immediately after, there was the feeling that the country, its people and remaining institutions, had reached its Zero Hour (*Stunde Null*, Eich's *Stunde X*). He was not alone in having the sense that the old world and society had been brought so low that it stood at nothing. Eich had seen everything that it had believed in, or was meaningful to it, either undermined and perverted, or destroyed and rendered illegitimate and complicit in the destruction of that world.

Despite feelings of disillusionment, of staring into an abyss, of always being confronted by a void, never far away, Günter Eich explored a greater reality, and attempted to access and put across its meaning. Using ordinary people and situations, he connected them with extraordinary dream-events which happened to recognizably ordinary people in order to make metaphysical responses to the situation in which he found himself and the world. There are hidden systems and structures. Nature speaks with inaudible voices that should be listened to: the world itself is language, an original and prototypical 'urtext' of things as they were originally intended to be. Eich considered himself to be their unwitting translator. *Träume* shows that these concerns existed from the beginning of Eich's resurrected career.

The genre of the radio play is an ideal vehicle for this mingling of realities and things known and unknown, heard and not heard. The use of voices, of characters and narrators, can focus on both the everyday reality as well as the overarching ones that the mundane actions are embedded in. Eich's gifts as a poet also allow his narrative voices to be very different to those speaking in dialogue or monologue. This hints at the interconnections and hidden structures, the system behind the world that the everyday characters, going about their business, may not perceive, occupied as they already are with their own reality.

In the conclusion to *Träume* as he finally left it, Eich created a memorable and inspirational image, and challenged the listener to do something for himself about the world as it is in reality, to be somehow the troublesome sand in its mechanisms, its system. This still leaves the listener under no illusions. For Eich that would be the worst situation that it would be possible to be in. At the end Eich shows a new beginning through self assertion and standing up against the system of the world, the gear-wheels that revolve and churn remorselessly even when there are people getting in their way. This displays Eich's preoccupation with attempting to bring meaning back into a society and world that had lost it. *Träume* is not a comfortable play, but it does show a way forward. Günter Eich's challenge to be truly awake is as relevant now as it ever was.

Against the Spirit:
A look at Hugh Walpole's
The Killer and the Slain

Death, and the passage of time, is the greatest leveller of literary reputations. The days when Hugh Walpole (1884-1941) was world-famous as a prolific and best-selling novelist are long over. For almost three decades he was one of the leading figures in British literary life. He commanded large advances and everything he wrote got published. His lecture tours in the United States were sell-outs. He received a knighthood in 1937. And yet this author of well over thirty novels, several collections of short stories and essays, and a diverse range of other books has fallen into almost complete obscurity. His main legacy today is rank after rank of green-bound volumes inhabiting the lowest shelves of second-hand bookshops.

Hugh Walpole was an immensely talented and fluent writer, who seldom ever rewrote a sentence, and whose work didn't particularly suffer because of it. His best-known and most popular works were the five completed novels (with a sixth still unfinished at the time of his death) of the Herries Chronicle – wide-screen historicals telling the story of a Cumberland family from the sixteenth century onwards. And there were the four novels in his series Scenes from Provincial Life, which were upmarket melodramas set in the cathedral city of Polchester, which could be described as Trollope with attitude.

Walpole's short stories have fared rather better than his

novels. Many of them are ghost stories or otherwise macabre tales. The best of them have appeared regularly in anthologies of classic short horror fiction. A large new collection, *Tarnhelm* (subtitled *The Best Supernatural Stories of Hugh Walpole*) was assembled and published in 2003.[1]

The rest of his other full-length fiction can generally, if very loosely, be categorised as either 'romantic' – long, flowing novels that deal with aspects of love, friendship, and relationships between suitable and unsuitable people – or 'macabre'. Although, of course, all of these categories are fluid: for example *The Inquisitor* (1935), one of the novels in the Scenes from Provincial Life series, also contains much romance and atmospheric menace.

In his lifetime Walpole described five of his novels as macabre, fantastic, or strange. These conveniently fall into three periods of Walpole's career. The two early-period novels were *Maradick at Forty* (1910) and *The Prelude to Adventure* (1912). Two were published in Walpole's mid-career: *Portrait of a Man with Red Hair* (1925) and *Above the Dark Circus* (1931). These first four were also collected in the omnibus volume *Four Fantastic Tales* (1932). From the later part of his career came *The Killer and the Slain* – which was actually the last novel that Hugh Walpole lived to complete, and which was published posthumously in 1942.

***

In his Preface to *Four Fantastic Tales*, Walpole reminisced about his own attitude to the fantastic in his work, and the circumstances that surrounded the four novels:

> This fantastic impulse gave, I remember, my friends and well-wishers a great deal of pain and has indeed continued to give them pain ever since. It is forever cropping up, for a man *is* what

he is, and the notion that artists could, if they wished, be something very different if they only gave their minds to it and listened to their critics, is altogether a false one.

I was, unfortunately for myself, writing at a time when Realism was the only critical colour for the novel, and so it has been ever since. Stories about the Devil *must* seem absurd to a generation that has known the Great War and the Economic War that followed it. Hard facts have been too real to be disregarded.

Nevertheless, I have been unable to keep fantasy out of my books. I am incurably romantic-minded – and now, at this stage, after publishing novels for twenty-five years, and there is nothing to be done about it.[2]

Walpole then moved on to place these novels in their literary context as he saw it. He listed several authors who influenced him and whose work he admired. These included E.T.A. Hoffmann and Nathaniel Hawthorne, both of whom had written much that could be described as fantastic or gothic. Walpole especially mentioned Henry James' 'most marvellous of ghost stories' *The Turn of the Screw*. The Preface continued:

All of these authors ... are concerned quite nakedly with the powers of Good and Evil. It is not just now the fashion to believe in Good and Evil; at any rate no one pays them the compliment of decorating them with capital letters... Hoffmann and Hawthorne are, I suppose, little read today and the *Scarlet Letter* is considered an absurd melodramatic emphasis on an everyday fact. It has been, indeed, an odd experience in writing these books to work *against* the spirit of the period. It has been the odder for me because I could, I always feel, be an honest and matter-of-fact realist if I wanted to... It is a matter of reconciling two opposite worlds, a feat possibly too difficult for me, but one well-worth attempting.[3]

Therefore it can be seen that common themes run through these five novels, despite the fact that over thirty years separates the first published from the last. The strange and unusual in people and the situations in which they find

themselves is juxtaposed with their usually ordinary surroundings and situations of other characters that they interact with. None of these novels could be described as supernatural, and yet there can often be the feeling that it is just around the corner, waiting to take over the story. Walpole's skilful use of gothic atmosphere and psychological tension heightens this aspect. And the sudden release of the tension, usually in an outburst of physical violence, is a feature that occurs, not only in the 'fantastic tales' but also, as for instance in *The Inquisitor*, where it takes on a communal life of its own.

Contemporary comments and reviews were often uneasy about this mixture of themes. Walpole was accused of 'having no idea of the difference of the respective functions of comedy and melodrama' whilst Henry James affectionately chided his young protégé for not being able to tackle and face the subjects that he had set himself in his work.[4] The later novels sometimes produced queasy reactions. *Portrait of a Man with Red Hair* was initially rejected by the editor who originally bought the story on the strength of its synopsis. He described the finished story as 'distinctly gruesome and unpleasant' and did not accept what he considered to be its sadism and 'queerness'.[5] However, Walpole himself was clearly happy – if he really had any choice as a creative artist – to make use of such a range of material, with all the reactions that resulted. And in any case, the books sold!

In this essay I intend to survey the final novel that Walpole wrote, and intentionally wrote 'against the spirit of the period'.

***

The Killer and the Slain had been planned as early as 1937. Hugh Walpole had the enviable ability to work mentally on his next novel, while actually writing down onto paper (he wrote in longhand) his current one. Therefore, when he came to actually write a book, he generally wrote fast and effortlessly, and if he had to spend time away from the current novel – when on a lecture tour, for instance – he was always able to pick up from where he had left off with no apparent problems.

By the time Walpole actually came to set pen to paper in 1940, Britain was at war with Nazi Germany. The world in which Walpole had come to maturity and fame as a novelist was under real attack, and threatened to its foundations. *The Killer and the Slain* was largely written in London, during the Blitz. Walpole confided: 'all these months of fear, uncertainty, and restlessness are behind it.'[6]

The Killer and the Slain was subtitled *A Strange Story*. Significantly, the novel was dedicated to Henry James, 'the great author of *The Turning* [sic] *of the Screw*'. Walpole had always venerated James, and James' influence in the literary world preceding the First World War had been of immense help to Walpole in his early career. It is entirely possible that, during a second world war, surrounded by death and destruction and in immediate danger himself, Walpole was reminded of his friend's death during the first (James had died in 1916). And although the novel was initially planned several years earlier, Walpole always wrote very much in the present, on a day-to-day basis. Perhaps he thought that it was all too possible that he might be killed at any time during the air-raids (or in the then still possible and feared German invasion), and so made a conscious decision to honour a vitally important past friendship.[7]

Walpole's novel does not have the incredible subtlety and probable multiple meanings that characterises *The Turn of the Screw*, but it shares much of the same atmosphere of psychological (and physical) terror, doom, and confusion that James' masterpiece evokes. As he admitted, Walpole put himself wholeheartedly into the novel, in more senses than one. Although *The Killer and the Slain* is a short novel (257 pages) when compared to most of his output, it is an intense and complex read, to say the least. And in those respects at least, Walpole certainly does come close to emulating the earlier work of his dedicatee.

John Talbot is a quiet and gentle man, a man who seems to be ineffective on almost every level, and in just about every aspect of his life, who commits a murder. This comes as no real surprise. The book is presented as a first-person narrative written-down and narrated by Talbot himself in order to establish his sanity and so justify himself.

On the very first page, then, Talbot tells the reader that he will confess to a crime. This is the technique of 'confirmation rather than revelation' that H.P. Lovecraft made use of so effectively.[8] Thus the reader sees Talbot gradually turning, morally and physically, in all ways, into the man he killed. Walpole wrote that the theme 'has obsessed me, as no idea for a book ever has before... It will undoubtedly write itself, and should be *my* best macabre and one of the best *if* it comes out right...'[9]

It was when he was ten years old, and at school, that Talbot first met James Tunstall, who he would murder all those years later. Tunstall appoints himself Talbot's protector, and constantly proclaims his liking for the other boy. Significantly, they shared the initials JOT. But Talbot is repelled:

> It wasn't as though I were frightened of him exactly, and yet I can see now that there was some sort of secret fear mixed in my feelings about him. Not so much fear, perhaps, as a consciousness of some bond between us. He felt that as well as I.[10]

Tunstall is everything that Talbot dislikes – but the more he tells Tunstall that, the more Tunstall tells him in return that Talbot in reality really does like him.

For the ten years after leaving school, they lose touch. Talbot becomes a very moderately successful novelist. He marries, and the marriage is happy enough, but from the beginning Talbot realises that his wife Eve doesn't quite love him, and won't quite give all of herself to him. And on the day that their son is born, Tunstall returns.

Now also married, and a successful artist, Tunstall's circumstances seem to mirror Talbot's – they are opposites. His former fascinated repulsion soon returns, but Tunstall isn't having any of it:

> 'It isn't as easy as that – not nearly as easy. I have you in my hand just as I had when we were at school. You say that you don't like me and never did. That may be. I'm the other side of yourself, Jacko, the side you're not very proud of. Stevenson wrote a story about that once. But this isn't Jekyll and Hyde. That

was just a story. This is *real*, Jacko – a real alliance. We're like Siamese twins and always were.'[11]

This is a nightmare: to meet someone who claims to know what you really are, and who you really are. Talbot had thought that Tunstall had gone out of his life for ever, but he was back. And it was even more of a bad dream for Talbot because he was aware that Tunstall really did seem to know him for what he really was.

Eve likes Tunstall, and can't understand her husband's loathing of him, even though he tries to explain its long history. Talbot meets and likes Leila, Tunstall's wife. So the two men's lives become more intertwined than ever. Talbot dislikes what he thinks of as Tunstall's flirting with Eve. Even Archie, their son, seems to prefer Tunstall's company to his father's. Many other things, which would be of minor importance in any other context, mount up. Eventually Talbot experiences a sort of revelation:

> It did not matter any more what he said or did, how he behaved. I was not jealous, nor angry. I was at peace with myself, as one is when at last one yields to a temptation against which one has long been struggling. Above all, I felt now a strong bond between himself and myself.[12]

Not long afterwards, and with a little planning, the opportunity presents itself. Talbot meets Tunstall in a secluded spot, and murders him. The crime that Talbot told us about right from the outset has taken place.

The bond between the two men continues, even though one is dead and his killer is still alive. Talbot starts to confuse aspects of his life with Tunstall's, and apparently even sometimes mentions things that only Tunstall could have known about. And Talbot's life undergoes change, as his habits alter dramatically and start to become more like those of his dead enemy.

So far, the story has been clearly told by John Talbot, as if he has been looking back, in a partly detached way, at the series of momentous and terrible happenings that he has been describing. This is Part I of the novel, and is told as a single continuous narrative (divided into chapters). Part II consists of three narratives, each one carrying on from the one before, but also with stylistic and other differences, that further show the changes that Talbot is undergoing.

For a start, there are physical changes:

There was a long old eighteenth-century mirror hanging on the right side of the window. In this I examined myself. Was I physically changed or no? I was stouter, heavier in the chest, the belly, the thighs. My face was fuller and rounder. There was nothing in that. I had always had a tendency to stoutness. Then as I looked in the mirror I had a crazy hallucination that another naked figure was behind mine, a figure of exactly my height, heavier and stouter, the features of the face coarser and bolder, the hair thicker. And as I looked they merged and became one figure.[13]

And there is the mental cost of his crime, as Talbot becomes convinced that his hallucination is that Tunstall possesses him: 'Occupying me body and soul'. Talbot starts to appear and act like the dead Tunstall.

Narrative two, although also written by Talbot, starts as if it were written by an entirely different man. The style is different. For example, Talbot is harsher and rougher in his language and views. His lifestyle has fully changed by now, and Talbot now actively pursues activities that he once despised and loathed in Tunstall. He comes to hate the sight of Richard, Tunstall's brother-in-law, who reminds him of the sort of man he used to be. Talbot declares that he is no longer afraid of Tunstall – just at the time when, perhaps he should be most afraid. Tunstall's widow notices the changes: 'You are moving, John, to some awful catastrophe. Those words aren't too strong. You are possessed as Jim was possessed. It is the same evil.'[14]

Finally, the opportunity comes, and roles do seem to reverse themselves. Talbot calls Richard by the nickname that Tunstall used to call him, and which he detested: 'Jacko'. Finding themselves near the local disreputable pub, the two men apparently and unwittingly begin to re-enact a pivotal encounter that Talbot once had with Tunstall. And after Richard leaves, not having allowed himself to react in the same way that Talbot had, Talbot casually confesses to one of Tunstall's seedy friends that he had killed him. Shortly afterwards, Tunstall's dog, Scandal, whom he had 'inherited' and had become deeply attached to, is run over and killed by someone driving a car just like Richard's. Talbot's attitude changes:

...a strange urge has been strengthening in me to take revenge on this filthy crowd of human beings who have insulted and derided and tried to murder me – who have killed the only friend I had.[15]

Narrative three is still more different in tone. Again it is written as if by a 'possessed' man, but one possessed by even more anger and potential violence. Pursuing Richard and his sister to London, Talbot's declared war begins to take shape. It will not be a 'phoney war' like the one currently under way. (The 'Phoney War' was, for the United Kingdom, that period of World War II between the invasion of Poland in September

1939 and the invasion and fall of France in the spring and summer of 1940.) Entering the dining-room of his boarding-house, Talbot thinks:

> I ate because I was hungry, but as I looked at them sitting around the table and mincing their words I thought how pleasant it would be to tie them to their chairs with green window-blind cord and shoot them, slowly, quietly, one after the other. You would gag them first with their soiled table-napkins... How delightful for the others to watch while their friends depart! [16]

Walpole is adept at depicting heightened mental states, whether of ecstasy, hatred, or any sort of mixture in between. *The Killer and the Slain* contains many odd moments of rather sadistic violence, whether real or dreamed. This is a characteristic of much of Walpole's work, and also appears in the two middle period macabre novels *Portrait of a Man with Red Hair* and *Above the Dark Circus*. The effect is as unsettling as the author no doubt intended.

Talbot goes on phantasmagorical journeys through the dark war-time London streets, searching for Richard. Talbot's identity waxes and wanes as he narrates his fights, mental and physical, with the outside world, and with who and what may or may not be now within him, possessing him. When the end finally comes, it is no surprise that it is the release of death, and an expected transformation does indeed take place. It is a sort of peace that Talbot has restored to him.

While Hugh Walpole was writing *The Killer and the Slain*, it was as if peace was eluding him, as much as he seemed to also be eluding it. His flat in Piccadilly was bombed, but he couldn't stay away from London. Walpole used the novel as an outlet for his nervous emotions: 'Meanwhile what a lot of nastiness, and pity for my own nastiness, I have in me! It's all coming out in this work.'[17]

The Killer and the Slain is in many ways the most personal and revealing book that Walpole ever wrote. He was able to channel much that he liked and disliked in himself, perhaps contrasting opposing elements within, and setting it all against a world facing destruction. In the novel a resolution of sorts is reached and a wholeness is restored.

It is fitting that *The Killer and the Slain* was the last book that Hugh Walpole lived to complete. Although he never saw it in print, it symbolised the ascendancy of that aspect of his life and literary career that went 'against the spirit' – by far the most interesting part, and the part by which he is best remembered today.

Notes

1.   Tartarus Press 2003, 363pp
2.   Hugh Walpole, *Four Fantastic Tales*, p.viii
3.   Hugh Walpole, *Four Fantastic Tales*, p.ix
4.   Rupert Hart-Davis, *Hugh Walpole*, p.77. Both comments were about *Maradick at Forty*.
5.   Rupert Hart-Davis, *Hugh Walpole*, p.239
6.   Rupert Hart-Davis, *Hugh Walpole*, p.438
7.   Rupert Hart-Davis, *Hugh Walpole*, p.433
8.   As in, for example, 'The Whisperer in Darkness'. Fritz Leiber used the phrase in his ground-breaking essay on Lovecraft 'A Literary Copernicus', and always attributed it to Henry Kuttner.
9.   Rupert Hart-Davis, *Hugh Walpole*, p.386
10.   Hugh Walpole, *The Killer and the Slain*, p.9 [Valancourt Books 2014]
11.   Hugh Walpole, *The Killer and the Slain*, p.29
12.   Hugh Walpole, *The Killer and the Slain*, p.52
13.   Hugh Walpole, *The Killer and the Slain*, p.112

14. Hugh Walpole, *The Killer and the Slain*, p.152
15. Hugh Walpole, *The Killer and the Slain*, p.159
16. Hugh Walpole, *The Killer and the Slain*, pp.161-162
17. Rupert Hart-Davis, *Hugh Walpole*, p.433

A Work of Love and a Lasting Creation: An Estimation of Harry Otto Fischer

Chronologies and Creations

Harry Otto Fischer was born in Louisville, Kentucky, on 9 July 1910, the son of Bettie Biery and Jake Fischer. Harry O. Fischer is known today solely for his friendship with Fritz Leiber (1910-92) and the unique and ground-breaking series of stories that it engendered. Although Leiber's fame as one of the greatest and most creative writers of fantasy and horror fiction has completely overtaken Fischer's short-lived early promise, Leiber never ceased to give credit to Harry Fischer and their enduring friendship for the impetus that the young Fischer gave to the very slightly younger Leiber.

Fischer's mother was a Christian Scientist who, according to Fischer 'filled her son with the assurance that whatever he did and whatever happened to him, he could never be really hurt.'[1] The boy played the most dangerous games, leaping from upstairs windows. And when he did injure himself, his mother was always able to miraculously nurse him back to health. A slight and occasional stammer developed after Fischer was hit by a baseball bat, and his forehead 'laid open'. Another time, his hand was seriously mangled in a ticket machine, and was to be amputated. Fischer's mother disregarded the advice of the doctors, and patiently used basic medical skills to heal and eventually completely restore the hand. [2]

Perhaps seeds were being sown. Reminiscing in 1980, Fritz Leiber wrote:

But one thing I *am* sure of about Harry's accident run, it was the very stuff of weird adventure stories (for a serious accident *is* the basic weird adventure story: the encounter with danger, playing with it, the brush with death and crippling, attendant strange circumstances, the escape and recovery) while his active childhood in an extended family provided just the sort of colourful, workaday, real living stuff that such a story needs for background.[3]

Harry Fischer became a student at the University of Louisville, and planned a medical career. It was while he was on a visit to Chicago in 1930, that Fischer was introduced to Fritz Leiber. Leiber was a student at the University of Chicago, and they were introduced by Fischer's Louisville friend Franklin MacKnight, who was a friend of Leiber's as well as a fellow student at the university. (MacKnight also did the service of introducing both men to the fiction of H.P. Lovecraft. Thus more seeds were sown...) Fischer and Leiber became instant friends:

...it took only one afternoon for me to decide that there was a blood-brother; a shard from the long-shattered completeness we were once part of; well met in many past embodiments. So I decided here is a man I must make into a firm friend and companion.[4]

Fischer had literary ambitions, and Leiber was soon infected with the bug. They conducted a voluminous correspondence, with news and commentary, talk of the books they had read, and fragments of poetry and fiction. 'We explored several other imaginary worlds before that of Lankhmar came dimly into view.'[5]

By 1934, both men had graduated from university. Harry

Fischer lived in Louisville, Kentucky, and the correspondence continued unabated. In the summer of 1934, Fischer wrote: 'I am static for fear that any motion would be fatal. The gods have laid my soul aside to moulder for a time.'[6] Leiber responded, trying to cheer up and encourage his friend: 'We still have those great foreknowledges of ourselves that you call adolescent fantasies. But they will become mouldy and rotten and the trolls will creep into them greedily if we do not act soon. Our dreams will become the nests of the little gray ones, unless...'[7]

That threatening 'unless' obviously gave Fischer's imagination the boost it needed. In a September 1934 letter, Fischer first mentioned Fafhrd and the Gray Mouser. He fictionalised himself as the tiny Mouser, while the tall Leiber was Fafhrd:

> For all do fear the one known as the Gray Mouser. He walks with swagger 'midst the bravos, though he's but the stature of a child. His costume is all of gray, from gauntlets to boots and spurs of steel. His flat, swart face is shadowed by a peaked cap of mouse-skin and his garments are of silk, strangely soft and course of weave...Until one night, the market night, the huxters all acry and horns blaring wares and smoky, stinking torches flared yellow-red in the foggy air – for the walled city of Tuatha De Danaan called Lankhmar was built on the edge of the Great Salt Marsh – there strode into the group of lounging bravos a pair of monstrous men. The one who laughed merrier was full seven feet in height. His light chestnut hair was bound in a ringlet of pure gold, engraved with runes. His eyes, wide-set, were proud and of fearless mien.[8]

Reminiscing in 'The Grey Mouser and the Game', Fischer looked back at himself:

When was I not the subtle, sleek, sly, sinewy, smart, slightly smudged and highly intelligent Mouser? Something of a cat has always been a part of me (my mother was a Witch) and I affected a coarsely weaved silken gray scarf and a shirt of the same sort. I was big-eyed and almost monstrously intelligent![9]

Fischer and Leiber continued to crystallise their 'fictional' characters. Leiber sometimes thought that they were in a friendly rivalry. Fischer's wide-ranging literary interests and invention served to galvanise Leiber's own imagination and wish to excel at something. By late 1935 Leiber was also starting to write solo fiction about Fafhrd and the Gray Mouser – his first attempts eventually saw publication as 'Adept's Gambit' in his book *Night's Black Agents* (1947). In the Foreword to that classic first collection, Leiber quotes extensively from Fischer's original letter, and never ceased to credit his friend with a co-creator's role.

By 1936 Leiber was including maps and drawings in his letters to Fischer, and soon Fischer's wife Martha (he had married Martha McElroy in 1935) was creating detailed maps of the world which became known as Nehwon. Fischer recalled that she was 'guided by several of Fritz's tales and some of my fragments and her own violent imagination.'[10]

There is one letter to Fischer collected in Lovecraft's *Selected Letters V*. (Dated by August Derleth as having been written in late February 1937, it is a poignant letter from the point of view that HPL mentions the forthcoming forty-seventh birthday that he never lived to reach.) Lovecraft echoes Fischer's feelings of being an outsider:

I can well comprehend the vague impression of aloneness or differentiation which you have always had in some degree. Such, I imagine, is always the concomitant of a very active imagination

& highly individualised personality. The bulk of the human race lives very little in the imaginative realm; hence can seldom grasp the goals, motives, & aspirations of anyone with whom subtle perspectives, symbolic associations, & obscure mental correlations form important emotional factors. Such a one must inhabit a quasi-solipsistic world of his own even more completely than the average individual, & he is always fortunate when he encounters others of a cast sufficiently similar to appreciate the existence, general principles, & typical laws of his private universe.[11]

Little wonder that both Fischer and Leiber considered Lovecraft to be a sort of mentor! An accomplished creator of private universes himself, HPL understood the impulses that drove the creation of fantastic fictional worlds.

After their marriage in 1935, Harry and Martha Fischer bought an old car and caravan, and tried to earn a living by travelling and staging puppet shows. As the United States was still firmly in the grip of the Depression, their venture was doomed to failure. Returning to Louisville, Fischer started to work in 'his box job', which left an ever-decreasing amount of time for writing fiction, and which helped to ensure that it was Fritz Leiber, who had occasional financial help from his father, who could afford to devote more time to breaking into the fantasy fiction market, and so 'became the Mouser's and Fafhrd's historian rather than he [Fischer], as might have been expected from his earlier maturing literary talent.'[12]

In his last, and unfinished, letter to James F. Morton, Lovecraft endorses Fischer and Leiber's joint work (increasingly Leiber's own after 1937). Commenting on the draft of 'Adept's Gambit' sent to him by Fritz Leiber, HPL wrote:

This novelette is part of a very unusual myth-cycle spontaneously evolved in the correspondence of young Leiber and his closest friend – Harry O. Fischer of lately-inundated Louisville. Fischer has also come within my congested epistolary circle, and is in some ways even more remarkable than Leiber – he has more imaginative fertility, though less concentrated emotional power and philosophic insight....Fischer's parts of this cycle are vivid but unformulated and disjointed, so that at present Leiber – the better craftsman – is the only publicly visible author of the pair.[13]

The letter was only published for the first time in 1976, and Leiber testified to his pleasant surprise in reading Lovecraft's positive remarks, even though he felt that the older man overestimated Leiber's contributions when compared to Fischer's. Leiber felt that Fischer was the better craftsman, but also points out that it was his own 'obsessive stubbornness of intent' that ensured that the stories were eventually finished and found publication. Fischer's talents were not in this direction, and, as has already been mentioned, the Fafhrd and Gray Mouser characters and stories became Leiber's by default (and hard work).

By the summer of 1937, Fischer and Leiber were not only thinking in two-dimensional terms: writing fiction and drawing maps on paper. They began creating the 'Great Game'. Decades before *Dungeons & Dragons*, the friends laid out a 38″ x 74″ area of squares and built the Lankhmar Game:

...there were three levels and Citadel Walls and Mountains... It was made of heavy corrugated paperboard, glued and coloured... Fritz and I searched the dime stores (they were indeed 5 and 10¢ in those days). We got corks and round toothpicks and inks (we used nothing but inks for colours). And so it grew... We used brilliant inks and spared no pains... The Mouser's sling was a rubber band! Movarl had a green salt-shaker top for his headpiece! Fafhrd's sword was steeled with tin-foil! And we were young and there! We pasted on the Icy Wastes; smeared the blues of the Inner Sea; cut out the Sinking Land; ruled the squares and glued on Citadel walls and mountains.[14]

As Leiber continued with his solo Fafhrd and Gray Mouser stories, Fischer also continued to contribute ideas to the growing saga. By this stage it was probably already very difficult (if not impossible) to truly disentangle precisely which settings, ideas, characters, etc., came from which man. They continued exchanging letters, and fragments of fiction, and ideas, continued to be written down. Some twenty-five years later Leiber eventually incorporated 10,000 words of Fischer's work, unchanged, in 'The Lords of Quarmall' (collected in *Swords Against Wizardry*).

Harry Fischer spent his working life advancing in his 'box job' – being involved in the design and manufacture of corrugated cardboard packaging. (It would be worth knowing whether this career move was sparked by the construction of the Lankhmar Game, or whether he was using an already existing interest or leisure activity!)

Fischer published little fiction or other writings of his own. A children's fantasy, about a family of likeable witches, 'The Finzer Family' was serialised in the fanzine *The Dragon* (1977). 'The Childhood and Youth of The Gray Mouser' appeared in *The Dragon* in 1978, and covers the earliest years of the Gray Mouser's life up to his meeting with Fafhrd as already chronicled in 'The Unholy Grail' (1962; collected in *Swords and Deviltry*).

Leiber used part of Fischer's name for the character Georg Reuter Fischer (as well as his own middle name of Reuter) in the Lovecraft tribute 'The Terror from the Depths' (1976). The final collection of Fafhrd and Gray Mouser tales (*The Knight and Knave of Swords*) was published in 1988, two years after Harry Otto Fischer died in Naples, Florida, on 30 January 1986.

Friendships and Fiction

For all their setting in the secondary world of Nehwon, the Fafhrd and Gray Mouser stories cannot be entirely separated from the mundane worlds of this dimension, nor from the characters and experiences of their authors. Reminiscing in 'Fafhrd and Me', Fritz Leiber observes that a December 1936 letter to Fischer

> ...tells more about the real origins of the intrigue-ridden, pleasure-sated, sorcery-working, thief-ruled city of Lankhmar, its fat merchants and cut-throat rogues, its gilded courtesans and shrewd mountebanks, and its linkages to a certain city in our own world, then perhaps even Sheelba knows.[15]

Leiber paints Fischer a brief but sharp word-portrait of a chaotic and confused Los Angeles, where he was living in 1936. Then Leiber made his main point: 'Fantasy must be *fertilised* – yes, *watered and manured* – from the real world.' Thus when Leiber started to make a concerted attempt to sell Fafhrd and Gray Mouser stories, he spiced-up the narrative style and formulated the main characters not as super-heroes, larger than life, but as 'earthy characters with earthy weaknesses, winning in the end mostly by luck from villains and supernatural forces more powerful than themselves...'[16] And so 'Two Sought Adventure' was published in the August 1939 issue of the prestigious new magazine *Unknown*.

From the very beginning, the characters of Fafhrd and the Gray Mouser deliberately contained aspects of the creators' own characters and many of their physical characteristics as well. This was started by Fischer, and Leiber was clearly happy to go along with his friend, as he continued to return to the world of Nehwon, in story after story, over fifty years.

As described above, Fischer's main contribution to the series was contained in the approximately 10,000 words that Fritz Leiber later included in 'The Lords of Quarmall'. In his Introduction to *Swords Against Wizardry*, Leiber even gives precise details (page numbers and paragraphs) as to which parts were Fischer's contributions. As the stories are episodic anyway, the transitions between Fischer's episodes, and the sections that Leiber wrote, are quite seamless. Thus Leiber was able to draw attention away from any real differences in the collaborators' styles.

Fischer and Leiber were joint Guests of Honour at GenCon X in August 1977. During a question-and-answer session, Fischer revealed that 'the only thing in the entire series that he didn't particularly care for was Fritz Leiber's version of the Mouser's boyhood in "The Unholy Grail"'.[17] Challenged by Leiber to write his own version, Fischer said that he already had! This was 'The Childhood and Youth of The Gray Mouser' – a short and witty account that fits into the chronology of 'The Unholy Grail'. It sets the scene – afterwards – for the introduction of the Gray Mouser. The story shows once again that Harry Fischer could easily have made a name for himself as a writer of fantastic fiction, if circumstances had turned out differently.

It seems likely that Harry Otto Fischer's destiny is to always be remembered only in connection with his friend Fritz Leiber. Leiber completely eclipsed Fischer in the pursuit of a literary career – as he towered over the heroic fantasy and horror fiction genres for forty years. Leiber wrote masterworks in each of the three apparently diverse fields of fantasy, supernatural horror, and science fiction. Leiber's contributions to just any one of these genres would have served any other author well. But in the Fafhrd and Gray Mouser stories, just one aspect of the work of a unique and multitalented artist, the name of Harry Otto Fischer will also live on as their 'onlie begetter'.

Bibliography

Byfield, Bruce, *Witches of the Mind: a Critical Study of Fritz Leiber*, Necronomicon Press 1991

Fischer, Harry Otto, 'The Childhood and Youth of The Gray Mouser', *The Dragon*, August 1978

Fischer, Harry Otto, 'The Grey Mouser and the Game', *The Dragon*, September 1978

Leiber, Fritz, Fafhrd and Me, *The Second Book of Fritz Leiber*, DAW Books 1975

Leiber, Fritz, Mysterious Islands', *Foundation* 11-12, March 1977

Leiber, Fritz, 'Obituary' (Harry Otto Fischer), *Locus* #302, March 1986

Leiber, Fritz, 'The Original Fafhrd and the Gray Mouser', *Fantasy Newsletter*, December 1980

Lovecraft, H.P., *Selected Letters V* ed. August Derleth and James Turner, Arkham House 1976

Notes

The title of this article is a quotation from 'The Grey Mouser and the Game', p.8

1.   Fritz Leiber, 'The Original Fafhrd and the Gray Mouser' p.4
2.   Fritz Leiber, 'The Original Fafhrd and the Gray Mouser' pp.4f
3.   Fritz Leiber, 'The Original Fafhrd and the Gray Mouser'p.5
4.   Harry Otto Fischer, 'The Grey Mouser and the Game' p.8
5.   Fritz Leiber, 'Fafhrd and Me' p.97

6.   Fritz Leiber, 'Fafhrd and Me' p.93
7.   Fritz Leiber, 'Fafhrd and Me' p.93f
8.   As reproduced in *Night's Black Agents* p.7f (Sphere edition 1977)
9.   Harry Otto Fischer, 'The Grey Mouser and the Game' p.8
10.   Harry Otto Fischer, 'The Grey Mouser and the Game' p.8
11.   H.P. Lovecraft, *Selected Letters V* p.418f
12.   Fritz Leiber, 'Fafhrd and Me' p.108
13.   Fritz Leiber, 'Mysterious Islands' pp.31f; H.P. Lovecraft, *Selected Letters V* pp.433f
14.   Harry Otto Fischer, 'The Grey Mouser and the Game' p.8
15.   Fritz Leiber, 'Fafhrd and Me' p.102
16.   Fritz Leiber, 'Fafhrd and Me' p.103f
17.   Harry Otto Fischer, 'The Childhood and Youth of The Gray Mouser' p.28

Francis Brett Young and *Cold Harbour*

Cold Harbour has had only one claim to fame since it was published: that it drew almost unreserved praise from H.P. Lovecraft, who was usually sparing in his admiration, but unstinting and loyal when he felt it to be deserved. In his ground-breaking essay 'Supernatural Horror in Literature', Lovecraft wrote:

> Much subtler and more artistic, [than Gerald Biss' novel of lycanthropy *The Door of the Unreal*] and told with singular skill through the juxtaposed narratives of the several characters, is the novel *Cold Harbour*, by Francis Brett Young, in which an ancient house of strange malignancy is powerfully delineated. The mocking and well-nigh omnipotent fiend Humphrey Furnival holds echoes of the Manfred-Montoni type of early Gothic 'villain', but is redeemed from triteness by many clever individualities. Only the slight diffuseness of explanation at the close, and the somewhat too free use of divination as a plot factor, keep this tale from approaching absolute perfection.[1]

The author of the novel that had earned such praise was born in Halesowen on 29 June 1884. The son of a doctor, Francis Brett Young had wanted to study literature but dutifully read medicine at the University of Birmingham. He married in 1908. The attraction of a literary career remained strong, and after qualifying as a doctor he wrote whilst in General Practice. Thankfully, as with another doctor turned author, Arthur Conan Doyle, Brett Young was eventually able to make a living by his considerable talents as an author.

Many years later, reminiscing in the Preface to his novel *The House Under the Water* (1933) Brett Young described what had first excited and later inspired him:

> If it be true that the child is the father to the man, it is even more true to say that the child is father to the writer. In every childhood there are, I suppose, certain features in the physical environment which exercise a preponderating effect on the imagination. Such, for me, without doubt, was the building of the Elan Valley reservoirs which impounded the wild waters of the Rhayader Massif in Radnorshire, diverting them from their natural outlet, which was by way of the Wye and the Bristol Channel to the Atlantic, into the sewers of a city which lay on the eastern side of the central watershed, and discharging them finally, by way of the Trent, into the North Sea.[2]

These childhood experiences remained with the aspiring author. Later they formed part of the overarching vision lying behind the great series of novels that occupied Brett Young throughout his literary career.

The majority of Francis Brett Young's novels were set in the West Midlands –Worcestershire and Warwickshire – but the boundaries were never too distinct, and his characters frequently went to earth in the nearby Black Country and Staffordshire Potteries, as well as the Border country of England and Wales. Although he sometimes gave foreign settings to his novels, Brett Young never departed far from his original design, returning again and again throughout his life to the lands through which the Severn and its tributaries flowed. Using the same areas popularised by A.E. Housman in *A Shropshire Lad*, Arnold Bennett's novels set in the Five Towns (Stoke on Trent), and the visionary rural novels of Mary Webb, Francis Brett Young joined the ranks of novelists and poets who wrote in the English regional tradition.

Brett Young was able to invest his Midlands and Border settings with much of the verisimilitude of Thomas Hardy's Wessex. And as Hardy did for his Wessex, Brett Young evolved a consistent landscape of the imagination. He  populated the country with many of the cities, towns, rivers, hills, and other physical features of reality, but also planted it with their fictional counterparts and others of his own invention. The books reprinted in the Severn Edition have attractive stylised maps for their endpapers which show many of the places described in the novels. The line of the Garon Water Scheme aqueduct (the fictional version of the tremendous Elan Valley aqueduct) marches across the map from west to east: the hidden artery of Brett Young's world. Perhaps a map can make it deceptively easy to assume links between real places and invented ones; but the printed landscape is also rendered nebulous enough to be a reminder that it a depiction of 'blue remembered hills' as much as the Ordnance Survey.

Francis Brett Young's first novel, *Undergrowth* (1911) was written in collaboration with his brother. In his later reminiscences he described *Undergrowth* as a 'superficial and amateurish attempt, deeply influenced by the writings of Mr Arthur Machen. The Machenery was obvious, and the treatment was vitiated by a vague and rather shallow mysticism.'[3] But Brett Young had begun as he so often meant to go on. Intimations of the strange and macabre, of the visionary, were never be to entirely absent from his fiction. His unique and painstakingly conceived visualization of his native region – sublime in its beauty and ugliness – filled the pages of his many novels, and worked in the lives of a gallery of vividly-drawn characters, who ranged from the rather sentimental to the truly monstrous. Characters and places occurred and reoccurred, with minor details and incidents in one novel becoming important in another.

***

The First World War saw Francis Brett Young serving in German East Africa (now part of modern Tanzania) fighting the forces of the larger than life Paul von Lettow-Vorbeck. These experiences provided him with plenty of material. South Africa later also became a source for some of Brett Young's later fiction.

Cold Harbour was first published in 1924. The entire novel is told as a series of interlocking narratives, recollections, and speculations in the tradition of Arthur Machen's *The Three Impostors*. An urbane Prelude sets the scene, and the oral storytelling has the effect of immediacy, focussing the reader on the gradually increasing menace, the wrongness of Cold Harbour, its inhabitants, and its history.

A small group of friends and acquaintances is enjoying the warm Mediterranean night on a terrace in Capri – an autobiographical touch, as the Brett Young lived on the island throughout the 1920s. The after-dinner conversation is agreeable and pleasant. The intimacy and safety of the story's framing setting contrasts with the recent experiences of two of the guests, Ronald and Evelyn Wake, and with what turns out to have been their accidental encounter with Cold Harbour and its owner. The atmosphere of the old house in the West

Midlands, and its ancient setting, attractive as it seemed on the surface, has reached down the hundreds of miles to the warm peace of the Italian coast, and spread its damp chill English spell.

The Wakes are a young couple, returning from a holiday in Wales. Their car breaks down on the far outskirts of Birmingham (Brett Young's constant 'North Bromwich'). The setting is sublime industrial Black Country: 'And then this apocalyptic light! It was like a landscape of the end of the world... Its beauty was singularly inhuman and its terror – for it was terrible, you know – elemental.'[4] Unable to continue their journey, the Wakes follow a sign to the Fox Inn, take shelter there, and decide to stay the night. They have the feeling that having to turn off the main road 'had switched [them] into another plane, dimension, whatever you like to call it, of existence, in which the support of ordinary earthly reason were denied.'[5] At the inn the Wakes also meet Humphrey Furnival, the owner of Cold Harbour, which is close by. Furnival tells them about Cold Harbour, and invites them to visit him and the house.

Furnival turns out to be a whirlwind of a man: genius, scholar, bigot, artist, masochist, sadist. Once considered to be one of the finest mining engineers in the country, he had been discredited after a colliery disaster. Yet after several years away licking his wounds Furnival had returned and immured himself and his family at Cold Harbour, almost within sight of the ruined pit, the cause of his downfall. Brooding, Furnival has turned in on himself, and effectively made his house into an extension of himself, partially merging personalities with Cold Harbour and its hidden, violent, and scandalous past.

Later, when the Wakes had been able to take their leave, they felt 'as though the whole course of our lives had been changed, as if they'd been thrust out of their normal, peaceful orbit by a blow from something dark and invisible whirling out of space.'[6]

Cold Harbour deserves to be much better known for its portrayal of one of the best described and most demoniacal 'haunted' houses in the literature, as well as for the threatening complexities of the character of Humphrey Furnival – one of the more repulsive and yet compelling of villains. And what is perhaps more chilling is the lack of certainty in this judgement. Furnival certainly is a bounder of the first order and a severely warped man. But if it is overbearing genius and pride that brought him down, his boundless ambition that allowed him to overestimate his great gifts and allow forces of corruption in to distort them, then he also becomes all the more deserving of sympathy and pity. Furnival comes to resemble someone like Lawrence Wentworth in Charles Williams' *Descent into Hell* (1937) – another novel of self-damnation that lingers on in the minds of those who know it.

Cold Harbour is an excursion into a hell on earth, particularly so because it was possibly created, and certainly sustained, by what is good in humanity going wrong, and becoming tainted and out of true. Francis Brett Young shows this process with meticulous and exquisite clarity – the compassionate precision of a medical man. And where Brett Young isn't precise, his diffuseness gives glimpses of spaces as it were between the walls of reality we build and experience around ourselves.

***

In 1929, Francis Brett Young and his wife returned to England, and lived in the Lake District. They remained there until 1932, when they purchased Craycombe House, a small estate set in the Worcestershire countryside in which Brett

Young continued to set his expanding series of novels. In 1944 Brett Young suffered a heart attack. Shortly afterwards, the Brett Youngs visited South Africa again, and settled there. Francis Brett Young died in Cape Town on 28 March 1954.

As is the case with many popular writers, Francis Brett Young's work lapsed into obscurity after his death, from which it has only since occasionally, and fitfully, emerged. This is a great pity. Brett Young's novels were often over-sentimental and sometimes too leisurely in pace for more modern tastes. However, at their best they do display a consistent literary vision, with a core of power that persists long after the book has been closed.

Nowhere is this shown to better advantage than *Cold Harbour*. It transports us into a strange world embedded within our own recognizable world. It might be dangerous – and it is certainly alluring. Its power is drawn from Brett Young's ability to suggest and then define the uncanny and dark places that can exist up any apparently quiet country lane, even within a few miles of the centre of a crowded city like Birmingham.

Cold Harbour is one of those novels that encourage us to get out an Ordnance Survey map in order to verify topographical details. (Working with contemporary maps, I have on more than one occasion explored the area that Brett Young had used as the setting for his novel. Although the potent sense of place that is such a feature of *Cold Harbour* is still to be felt, urban sprawl and road traffic that has increased out of all recognition, has made a great many changes to the landscape since the 1920s!)

After reading *Cold Harbour*, if Ronald Wake's experience of the house that 'on the plane of practical geography it doesn't exist... I find it difficult to persuade myself that it had a more real existence than one of those landscapes that repeat themselves in dreams…'[7] seems true for us, then nevertheless we are always haunted by the feeling that he might just be wrong.

Notes

Page numbers for *Cold Harbour* refer to the Ash-Tree Press edition of 2007.

1.   H.P. Lovecraft, 'Supernatural Horror in Literature' in *The Annotated Supernatural Horror in Literature* ed. S.T. Joshi, Hippocampus Press 2000, p.56. (Manfred and Montoni appear, respectively, in the 18th century Gothic classics *The Castle of Otranto* by Horace Walpole and *The Mysteries of Udolpho* by Ann Radcliffe.)
2.   Francis Brett Young, *The House Under the Water* (Severn Edition reprint 1949) p.vii
3.   Francis Brett Young, *The House Under the Water* (Severn Edition reprint 1949) p.viii
4.   *Cold Harbour* p.10
5.   *Cold Harbour* p.16
6.   *Cold Harbour* p.117
7.   *Cold Harbour* p.47

Interpenetrations:
Ecstasy and Boundaries in the
Works of Arthur Machen

'Holiness requires as great, or almost as great, an effort [as sin]; but holiness works on lines that *were* natural once; it is an effort to recover the ecstasy that was before the Fall. But sin is the effort to gain the ecstasy and the knowledge that pertain alone to angels, and in making this effort man becomes a demon... In brief, he repeats the Fall.'[1]

The works of Arthur Machen published during a period of over forty years from, say, *The Great God Pan* (1894) to the best of the stories in *The Children of the Pool* (1936), contained and set forth a core set of beliefs and opinions which remained remarkably consistent during the course of a long life and literary career. And as such, these works – both fiction and what must be labelled nonfiction – can also be considered as expressing what may be termed a philosophy. Although I intend to concentrate here on Machen's fiction – which by no means comprised the main part of his literary work and certainly did not provide him with any form of secure livelihood – it is not always very distinguishable from his nonfiction.

Machen's three volumes of autobiography and many articles, written in the same style as much of the fiction, can seem to fuse reality with invention and a dreamlike speculation, making the boundaries between them as insubstantial and misty as a vista dimly discerned through one of the London fogs of the period. During the opening weeks of the First World War Machen deliberately crossed the border with 'The Bowmen'; he also wrote his wartime novel *The Terror* in his best documentary and reportorial style, and it first saw serialisation in the newspaper he worked for.[2] That Machen produced vast amounts of newspaper journalism for his employers makes the use of the term 'story' for his output both as a reporter and as a writer of fiction doubly ambiguous – and therefore all the more appropriate.

THE GREAT GOD PAN

Arthur Machen

Arthur Machen's beliefs and opinions, his philosophy, was reflected in his work through themes and imagery that also recurred over the decades. Themes flowed into and merged with each other like the London streets and districts, or twisting lanes winding over wild Welsh hills, both of which appear and reappear as images. Many stories concerned the consequences of the abuse of what should be the natural order: *The Great God Pan* and 'The White People' are two examples. Machen distrusted the world he knew, considering it not to be natural but having fallen away from what it should be. Machen reserved a special distrust and scorn for the scientific progress of the nineteenth century and after, which he regarded as having led the world astray from the spiritual to the idolisation of the material.

Adherence to the Anglo-Catholic version of Christianity gave Machen added justification for his exaltation of the spiritual over the material, and so his revolt against the materialism of contemporary life. Machen saw humanity as a 'sacrament': an inner soul manifested in an outer body. This was a natural unity not to be broken, but which was always under threat. The worst 'sorcery' (which for Machen could often be equated with science) was that which destroyed the sacred link. In 'The Inmost Light' Dr Steven Black's experiment on his consenting wife left her 'what was no longer a woman' and in consequence led to what amounted to his self-damnation and exclusion from the human race – crossing, with no possibility of return, the most important boundary of all.[3] The long discussion between Ambrose and Cotgrave that forms the opening of 'The White People' showed the way Machen meant to go on, as well as where he had already started from: 'Sorcery and sanctity,' said Ambrose, 'these are the only realities. Each is an ecstasy, a withdrawal from the common life.'[4]

Machen had already written an entire book, *Hieroglyphics* (1902), in order to expound his theory of literature. He contended that it is the presence of ecstasy that distinguishes 'fine literature' from something which, no matter how clever or interesting, will not be fine literature.[5] Ecstasy (*ekstasis*, to be or stand outside the self, to be put out of place) is a movement or separation; for Machen efforts towards the recovery of ecstasy represented efforts towards holiness; a high calling for fine literature and those able and willing to create it. But when the 'wrong' sort of ecstasy is sought, then the result is sin; the reader will not get fine literature but may nevertheless be enabled to dally with sin and all its alluring glamour at second-hand, and to come close to the demonic without actually quite going all the way. There is a boundary. If it is crossed, someone would be lead from sanctity to sorcery – trespassing from one reality in to another reality – and the house of life would be riven asunder and the primal Fall repeated.[6]

The crossing of boundaries to ecstasy – whichever boundaries to whichever sort of ecstasy – is possibly the most important preoccupation in Arthur Machen's work. The borderlands are where chaos and order meet, the ragged edge of reality and illusion (or perhaps true reality) where lives are touched and transmuted. By sheer indomitable will Machen attempted to impose order on life as he saw and lived it. He sought and showed hints of what he perceived as lying behind its commonplaces and confusions, sharing his views and insights with those who were able to discern his design. This is Arthur Machen's distinct, and lasting, contribution to fantastic literature.

***

Boundaries are where things happen – both mentally and physically. Significant events occur on or close to boundaries. Borders can symbolise tensions, and express them where they count: in coexistence, whether easy or not; exchanges hopefully leading to mutual enrichment; domination from one side or the other and possible destruction. Boundaries exist between states of life and environments. All of these are apparent in the life and work of Arthur Machen.

He was born and brought up in rural Wales and lived and worked for most of his life in London. His county of birth is itself a shifting borderland: a home at different times included in Wales as Gwent or in England as Monmouthshire. Machen spent his last years in the compromise of Old Amersham in Buckinghamshire, with its surrounding countryside and yet nearness to the suburban Metroland of Amersham-on-the-Hill and its station at the far end of the Tube. In his work these sort of differences in setting and background are received (or come to terms with) to some extent by Machen's technique of heightening the colours and deepening the shadows of the settings of his stories. There are places for ambiguities and seeing things, even if through a glass darkly: 'And as I think the pure provincial can never understand the quiddity or essence of London, so I believe that for the born Londoner the country ever remains an incredible mystery.'[7]

Machen loved and revered his native rural Wales all of his life: yet as a place of residence he left it behind at the age of 19, never to return except for visits of longer or shorter duration. Machen's work is largely set in the countryside, yet he is as much an urban writer as a rural one. The city – London – is seen as a bright place of challenge to someone from the country. The country is seen as an idyllic place of retreat and escape. And yet neither is really the case. At times London was the 'grey temple of an awful rite' and circled by boundaries to be crossed for which every crossing required an initiation that was 'eternal loss.'[8] And, as has just been seen, the country, the 'strangely beautiful' rural Wales, is also 'full of mystery.'[9]

Machen seems constantly to have held his rural and urban sympathies in tension. No doubt this was a mixed attitude, held because of, as well as despite of himself. To say that, in terms of his literary career and output, it was a creative tension would be an understatement. Perhaps it was the product of alienation, or a seeking for something that never quite existed or was realised in Machen's life. He recalled his rural past with fondness, but it could be dull. The urban present was lively, and Machen celebrated that in his work. And to a mind such as his, always probing at the boundary between 'sanctity and sorcery' there was still the ever-present possibility that either the rural scene or London could swallow someone and leave them remaining alive but no longer really a human being:

> He had found himself curiously strengthened by the change from the hills to the streets. There could be no doubt, he thought, that living a lonely life, interested only in himself and his own thoughts, he had become in a measure inhuman.[10]

Machen's work spanned boundaries, the 'twilight zones' between the more customary ways of seeing and experiencing places. In both fiction and nonfiction Machen conjured up a rightly renowned sense of place in which to described characters as well as his narrative 'I' as exploring the boundaries. Passages from a volume of autobiography, such as *Far-Off Things,* and a work of fiction (which nevertheless contain strong autobiographical elements), such as *The Hill of Dreams,* resemble each other closely and are often in effect interchangeable. Machen described how, after moving to London, he 'began the habit of rambling abroad in the hope of finding something that could be called country' and into regions that he recalled as a 'sort of nightmare.'[11]. And in the same way Lucian Taylor 'tried to make for remote and desolate places, and yet when he had succeeded in touching on the open country, and knew that the icy shadow hovering through the mist was a field, he longed for some sound and murmur of life, and turned again to roads where pale lamps were glimmering...[12]

During Machen's lifetime, as the nation's population grew, its work patterns changed, and the transport infrastructure developed, the phenomenon of urbanization became more noticeable than ever. As far as London was concerned, Machen was present during the time of its greatest expansion, from the growth of the later nineteenth century through to the tremendous explosion of urban sprawl after the First World War. This led to the swamping of Middlesex and large areas of other surrounding counties, with open spaces, fields, woodland, and much productive agricultural land in particular being covered with houses and roads. But it was the Victorian expansion of London, especially in the 1880s and 1890s that formed the background to so much of Machen's work, and especially the stories written during his great creative decade of 1889-99 (although in some cases they were not published until years later).[13]

> In a confused vision I stumbled on, through roads half town and half country, grey fields melting in to the cloudy world of mist on one side of me, and on the other comfortable villas with a glow of firelight flickering on the walls, but all unreal...[14]

This example illustrates the sort of landscape Machen must have seen again and again on his constant wanderings around the western outskirts of a fast-growing London. It was the ragged place where town and country meet, the jagged line of a jumble of new streets and ravaged fields, and a place ideal for outrageous coincidences to occur with regularity, to form the setting for adventures stranger than can be imagined. The Prologue to *The Three Impostors* is a notable example. Two of Machen's cast of idler characters, Phillipps and Dyson, whose very idleness always allows them the time for things to happen to them and to pursue them, while exploring the 'forgotten outskirts' of London see a deserted house from the road and wander up to it. It is in such a setting that a boundary into dark enchantments is crossed: 'I yield to fantasy; I cannot withstand the influence of the grotesque ... I cannot regain commonplace, I look at that deep glow on the panes, and the house lies all enchanted; that very room, I tell you, is within all blood and fire.'[15]

Here the house appears to stand as a stable remnant of the past – pleasant to look at, and in an apparently tranquil setting. But even this 'picturesque but mouldy residence' is not what it might seem. It lies on a boundary and is itself a boundary. It is a place where past and present comes together and where the future decays into the present on its way to becoming past. The stationary house can be seen as enclosing the boundary, and containing within it its own decay as it moves in transition backwards from its future. The house, seemingly serene, is a trap: in reality the setting for strange and terrible happenings.

Arthur Machen's boundary zones are places for seeking and finding: seeking that which should not be sought, and coming to terms with that which should not have been found. Where the edges meet or overlap sanctity and sorcery are closer to each other than can be healthy, and the commonplace is decisively lost: '...a veil seems drawn aside, and the very fume of the pit steams up through the flagstones, the ground glows, red hot... I see the plot thicken; our steps will henceforth be dogged with mystery, and the most ordinary incidents will teem with significance.'[16]

The subtitle of *The Three Impostors* is *The Transmutations*, which as S.T. Joshi points out, gives an indication of the different types and levels of transmutation that this complex novel reveals. Both human beings and landscapes are portrayed as undergoing transmutation; this usually involves entering the borderland, crossing boundaries and the sweeping away of previous conceptions.[17]

***

Boundaries and ecstasy belong together; they intermingle with each other and transform those who seek and encounter them. Towards the end of his active literary career Machen wrote what was perhaps his most effective use of the theme of crossing borders and the transformation through ecstasy of those who do so. This is the idea of interpenetration or *perichoresis*, which literally means the area or space around about: in this case perhaps the boundary between the worlds, between reality and illusion, or two orders of both. Machen's work abounds in ideas of an unseen world pressing in on ours – and actually interpenetrating with it in usually the most unexpected and unlikely places, such as 'ordinary' London suburbs, and with the most dire results.

As discussed above, buildings and roads in the shifting transition zone between town and country can be considered boundaries between the worlds. This also forms a connection with Machen's Christian faith and acceptance of a 'Platonic' view of the universe. In this view the world as seen and experienced by human beings is in fact only the shadow of a perfect and unchanging reality, and usually veiled from sight; even so, there may be traffic between the two. According to the American critic Joseph Wood Krutch, Machen had 'only one plot, the Rending of the Veil'.[18] Machen explored the concept of another dimension of reality – or, rather, reality itself – beyond the veil, the veil sometimes being rent asunder and the other side interpenetrating rarely with our world, and being perceived by a few people in the right place at the right time: '...we stand amidst sacraments and mysteries full of awe, and it doth not yet appear what we shall be. Life, believe me, is no simple thing...'[19]

It is in the late story 'N' where the idea of interpenetration, *perichoresis*, is most strikingly developed. 'N' is a key story in Arthur Machen's large and varied output.[20] But perhaps because it was a new story specially written in 1935 for *The Cosy Room and Other Stories*, a collection of otherwise reprint fiction published the following year, it can easily be overlooked and not accorded the importance it deserves. Three of Machen's company of habitual talkers, middle-aged and elderly men, meet from time to time in the rooms of one of them. They speculate as to why, over the years, there have been persistent hints and rumours of gardens and panoramas of 'unearthly' or 'astounding' beauty to be glimpsed behind the ordinary streets and through the windows of a place they think they know intimately, the thoroughly ordinary north London suburb of Stoke Newington.

One of the characters recalls a 'shabby brown book' by the Reverend Thomas Hampole, *A London Walk: Meditations in the Streets of the Metropolis* (which had first been mentioned in *The Green Round*, published in 1933). In his book Mr Hampole refers to a conversation he had as a young clergyman with Mr Glanville, a member of his congregation who tells him about 'a consequence, not generally acknowledged, of the Fall of Man.' His doctrine was that the universe was 'originally fluid and the servant of his spirit, became solid and crashed down upon him overwhelming him beneath its weight and its dead mass.'[21] During a last visit to Mr Glanville at his rooms, Hampole is invited to look at the view from his window. It is not what he expected to see in Stoke Newington; Hampole 'uttered an inarticulate cry of joy and wonder.' Hampole immediately feels a 'swift revulsion of terror' and rushes from the house.[22] Clearly a boundary had been removed, and Hampole's initial ecstasy was exposed as a manipulation from the demonic.

Through the skilful use of linked narratives, interconnected memories, pub anecdotes, second-hand reportage, Machen carefully constructed a documentary verisimilitude that is pervasive as well as being persuasive. When the men meet again and consider everything they have found out, the most likely explanation, it is hazarded, is 'that there is a *perichoresis*, an interpenetration. It is possible, indeed, that we three are now sitting among desolate rocks, by bitter streams.' The final words that follow are as redolent with horror, understated menace, and intriguing possibility as anything Machen ever wrote during the heyday of his literary career around the turn of the twentieth century.[23]

At that time, in *Hieroglyphics*, Machen used the device of the narrator's visits to another of his talkative characters, a reclusive elderly man in his retreat, an old house in the 'almost mythical region' of Barnsbury, then very much on a boundary at the northern edge of London. They discuss – or rather, the hermit tells the narrator – what it is that makes true literature. As has been seen, the deciding factor is the presence of ecstasy; in his book Machen put forward an entire literary theory, exploring the roots of ecstasy and defining another kind of boundary.[24]

Machen sought the ecstasy which brings the boundary experience home at the deepest level, and makes the world and life within it into a place of darkness and glory, coexisting and interpenetrating with somewhere else through rendings of the veil:

I recall the presence of that hollow, echoing room...and the tone of voice speaking to me, and I believe that once or twice we both saw visions, and some glimpses at least of certain eternal, ineffable Shapes.[25]

In the final analysis Arthur Machen's best work, his fiction of boundaries, seeks to test and cross those boundaries, explore the consequences, and enhance, embrace, and communicate ecstasy.

Notes

1. 'The White People' (1906) in *Tales of Horror and the Supernatural*, Tartarus Press 2006, p.114
2. *The Terror* was first published in *The Evening News* (London), October 16-31, 1916 and in book form by Duckworth in 1917.
3. 'The Inmost Light' (1894) in *Tales of Horror and the Supernatural*, Tartarus Press 2006, pp.175-176
4. 'The White People' p.111
5. *Hieroglyphics* (1902) Martin Secker (New Adelphi Library) 1926, p.18
6. 'The Novel of the White Powder' (1895) in *Tales of Horror and the Supernatural*, Tartarus Press 2006, p.56
7. *Far-Off Things* (1922) in *The Collected Arthur Machen* edited by Christopher Palmer, Duckworth 1988, p.90
8. *The Hill of Dreams* (1907), Tartarus Press 2006, p.167
9. *The Three Impostors* (1895), J.M. Dent 1995, p.55
10. *The Hill of Dreams* p.135
11. *Far-Off Things* in *The Collected Arthur Machen* p.146
12. *The Hill of Dreams* p.157
13. S.T. Joshi, *The Weird Tale*, University of Texas Press 1990, pp.39-41. Joshi provides a list of the dates of writing, first publication, and first collection in book form.
14. *The Three Impostors* p.47
15. *The Three Impostors* p.6
16. *The Three Impostors* p.13
17. S.T. Joshi, *The Weird Tale* p.25
18. Joseph Wood Krutch, 'Tales of a Mystic' in *Nation* CVX (September 13, 1922), p.259. Cited in Wesley D. Sweetser, *Arthur Machen*, Twayne Publishers 1964, p.78.

19.   *The Three Impostors* pp.50-51

20.   Thomas Kent Miller rightly draws attention to its importance in 'Some thoughts on "N"' in *Faunus* No. 26, Autumn 2012, pp.21-38

21.   'N' (1936) in *Tales of Horror and the Supernatural*, Tartarus Press 2006, p.294

22.   'N' pp.295-296

23.   'N' pp.305-306

24.   '"The Secret and the Secrets": A Look at Machen's *Hieroglyphics*' in *Faunus* No. 5, Spring 2000, pp.3-12

25.   *Hieroglyphics* pp.5, 8

Old England, New England:
M.R. James, Mary Wilkins Freeman,
and Sarah Orne Jewett

Montague Rhodes James (1862-1936) had a special fondness for some of the works of two American women novelists and short-story writers, now somewhat forgotten. In this essay I wish to consider some of the reasons why James, one of the greatest writers of supernatural fiction, responded so warmly to the stories of his near contemporaries Mary Wilkins Freeman (1852-1930) and Sarah Orne Jewett (1849-1909). In particular, given M.R. James' reputation for not liking women, I wish to consider the place of some of the fiction of the two women – proto-feminists of their time if ever there were any – in M.R. James' estimation, if not also in his heart.

There has been plenty of speculation on the reasons for the scarcity of women in James' life, and of female characters in his fiction, although in both instances this is a sweeping generalisation. M.R. James never married, and the vast majority of his working and social life was spent, by its very nature, in almost exclusively male company. Even so, the image of Dr James as a 'confirmed' bachelor, actually disliking women, would be an all-too easy one to adopt. Whatever the reality actually was – and it certainly was not the image just described – James did have a special place for two particular women and some, at least, of their works.

Growing up and forming a range of life-long attitudes at the time he did, M.R. James could well have considered himself to be a quintessential Englishman. His lifetime coincided with the zenith of Great Britain's imperial ambitions and superpower status, and his working life was spent entirely in those educational bastions of the Establishment, Eton and Cambridge. On occasion he may very well even have had a slight English disdain for citizens of that new, brash, and still frontier country, the United States of America – and extended the same feelings to its literature as well (an attitude far from dead for many present-day English people!).

On 12 January 1928, M.R. James wrote to Nicholas Llewelyn Davies discussing the American writer H.P. Lovecraft's major study 'Supernatural Horror in Literature'. James had received a copy of W. Paul Cook's amateur magazine *The Recluse* containing the essay. Presumably either Lovecraft or his publisher had sent James the copy – certainly in Lovecraft's case it would have been the action of a sincere admirer to one of his respected masters. That time, the result did conform to stereotype. James was at his most waspish and disdainful in his dismissive comments on Lovecraft's work, even describing his style as being 'of the most offensive'. Nevertheless, James did agree with many of Lovecraft's judgments, including his praise of the New England writer Mary Wilkins Freeman (or Mary E. Wilkins as she was known and published as before her marriage).

Freeman wrote a respectable number of excellent supernatural stories set in New England, as part of her prolific output of stories and novels. Further on in his letter, James characterises the contents of Wilkins' collection *The Wind in the Rosebush* (1903) as 'quite successful domestic New England: I like it'. This confirms that James was fond of stories with a distinctive New England setting. In addition, in Gwendolen McBryde's *Letters to a Friend* (1956) he is recorded as reading and re-reading one of the best New England novels, *The Country of the Pointed Firs* (1896) by Freeman's close contemporary, Sarah Orne Jewett.

Whilst both Freeman and Jewett wrote supernatural fiction, I think it is true to say that Freeman is the better known of the two for her contributions to that genre (her work was also admired by Arthur Machen).

And while both wrote mainstream stories of domestic New England, Sarah Orne Jewett is the best known of the two for making that territory her own.

Always partial to a good ghost story, it certainly was to be expected that M.R. James would be acquainted with Freeman's supernatural fiction. This displayed the same

regional awareness and knowledge, and the same types of New England character that occurred throughout her regional fiction. Freeman's work was typically centred on middle-aged or elderly women, usually single through being widowed or simply through never having married, and who somehow came into conflict with the expectations of their friends, or established custom.

COLLECTED
GHOST STORIES
MARY E. WILKINS-FREEMAN
With an Introduction by EDWARD WAGENKNECHT

Eventually a problem is resolved, and the elderly female view is vindicated, or its New England stoicism is brought to the fore in what may or may not be defeat.

Freeman's supernatural fiction is very similar in tone and

themes. Eleven stories were gathered in *Collected Ghost Stories* (1974) which contained all her significant supernatural stories (not all are ghost stories). It is worthwhile to examine a selection of the more obviously 'ghostly' of these stories by Freeman, before taking a look at Jewett's novel, and then speculating a little as to just why M.R. James was so pleased by them.

While 'A Symphony in Lavender' is not the best story in *Collected Ghost Stories*, it is, perhaps, one of the most characteristic. A single lady comes to visit her friend Mrs Leonard. Across the road is the Munson house, inhabited by 'a maiden lady' – Miss Caroline Munson, and her servant Margaret. The narrator is soon invited to tea – a visit within a visit.

> Indeed, Miss Munson did make me think of a flower, and of one prevalent in her front yard, too – a lilac: there was that same dull bloom about her, and a shy, antiquated grace.[1]

Everything about Miss Munson and her house is graceful and old. All is calm and quiet and poised: the perfect idea of New England. During the length of her visit, the narrator gets to know Miss Munson as well as it is possible for anyone to. She is invited to the Munson house for tea on many occasions.

> All that I could think of sometimes, when with her, was a person walking in a garden and getting continuously delicious sniffs of violets, so that he certainly knew they were near him, although they were hidden somewhere under the leaves, and he could not see them.[2]

Then, the day before she is due to leave, Miss Munson confides to the narrator a dream that she once had. She is walking down a street carrying a basket of lilies and roses, when an attractive young man, an artist, asks her for a lily. She begins to hand him the flower, when she begins to sense something at once repulsive as well as beautiful in him:

> I wanted at once to give him the lily and would have died rather than give it to him, and I turned and fled, with my basket of flowers, and my dove on my shoulder, and a great horror of something, I did not know what, in my heart.[3]

The sexual symbolism is unmistakeable. A year later, Miss Munson continues, she really did meet in the street the man she had dreamed about. She walked on past, very disturbed. She soon found out that the stranger was indeed an artist, and staying in the locality. They met, and fell in love. When he asked Miss Munson to marry him, she looked into his face, and experienced the same horror that she had felt in her dream.

A year later, when the narrator returned for another visit, she learns that Caroline Munson had died during the winter, and was laid to rest dressed in lilac, as she had requested.

Amongst all the lavender and lilac, in this story there is a woman who was confronted by a stark choice. She could marry – presumably the expected thing. Or she could remain single. The power of love and attraction is revealed as being decidedly ambiguous. Should she choose certainty (spinsterhood) or adventure within normality (marriage)? Either way her life could be seen as being diminished. She would be a no-sayer. And yet... Freeman turns the categories of certainty and uncertainty and adventure on their heads. Like Louisa Ellis, the heroine of one of Freeman's best-known stories, the non-supernatural 'A New England Nun' (reprinted in *Short Fiction of Sarah Orne Jewett and Mary Wilkins*

Freeman, ed. Barbara H. Solomon), Miss Munson makes up her mind, and decides to take whatever the future will bring, on her own terms, and not anyone else's. But in this case with the possibility of supernatural intervention!

'A Far-Away Melody' concerns the twin sisters Priscilla and Mary Brown. Now over fifty, these plain, hard-working, independent women are hanging out washing on a fine spring morning. Suddenly Priscilla starts musing out loud about death:

> I wonder ... if it would seem so very queer to die a mornin' like this, say. Don't you believe there's apple branches a-hangin' over them walls made out of precious stones... An' I wonder if it would seem such an awful change to go from this air into the air of the New Jerusalem.[4]

Although they are religious women, and 'knew almost as much about the Old Testament prophets as they did about their neighbours', they never talked about such things, and certainly not about death and the next world.

Later, in the evening, Priscilla hears beautiful music wafting in through the window. No-one else can hear it, neither Mary nor Miss Moore, who is paying the sisters a visit.

Priscilla Brown dies suddenly that night. Mary now feels guilty for not believing what Priscilla said she had heard, and determines to wait to hear the ethereal music herself, so she can die and join her sister. Over the following months Mary grows weaker. Finally, nearly a year after Priscilla's death, she dies. Shortly before her death, she tells her niece: 'I've heard it! I've heard it! ... A faint sound o' music, like the dyin' away of a bell.'[5]

Perhaps Freeman's best, and most famous, supernatural story is 'Luella Miller'. The memory of Luella Miller still haunts the village, even years after her death. For fifty years her house lies empty, and is avoided. Only one person who really knew Luella Miller still survives – Lydia Anderson. She tells her story.

Luella was an attractive woman, who had no difficulty in making friends. Shortly after her arrival in the village, where she had come to be schoolteacher, one of her older pupils, Lottie Henderson, began to help Luella out with her teaching duties. Soon she was doing most of the work. Despite being in excellent health, after helping Luella for about a year, Lottie 'just faded away and died'.[6]

Luella also attracted a husband, Erastus Miller, who after their marriage began to get 'consumption of the blood' despite having always been strong and healthy before. He waited on Luella hand and foot until he died. Then the 'robust' Lily Miller, Erastus' sister, moves in. She, too, gradually grew feeble, and died.

Then Lily's Aunt Abby comes to look after Luella. She, too, gradually loses her health, and eventually dies. Then Dr Sam Abbot falls for Luella, who after Abby's death acts her most charming and innocent. But Abby's daughter speaks her mind:

There ain't nothin' weak about that woman. She's got strength enough to hang onto other folks till she kills 'em. Weak? It was my poor mother that was weak: this woman killed her as sure as if she had taken a knife to her.[7]

But Dr Abbot was too smitten to take notice. Lydia Anderson takes Luella to task: "'I don't know what there is about you, but you seem to bring a curse.'" The doctor dies in turn, as well as two girls who 'did' for Luella. Eventually the village wakes up to Luella's 'curse', and no-one will go near her. She declines, and grows weaker by the day. Afterwards, Lydia relates what she had seen:

> I saw Luella Miller and Erastus Miller, and Lily, and Aunt Abby, and Maria, and the Doctor, and Sarah, all goin' out of the door, and all but Luella shone white in the moonlight, and they were all helpin' her along till she seemed to fairly fly in the midst of them. Then it all disappeared... I knew what had happened. Luella was layin' real peaceful, dead on her bed.[8]

Although 'Luella Miller' is not a 'ghost' story as such, except perhaps for the scene at the end, it warrants mention in this context. I think that M.R. James, who wrote as many monster stories as he wrote ghost stories, would have savoured it. It was also a strikingly unusual story for its time. The vampire depicted as a being living off emotions rather than blood is now a well-used theme in the field. Freeman's character is a vampire who lives off its victims, but not through taking their blood. But it is still a parasite on humanity, a creature who leaves only death behind it. That this could occur in a small New England village makes this story special in Freeman's work, and an example of real domestic horror. Luella Miller is a monster, and is depicted as such. There are no illusions, except those of the townspeople that are slowly destroyed by the mounting death-toll amongst Luella's 'friends'. At the end, women unite against another woman, and effectively quarantine her to death, in order to preserve their world and restore it.

The ending of an illusion is a theme in 'The Wind in the Rose-Bush'. Rebecca Flint comes from Michigan on a visit to Ford Village. She comes to visit her brother's widow, his second wife, in order to collect her niece, the daughter of the brother and his first wife. Rebecca arrives at Mrs Dent's house, only to find that her niece is out. Mrs Dent puts Rebecca off with excuses as to the niece's non-appearance.

Strange things begin to happen. A rose-bush moves, despite there being no wind. The tune 'A Maiden's Prayer' is heard, but there is no-one at the piano. The shadow of a girl crosses the window, but there is no-one to be seen. And Mrs Dent denies any knowledge of these events.

Further excuses are given to Rebecca about her niece's whereabouts. Finally she decides to investigate for herself, but is prevented from doing so by a summons home. She leaves, instructing Mrs Dent to send her niece on to her in due course. She does not appear. Rebecca writes to Mrs Dent, but with no result. She eventually writes to the postmaster of Ford Village, who replies:

> Mrs John Dent said to have neglected stepdaughter. Girl was sick. Medicine not given. Talk of taking action. Not enough evidence. House said to be haunted. Strange sights and sounds. Your niece, Agnes Dent, died a year ago, about this time...[9]

The examples of Mary Wilkins Freeman's work that I have discussed or mentioned above, although characterised as being domestic, are far from domestic in the sense of being comfortable or being about pleasant things. Freeman is happy to show that life in small communities is often not at all idyllic, as nostalgia for rural New England and its villages and small towns and their positive qualities, might sometimes suggest. There are always victims, even in the most attractive or deceptively homely setting. They are victims of conformity, or the risks taken in reacting against it.

Freeman wrote about people encountering the undomesticated in their own domestic surroundings. She did so with feeling and understanding, and often a sharp edge of dry wit. These sorts of unimaginative and unaffected people also populated the fiction of Sarah Orne Jewett. Like Mary Wilkins Freeman, Jewett wrote novels and short stories with a New England setting, whether or not they were also supernatural. Although *The Country of the Pointed Firs* is not a supernatural novel, it does share the common New England

setting that both women used in their work. That world is a normal, ordinary and easily recognizable one.

Perhaps that is the main reason why M.R. James enjoyed *The Country of the Pointed Firs* so much. In her novel, Jewett described a complete and living place that the reader can enter into and inhabit, being welcomed there unconditionally just as the novel's narrator is. The small town of Dunnet Landing, Maine, together with its back country and offshore islands, is like a second home: intimate, friendly, quiet, and inviting.

Much of the novel is structured around visits made by the narrator to various inhabitants of the town. She is also taken around by the main character, Almira Todd. These are model visits, revealing depths hidden behind the outward New England calm and poise, and allowing the narrator to take part as a trusted friend rather than as a newcomer. M.R. James could have found his positive experiences and wishes reflected in *The Country of the Pointed Firs*.

As stated earlier, M.R. James is usually regarded as at best having an ambivalent attitude towards women. In his biography of James, *M.R. James: An Informal Portrait* (1983) Michael Cox describes the younger James as occasionally affecting misogyny, while he ended up as 'one of nature's bachelors'. Cox describes several of James' friendships with women, as well as a couple of potential near-collisions with matrimony. So while James was certainly not anything so distasteful as a woman-hater, he preferred to keep them at arm's length. Barbara H. Solomon has described *The Country of the Pointed Firs* as 'so thoroughly a woman's book about the world of women – old women at that'.[10] In Dunnet Landing it is the women who reign supreme. A typical Dunnet Landing woman (to say nothing of most of the female characters in the rest of Jewett's – and Freeman's – work) is unmarried, or a widow. The men are absent: most have died young, lost at sea, leaving their women to outlive them, and to continue their lives, playing both traditional male and female roles.

When men that do appear, they are fairly peripheral to the story, or are characterised as being somewhat incompetent, or lacking the fire and ambition of the women. *The Country of the Pointed Firs* can thus also be read as offering a fascinating (and safe) glimpse into a world of challenging and unconventional women.

A small community, where everyone knows each other, and their business, where everyone has their place, would be a setting that M.R. James would be familiar with. School and college life, and James' academic world, have their parallels with Dunnet Landing in this respect. It would have the allure that New England has always had to many English people: images of the blazing colours of trees in the fall, the white spires of churches against the blue sky, and so on. It would be sufficiently different from James' Cambridge to be worth escaping to, and yet also a little safe in this similarity of the sense of feeling a part of it. And in a work of fiction, there is no-one to offend or make demands.

As in M.R. James' world, Jewett celebrates age, and makes it clear that age is no barrier to usefulness or carrying on as usual. Almira Todd is 67; her mother, Mrs Blackett, is still active at the age of 86. A Jewett character is elderly, but shows the superiority over younger people of wisdom gained through age and experience.

Perhaps James found the world of Dunnet Landing and its people the place to have the best of all possible worlds: a vividly realised world away from his ordinary one, a home away from home, yet also a place that is also home.

The novel contains exemplars for people who live a single life, and who make the best of their circumstances and surroundings, if not actually triumph over them. The narrator experiences the unconditional acceptance and love of Dunnet Landing's inhabitants. These are basic Christian teachings, and, in theory at least, experiences. M.R. James never expressed as 'Christian' a world-view as might be expected. (Simon MacCulloch's major article 'The Toad in the Study: M.R. James, H.P. Lovecraft and Forbidden Knowledge' explores this theme in detail.[11]) Although James was a sincere Christian believer all of his life, perhaps some of the values of Jewett's novel may well have been more real and meaningful to him than many of those of orthodox Christianity, including the Bible.

Although *The Country of the Pointed Firs* is a determinedly realistic novel, it does contain two episodes that could be considered as involving the supernatural.

The first was originally a separate story. In Chapter VI, 'The Waiting Place', the narrator visits Captain Littlepage, who tells her about his sea-voyages. Eventually he mentions a strange town in the Canadian arctic that he himself had once been told about. The town lay further north than any ship had ever been, and was only visible from the sea, and could not be seen from the land, or reached by it.

[The town was] like a place where there was neither living nor dead ... when they got close inshore they could see the shape of folks, but they could never get near them, – all blowing gray figures that would pass along alone, or sometimes gathered in companies as if they were watching.[12]

The second episode is 'The Foreigner' (1900), one of four standalone Dunnet Landing stories usually published with the novel. Mrs Todd tells the narrator about the death of Mrs Tolland:

All of a sudden she set right up in bed with her eyes wide open... I looked the way she was lookin', an' I see someone was standin' there against the dark ... I couldn't tell the shape, but 'twas a woman's dark face lookin' right at us; 'twa'n't but an instant, as I say, an' when my sight came back I couldn't see nothing there.[13]

Just before Mrs Tolland dies, she asks Mrs Todd if she had seen something. Mrs Todd answers her: "'Yes, dear, I did; you ain't never goin' to feel strange an' lonesome no more.'"[14]

To never feel out of place, and alone, is a natural human desire. I think that the domestic yet strange world of Jewett's

Dunnet Landing – and Freeman's New England – helped M.R. James to fulfil that desire. And with the bonus of a few shudders along the way.

Notes

Page references to Freeman's stories are to *Collected Ghost Stories* (Arkham House 1974). Those to *The Country of the Pointed Firs* are to the W.W. Norton paperback edition of 1982.

1.   *Collected Ghost Stories* p.83
2.   *Collected Ghost Stories* p.84
3.   *Collected Ghost Stories* p.86
4.   *Collected Ghost Stories* p.72
5.   *Collected Ghost Stories* p.79
6.   *Collected Ghost Stories* p.41
7.   *Collected Ghost Stories* p.48
8.   *Collected Ghost Stories* p.53
9.   *Collected Ghost Stories* p.109
10.   Barbara H. Solomon (ed.), *Short Fiction of Sarah Orne Jewett and Mary Wilkins Freeman* p.5
11.   Simon MacCulloch, 'The Toad in the Study: M.R. James, H.P. Lovecraft and Forbidden Knowledge' in *Ghosts & Scholars* Nos. 20-23
12.   *The Country of the Pointed Firs* p.25
13.   *The Country of the Pointed Firs* p.184
14.   *The Country of the Pointed Firs* p.186

In Lonely Places:
The Essential Horror Fiction
of Karl Edward Wagner

Authors sometimes publish one collection of short fiction at some point during their writing career that seems to define and sum-up their output. For me, such modern classic and essential collections as *The Opener of the Way* (1945) by Robert Bloch, *The October Country* (1955) by Ray Bradbury, *Mr George and Other Odd Persons* (1963) by Stephen Grendon (August Derleth), *Demons by Daylight* (1973) by Ramsey Campbell, *Night Monsters* (1974) by Fritz Leiber, *Deathbird Stories* (1975) by Harlan Ellison, and Charles L. Grant's *Tales from the Nightside* (1981) bear this out. Presumably assembled by the authors themselves, such collections often function as 'The Best of…' books, and showcase the full range of their work. Or they can display a quantity of quality and characteristic work, showcasing the best short fiction that the author feels that they have produced up to the date of publication.

When Karl Edward Wagner (1945-94) died, he had published two collections of his modern short horror fiction. The first of these, *In a Lonely Place* (1983) certainly belongs in the list given above. It showcased the best of Wagner's work, and indeed contains virtually all of his short fiction that it is essential to have read.

As this essay is intended as an examination of Karl Edward Wagner's modern horror fiction, I feel that a survey of the contents of *In a Lonely Place* amounts to the same thing. Although there are good stories in the later collection *Why Not*

You and I? (1987) and the posthumous round-up *Exorcisms and Ecstasies* (1997), nevertheless, for Wagner's most characteristically concentrated and nerve-tingling fiction, his first collection remains head and shoulders above the later books in creative power and impact. Doubtless this decline was helped by Wagner's increasingly tragic personal life and his growing dependence on alcohol.

In a Lonely Place contains seven stories, all previously published in magazines or anthologies of original fiction. They were first published between 1973 and 1982, the decade which turned out to be Wagner's most creative from the point of

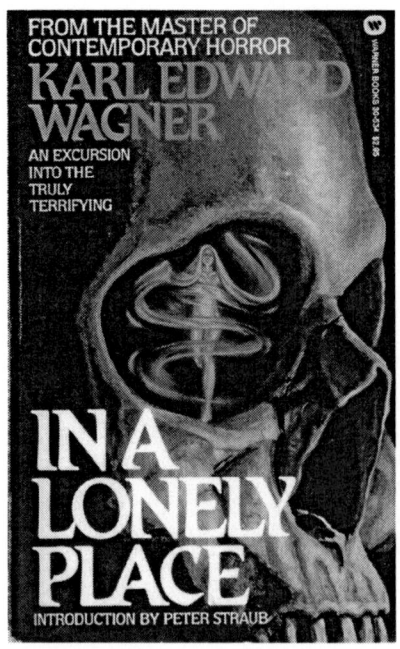

view of his own fiction. In 1980 Wagner had taken over from Gerald W. Page as editor of the annual *The Year's Best Horror Stories* reprint anthologies published by DAW Books, and edited fifteen volumes in a run that only ended with his death. Maybe it was a tribute to Wagner's skills as an editor and encourager of new talent, that the series was not continued under a different editor. Maybe, like August Derleth, Wagner will mainly be remembered and appreciated as an editor and publisher. In addition to his anthologies, Wagner's small press Carcosa Books helped to resurrect the reputations of such classic pulp-era authors as Manly Wade Wellman (1903-86) and Hugh B. Cave (1910-

2004), and reintroduced the thinking genre to the incomparable talent of artist Lee Brown Coye (1907-81). And, like Derleth, Wagner also produced a handful of stories of his own which deserve to be remembered. And these are contained in *In a Lonely Place*.

This survey will inevitably contain much in the way of plot -summary, and I hope that I have been vague and unclear, rather than giving away any particularly important or surprising plot twists. There are many, and spoilers are terrible things. I hope that this piece will encourage readers to seek out and experience for themselves the full impact of Wagner's work, and especially *In a Lonely Place*.

***

In a Lonely Place opens with an almost Lovecraftian 'Prologue', one which sets the tone for most of the book's contents:

> There is an atmosphere of inutterable loneliness that haunts any ruin – a feeling particularly evident in those places once given over to the lighter emotions... Such places are lairs of inconsolable gloom... These places are best left to the loneliness of their grief...[1]

The first story, 'In the Pines' was first published in *The Magazine of Fantasy and Science Fiction* (*F&SF*) in 1973, and the immediately preceding Prologue (placed so as to make it in effect the prologue to this particular story) is entirely appropriate. Like most of the stories contained in *In a Lonely Place*, it has the sort of well-crafted and evocative southern United States regional setting that was such a Wagner trademark. Set in Tennessee, in mountainous pine-covered territory, 'In the Pines' is simple in theme, and the eerie landscape as much a character as any of the human figures in it.

Gerard and Janet Randall arrive on vocation, to help them recover from the loss in a car-accident of their only son. Janet Randall was also severely injured in the accident, and her physical dependence on her husband has already helped to begin to erode the relationship between them. But what was worse, Gerard is convinced that Janet contributed to the cause of the crash – and that she is therefore guilty in no small part for their son's death, and the loss of their 'comfortable, well-ordered existence torn to twisted wreckage'.[2] Not least amongst the wreckage is their marriage. They hope that a vacation at a remote cabin can help them to sort things out...

Despite some early attempts to relax together, Gerard soon starts to avoid his wife. He sits up late drinking cheap Scotch, and explores the whole room full of accumulated debris that is the cabin's storeroom. Among the items left there over the years is an oil-painting of a woman:

> It was a lonely picture. She stood against a background of dark pines, cold and lonely about her. There was a delicacy about her and, illogically, an impression of strength... The eyes – soft blue, or did they glow? Did they express longing, pain? Or were they hungry eyes, eyes alight with triumph? Lonely eyes. Lonely face. A lonely picture.[3]

Randall's stress, his resentment and guilt, his longing for the past before the accident, have all rendered him extremely vulnerable. Soon his drunken dreams start to include Renee, the girl in the painting, and she starts to get progressively more real to him. During the day he further avoids his wife by exploring the area around the cabin, and finding out about its 'unlucky' history, and the violent and blighted lives of those who have lived there before. Discovering the fragments of an old diary, Randall unearths the history of the painting, and who the girl actually must be. Then, as Randall's obsession with her grows, all warnings are disregarded, and it also becomes clear *what* Renee must be. Except to Randall, who is lost for ever.

'In the Pines' is a fine example of regional horror fiction, where an apparently quiet and beautiful setting always hides (though not usually for long) an underlying horror that expands to fill the world of the character entering it. This is characteristic of Wagner's fiction, and this sort of theme recurs in several of the otherwise very different stories in the collection.

Contrasting with the deadly rural coolness of the pines is the urban dust and heat of 'Where the Summer Ends'. First published in Kirby McCauley's landmark anthology *Dark Forces* (1980), 'Where the Summer Ends' is set in a decaying and derelict area of Knoxville, Tennessee, where 'urban renewal' has done its worst and formerly upmarket and attractive districts have become, Innsmouth-like, something else entirely. Authors as diverse as Russell Kirk and T.E.D. Klein have also mined this urban twilight zone territory very effectively.

An elegiac tone is quickly replaced by hard reality as Jon Mercer, a student, visits Mr Gradie, a near-alcoholic dealer in second-hand furniture and collectables whose property is the last remaining lived-in, in an area of Knoxville whose heart has been torn out by depopulation and property demolition. And what is left is being strangled by the unstoppable kudzu vines.

> As he trudged along the skewed paving, he could smell a breath of magnolia through the urban miasma. That would be the sickly tree in the vacant lot across from Gradie's – somehow overlooked

when the house had been pulled down and the shrubbery uprooted – now poisoned by smog and strangled beneath the consuming masses of kudzu.[4]

Fascinated by the range of bric-a-brac in Gradie's yard, Mercer constantly buys as much as he can afford for his own collection. He and Gradie have gradually formed a friendship, and Gradie is willing, helped by Mercer's wine, to speculate on more than just the origin of the all-enveloping kudzu vines. Following the disappearance of one of his friends, and then his dog, Gradie continues tantalisingly to outline his theories about what lies under the impenetrable and indestructible plants. And when Mercer and his girlfriend glimpse an animal that is not quite a rat or a monkey, Gradie's semi-drunken speculations take on a sharper and more urgent meaning.

There is as much of Arthur Machen as H.P. Lovecraft in 'Where the Summer Ends' – with its secret 'people' living alongside us and unsuspected by the vast majority, and needing to keep their existence unknown. Again the setting plays as much a part as the human characters. Like Lovecraft's New England and Machen's London and Wales, Wagner's evocation of Knoxville enables the addition of a real depth and sense of living reality to the story's events. The setting is mundane, but the events are decidedly not mundane. Setting and events complement each other, and create a real world where it is possible to blur the lines between what can (or has) happened, and what certainly should not be able to happen. As that world is consumed, and the characters drawn into it, to be changed for ever – if they are able to escape.

'Sticks' (1974) was the first of several stories that Wagner first published in the highly-respected small-press magazine *Whispers*. Like 'Where the Summer Ends', 'Sticks' is another story that used Machen's and Lovecraft's theme of lingering survival. Reminiscent of such stories as Arthur Machen's 'The Shining Pyramid,' Wagner set 'Sticks' in upstate New York, and, like 'In the Pines' the scene is a rural one that forms an evocative background to action that unfolds over decades.

Exploring an abandoned and overgrown house, magazine artist Colin Leverett finds a number of delicately constructed 'lattice' structures:

> Sticks from trees and bits of board nailed together in fantastic array. They defied description; no two seemed alike. Some where only one or two straight sticks lashed together in parallel or at angles. Others were worked into complicated lattices of dozens of sticks and boards. One could have been a child's tree house – it was built in three planes, but was so abstract and useless that it could be nothing more than an insane conglomeration of sticks and wire.[5]

Leverett enters the house's cellar, where he finds what he thinks could a stone table. The cellar is built of huge and well-fitted stone blocks – like in H.P. Lovecraft's 'The Rats in the Walls,' the further you go from the sunlight, the deeper you go underground, the unnaturally older things get. There are hints of further vast chambers deeper underground, but Leverett barely escapes from the cellar when something rises from the 'table' and attacks him...

That was in 1942. After his return from the Second World War, Leverett resumes his career as an artist for pulp magazines, but his war experiences and others have permanently scarred him. Commissions fall away, and Leverett ekes out a living making and selling macabre sculptures, and having his work appear in selected galleries.

Years later, Leverett's friend Prescott Brandon

commissions a series of illustrations for a collection of cult
pulp horror-writer H. Kenneth Allard's short stories that he is
publishing. Leverett rises to the occasion, and his illustrations
are a hit, inspired as they are by his memories of the stick
structures that he saw decades previously. Contacted by an
archaeologist who is interested in the stick structures, Leverett
attempts to find the abandoned house, but the site has been
obliterated with the passing of the years. And then death
strikes, with Prescott Brandon's brutal murder, just as he had
published the final volume of Allard's stories.

Then Allard's unknown nephew turns up, with a
commission for Leverett to illustrate *Dwellers in the Earth*, a
collection of some of Allard's previously unpublished stories.
And he wants him to use the stick motifs again. But when the
drawings are completed, the nightmares begin.

Further Lovecraftian echoes, of 'The Rats in the Walls,'
'The Whisperer in Darkness,' and *The Case of Charles Dexter
Ward* appear in the dreams of stone underground places and
their inhabitants. Leverett grasps the true meaning of the stick
lattices, and attempts to get Allard to destroy the edition of
Dwellers in the Earth. But Allard isn't quite the person that he
said he was:

> 'Then you appeared, Colin Leverett – you with your artist's
> knowledge and diagrams of Althol's symbols. And now a
> thousand new minds will read the evocation you have returned to
> us, unite with our minds as we stand in the Hidden Places. And
> the Great Old Ones will come forth from the earth, and we, the
> dead who have steadfastly served them, shall be masters of the
> living.'[6]

As well as being a fine addition to a generally
undistinguished sub-genre, that of 'Cthulhu Mythos' fiction,

'Sticks' is Wagner's homage to H.P. Lovecraft and the artist Lee Brown Coye. Even as the possibility of horror mounts, the reader can smile at the in-jokes, recalling that Wagner was himself a publisher at the time, reprinting classic pulp horror fiction, and commissioning Coye to illustrate the books. 'Sticks' is an updating of the Machen/Lovecraft theme, a fine example of modern horror that also remains a distinctively Karl Edward Wagner piece, with its remote and run-down settings, and lead character who is decidedly partial to a drink.

'Sticks' also has its more cosmic side, as symbols rooted firmly in the earth and under it are manipulated in order to transform it totally. Like in T.E.D. Klein's novel *The Ceremonies* (1984), which was considerably expanded from 'Events at Poroth Farm' (1972), the rural eastern United States contains ancient and deadly forces that have only been temporarily absent from the scene.

The following year, 1975, saw *Whispers* publish 'The Fourth Seal,' perhaps the least obviously Wagnerian story in *In a Lonely Place*. A fine example of conspiracy theory fiction (hopefully!), 'The Fourth Seal' poses the idea that certain medical advances have been deliberately withheld, and that the medical profession and much else is under the hidden control of people whose aim is effectively to provide continuous employment for its members.

The rising young physician Dr Metzger is sounded out by Dr Thackeray, Chairman of Medicine at the hospital where he conducts his research, and where his latest results, should they be made public, would have the most revolutionary results. The elite get together:

> Dr Lipton laughed shortly. 'If only you knew half our efforts toward keeping cars and highways unsafe! Or the medications we

release for the public to abuse. Or the chemical additives we've developed...'[7]

A short and effective story, 'The Fourth Seal' shows that Wagner was at home in thoroughly modern settings where the supernatural is not an option, but where reality is still seriously skewed, with a paranoiac fantasy possibly ruling the world from behind the scenes. Everything that we ever knew is still wrong.

'.220 Swift' was first published in the other landmark horror anthology from 1980, Ramsey Campbell's *New Terrors* – a two-volume paperback original that showcased excellent works by existing talent, and hinted at much of the talent to come. Karl Edward Wagner's contribution (in Volume 1) returns to familiar territory – the rural landscapes of the Tennessee/North Carolina country, a fascination with underground passages and caves, and the survival of something inimical from the past that breaks out into the contemporary world, and changes everything.

Archaeologist Morris Kenlaw is looking for 'mines of the ancients' which he thinks were actually dug by Spanish conquistadores looking for gold.[8] An albino anthropology student, Brandon, believes that they are much older, and the Cherokee and other legends of spirits and serpents and other beings that lived in the caves do actually point to something – maybe 'the Yunwi Tsundi, the Little People who live deep inside the mountains.'[9]

Kenlaw and Brandon descend into a cave where they discover evidence of Spanish or Colonial exploration. Again Wagner's apparent fascination with huge underground spaces (and has already been pointed out, one used by Arthur Machen and certainly shared with H.P. Lovecraft) reappears as the two academics find that the caves go back and down further than they ever suspected, and show all the signs of not being natural tunnels.

Deep inside, Brandon realises that there is gold there, and Kenlaw attempts to kill him to keep the secret to himself. But he only succeeds in knocking Brandon unconscious, and so he disguises what he did so that it could seem to have been an accident. Attempting to escape the scene of his crime, Kenlaw then meets the surviving inhabitants of the caves.

Brandon recovers and is rescued by the same 'people' who killed Kenlaw:

> Brandon stared back at the vast circle of eyes. It occurred to him to wonder that he could see them; his first thought was that there must be a source of dim light from somewhere. It then came to him to wonder that these creatures had spared him; his first thought was that as an albino they had mistakenly accepted him as one of their race... And, in understanding at last, Brandon knew who he was, and why he was.[10]

The legends about the tunnels and caves under the mountains are true. An ancient race has survived. There is only one more legend to be utilised now, as Brandon returns to the surface once more, and meets his girlfriend:

> She cried out when she saw their faces, and instinctively pressed against Brandon for protection.
> 'Don't be afraid,' he soothed, gripping her tightly. 'These are my people. They've fallen far, but I can lead them back along the road to their ancient greatness.
> 'Our people,' Brandon corrected himself, 'Persephone.'[11]

'The River of Night's Dreaming' (1981) was first

published in *Whispers III*, a combination 'Best of' *Whispers* magazine and original anthology. A long and atmospheric opening – it really was a dark and stormy night – paints a picture of desperation and urgent survival against overwhelming odds. A nameless convict or mental patient barely escapes drowning when the prison bus crashes into the sea. She ends up struggling to the shore in a section of the city that she doesn't know, but which even so seems somehow wrong. Chased by something she can't quite ever make out, but which horrifies her, she finds shelter in the only house that seems to be inhabited.

Mrs Castaigne and her maid Camilla take the near-naked and freezing stranger into their home. The house also seems wrong. For example, the two women wear Victorian-style dresses:

> The sitting room was distinctly old-fashioned – furnished like a parlour in an old photograph, or like a set from some movie that was supposed to be taking place at the turn of the century. Even the lights were either gas or kerosene.[12]

When they ask her name, one 'suited to her surroundings' occurs to her – 'Cassilda Archer'. We have been advised. We are about to experience Karl Edward Wagner's homage to Robert W Chambers (1865-1933) and his bizarre and decadent world, and the fearsome *The King in Yellow* (1895).

Cassilda is encouraged to stay indefinitely, and she can scarcely escape, having no clothes left of her own and an alibi that wouldn't stand up against any threatened police enquiries. She seems to all-too easily slip into the vacant place left by Mrs Castaigne's vanished daughter, Constance. Cassilda's new life in Mrs Castaigne's house coincides with the continuing loss of her memory of any part of her life before prison. Her life is warm and faintly stifling, like the atmosphere of the house – the world is kept firmly at bay, but that world is still not right: Cassilda realises that she can hear horses' hooves outside. But it all seems somehow familiar as well.

Cassilda's main duty is to be Mrs Castaigne's companion, and to read to her when required:

> Taking up the book, Cassilda again experienced a strange sense of unaccountable *déjà vu*, and she wondered where she might previously have read *The King in Yellow*, if indeed she ever had.
> 'I believe we are ready to begin the second act,' Mrs Castaigne told her.[13]

We certainly are. There is a strong sexual charge in 'The River of Night's Dreaming'. Camilla points out that the two characters in *The King in Yellow* have the same names and 'are such very dear friends'.

Mrs Castaigne refuses to talk about Constance, but Camilla tells Cassilda that she became ill, had to be taken away after suffering nervous fits. Camilla's punishment for gossiping expands to take in Cassilda. Her life in the house now includes keeping a journal which frightens her when she realises what the date is, and yet all of the entries have been entered in her own handwriting. Cassilda's memories are of dislocation and yet being at home.

> There were too many elusive memories, memories that died unheard…Had she not read that? *The King in Yellow* lay open upon her nightstand. Had she been reading, then fallen asleep to such dreams of depravity? But dreams, like memories, faded miragelike whenever she touched them, leaving only tempting images to beguile her.[14]

Finally Cassilda's memories return in full and the circle is completed as her past catches up with her at last, and time and space unravel for the last time. Unless the terrible hint in an old copy of *The King in Yellow* found in a prison hospital means more than some staff members think:

> 'Harmless nineteenth-century romantic nonsense,' Dr Archer concluded. 'Send it back to the library.'
>
> The psychiatrist glanced at a last few lines before closing the book:
>
> *Cassilda*: I tell you, I am lost! Utterly lost!
>
> *Camilla* (terrified herself): You have seen the King...?
>
> *Cassilda*: And he has taken from me the power to direct or to escape my dreams.[15]

'The River of Night's Dreaming' is perhaps the single best story included in *In a Lonely Place*. Rich and moody, with a slowly growing strain of terror, nightmare, and madness, it is deeply disturbing and ambiguous about the things that we take for granted – who we are, where we have come from, what attracts and tempts us. The potential power of art to corrupt absolutely is made obvious.

The final story is 'Beyond Any Measure,' first published in *Whispers* magazine in 1982. There are some overlapping themes with 'The River of Night's Dreaming': dislocations in time and memory as experienced by a young woman far from home, the power of what might or might not be dreams, and a strong sexual and decadent element, although the story is firmly, this time, rooted in twentieth-century London.

Listte Seyrig, an American living in London, shares a flat with Danielle, who moves in vaguely occult circles. She reads books like Roland Franklyn's *We Pass from View* – a nice in-joke and tribute to Ramsey Campbell and his fictional book and author featured in *Demons by Daylight*'s 'The Franklyn Paragraphs'). When Lisette tells Danielle that she was mistaken in the street for someone else, warns her of the disaster to follow if she should ever meet her doppelganger herself.

Suffering from recurring nightmares, Lisette has been seeing Dr Magnus, who is convinced that they point towards proving his theory that the soul can be reincarnated, and that she is reliving the terrible events in someone else's life.

Under hypnosis the dreams become more detailed, various aspects of a horrifying past event gradually being revealed as dream succeeds dream. Despite Lisette's growing fright and reluctance to continue, Dr Magnus is eager to carry on, because if he can show that the dreams do not include anyone possibly connected with Lisette's past, then the dreams have no subconscious or genetic basis, and his theory is correct.

At a masked party, Lisette finally does meet her doppelganger, Beth Garrington:

> The lips beneath the mask curved in a pleasurable smile. Lisette gazed into the eyes behind the mask, and discovered that she could no longer feel her body. She thought she heard Danielle cry out her name.
> The eyes remained in her vision long after she slid down the newel and collapsed upon the floor.[16]

As in 'The River of Night's Dreaming,' the lead female character is invited to take refuge in a strange house. In this case, Lisette goes to stay with Beth Garrington after Danielle is murdered in the flat she and Lisette shared. Again, the 'refuge' is actually a doubtful one, and it means that the various strands from the past and present that haunt the characters are finally woven together, with catastrophic results for those involved. At Beth Garrington's house, the source of Lisette's dreams is revealed, and all of the accumulated hints that have built up throughout come together in a devastating climax in which Wagner keeps the reader guessing for the exact confirmation right until the final page.

***

In a Lonely Place was first published as an original paperback, and one rather undistinguished in appearance at that. In my experience it is now very hard to find. And yet it is entirely appropriate that such a range of dark treasures should be found within such a container so easily battered by time and ordinary wear and tear as a paperback book. The word endures.

Notes

Page references are to the first edition of *In a Lonely Place*, Warner Books, 1983

1.   *In a Lonely Place* pp.1-2
2.   *In a Lonely Place* p.7
3.   *In a Lonely Place* pp.9-10
4.   *In a Lonely Place* p.38
5.   *In a Lonely Place* p.71
6.   *In a Lonely Place* p.91
7.   *In a Lonely Place* p.114
8.   *In a Lonely Place* p.121
9.   *In a Lonely Place* p.129
10.   *In a Lonely Place* p.164
11.   *In a Lonely Place* p.167
12.   *In a Lonely Place* p.181
13.   *In a Lonely Place* p.194
14.   *In a Lonely Place* p.201
15.   *In a Lonely Place* p.208
16.   *In a Lonely Place* p.243

Somebody Pointed Earth:
August Derleth's Science Fiction

August Derleth is not best remembered for being a writer of science fiction. When compared with the quantity of macabre, mystery, and regional fiction that he wrote, his output of science fiction was minimal. During an active publishing career as a professional that lasted from 1926 until his death in 1971, Derleth's activities in the science fiction field mainly occurred in the late 1940s and early 1950s. Despite this being but a small part of his total output, Derleth's work in science fiction is worth examining, and so that is what I set out to do here. It will also survey his work as an editor, and publisher, of science fiction.

August Derleth's involvement with science fiction began when he was in his adolescence. He was a reader and early contributor to the magazine *Weird Tales*, founded in 1923. (His first story there, and his first published work, was the macabre 'Bat's Belfry' in the May 1926 issue.) During its first ten years or so, *Weird Tales* published much science fiction, for example the Interstellar Patrol stories of Edmond Hamilton (between 1929 and 1934), although the magazine soon came to concentrate on weird, macabre, and fantasy fiction.. As a reader of, and contributor to, many fiction magazines in several genres, Derleth would certainly have encountered these and similar tales. In his book *All Our Yesterdays*, Harry Warner states that Derleth was a reader of the science fiction magazine *Amazing Stories* (founded in 1926).[1]

During this period, Derleth wrote a great deal of fiction for

Weird Tales and other macabre and mystery magazines, as well as beginning what would soon become his Sac Prairie Saga. But he concentrated on these, and actually wrote almost nothing that could really be described as science fiction, until the early 1950s.

(The main exception to this was in Derleth's codification and use of H.P. Lovecraft's 'Cthulhu Mythos' background. During his lifetime, the fiction of H.P. Lovecraft (1890-1937) had moved from an essentially fantastic framework for his creations, to one in which his 'gods' were merely very powerful alien beings and concepts, that interacted with people on this planet unfortunate to encounter them. This was science-fictional enough to warrant publication in some science fiction magazines, although the bulk of Lovecraft's work still appeared in *Weird Tales*.[2] Derleth used Lovecraft's fictional background for much of his own work, as well as in collaborations with fellow Sauk City inhabitant Mark Schorer (1908-77), and the 'posthumous collaborations' with Lovecraft himself. These stories are essentially science fiction, but are told within a gothic and macabre framework, in which incantations, talismans, and dreams play a part. As such, these stories will not be dealt with here.[3]

***

The bulk of August Derleth's science fiction proper is to be found in the collection *Harrigan's File* (1975). Indeed, this book claims to contain 'all the science fiction Derleth ever wrote and prepared for publication'.[4] However, this is not quite the case, and a small number of other stories will be considered below.

In almost every case, Derleth's science fiction stories were first published in magazines. Each of the five issues of *Orbit Science Fiction* (1953-54) contained a Harrigan story, as did several other, mainly short-lived, magazines of that time. The early 1950s was a time of great expansion of the science fiction magazine field in the United States. It is not too difficult to imagine that Derleth took advantage of this by seeking, or being offered, the opportunities to publish in these growing markets.[5]

The stories collected in *Harrigan's File* all follow the same basic formula. The veteran newspaper reporter Tex Harrigan finds himself reminded about a strange or odd person that he

has encountered during his career. Then, usually over several drinks, he proceeds to recount his memory. The people that he has come into contact with usually turn out to have invented some sort of scientific device, or harnessed a theory, or claim to have had an unusual experience.

In the Harrigan stories, Derleth covered a very wide range of science-fictional ideas. It was as if Derleth had compiled a list, and set himself the task of taking as many commonplace science fiction themes as he could, and then writing a story around each one.

For example, there are contacts with aliens: 'McIlvaine's Star', (*If*, July 1952); 'The Man Who Rode the Saucer', (*Far Boundaries*, as by Kenyon Holmes). New mechanical devices are involved in 'Mark VII' (*Orbit Science Fiction*, September-October 1954), 'The Maugham Obsession' (*Fantastic Universe Science Fiction*, June-July 1953), and 'The

Mechanical House' (*Orbit Science Fiction*, July-August 1954) – this last offering a humorous glimpse of a tragic situation envisaged in Ray Bradbury's classic mood-story 'There Will Come Soft Rains' (1950). Time travel appears in 'The Penfield Misadventure *(Orbit Science Fiction*, November-December 1954) and 'A Traveller in Time' (*Orbit Science Fiction*, No 2, 1954). 'An Eye For History' echoes Robert A. Heinlein's 'Life-Line' (*Astounding Science Fiction* August 1939) and T.L. Sherred's 'E For Effort' (*Astounding Science Fiction* May 1947) in its use of a device built in order to see the past and future, with dire consequences. Derleth uses science fiction to indulge in some mild satire in 'The Detective and the Senator' (*The Saint Detective Magazine* August-September 1953) in which a Joe McCarthy character gets his just desserts! 'Protoplasma' uses the monster-out-of-control theme. There is further satire in 'The Remarkable Dingdong' (*Spaceway* April 1954) in which the editor of a science fiction magazine always seems to know the latest scientific developments – before anyone else. This must have been inspired by the editor of *Astounding Science Fiction*, John W. Campbell, whose publication of Cleve Cartmill's story 'Deadline' (March 1944) worried the FBI because of its apparent inside knowledge of aspects of nuclear research.

These and the other Tex Harrigan stories are science fiction only by virtue of the scientific (or pseudo-scientific) trappings used in them. Derleth's use of standard science fiction themes was not one that added anything to the body of literature that had already been published. Derleth gives no details as to the workings of his creations: they are simply there as gadgets, or props for the story that Derleth wishes to tell. In several stories Derleth shows his misunderstanding of such basic knowledge as the composition and size of stars, galaxies, and nebulae.[6]

This also, of course, reflects badly on the editors who published Derleth's work, without correcting his mistakes, thus reinforcing the criticism that science fiction literature is often badly-written and ignorant of real science.

In the Tex Harrigan stories, as in most of his work, Derleth's main concern is with people, situations, and places. He wished to show how 'odd' and 'queer' people live and react in certain situations. For example, in his early Steve Grendon stories, such as those collected in *Place of Hawks* (1935), Derleth deals with afflicted people confronting problems caused by knowledge of some mental or medical condition, as observed and narrated by the grandson of a Sac Prairie doctor. The village and rural background is also integral. In the same way, Derleth used that language and conventions of science fiction to tell stories about unusual and vulnerable people, and the situations that they found themselves in.

Five other stories, eventually collected in *Dwellers in Darkness* (1976) can also be classified as science fiction. They have much the same characteristics as the Tex Harrigan stories.

An alien incursion on Earth is the theme of 'The Island Out of Space' (*Amazing Stories* June 1950.) 'The Song of the Pewee' (*The Arkham Sampler* Autumn 1949) deals with a young nonconformist living in a regimented future. 'The Place of Desolation' (*Weird Tales* March 1952) has the narrator seeing visions of other times and dimensions from a house, in a way that recalls William Hope Hodgson's novel *The House on the Borderland* (1908), itself published in an omnibus edition by Derleth in 1946. 'Memoir for Lucas Payne' (*Strange Stories* August 1939) has the narrator meet the character Payne, who has invented a device that can make himself shrink, and stop him from growing old. 'Open, Sesame!' (*The Arkham Sampler* Winter 1949) has a professor unwittingly opening a way for the alien invasion of Earth.

Science fiction also appeared in Derleth's long-running series of Sherlock Holmes pastiches, the Solar Pons stories. There are two Pons stories, collected in an appendix to *The Solar Pons Omnibus* (1982) that can be described as fantastic, in a science-fictional sense. Both originally appeared in *The Magazine of Fantasy and Science Fiction*, and were collaborations with science fiction writer Mack Reynolds (1917-83). 'The Adventure of the Snitch in Time' (July 1953) concerns Pons' meeting with a client from the year 2565, and a parallel universe in which Pons is only fiction! In 'The Adventure of the Ball of Nostradamus' (June 1955), Pons takes action against a man who is murdering children whom he knows will cause worldwide problems when they grow up.

***

Derleth was also heavily involved in the editing and publishing of science fiction. He began with the publication of much of H.P. Lovecraft's work, including his science fiction, in *The Outsider and Others* in 1939. To do this he founded, with Donald Wandrei (1908-87), the publishing company Arkham House, which still exists today. Although Arkham House concentrated on weird and macabre fiction, it did publish science fiction in collections of stories by Wandrei and Clark Ashton Smith.[7] In 1946 Derleth published A.E. van Vogt's novel of mutant telepaths *Slan* (originally serialised in *Astounding Science Fiction* September-December 1940). Several science fiction short stories also appeared in *The Arkham Sampler*, Derleth's own magazine which ran for eight issues during 1948 and 1949.

Derleth's main contribution to science fiction publishing

lies in his anthologies. He was a pioneer anthologist. His earliest anthologies, *Sleep No More* (1944) and *Who Knocks?* (1946) contained mainly macabre fiction, but were contemporary with the first science fiction anthologies, such as Phil Stong's *The Other Worlds* (1941) and *Adventures in Time and Space* (1946), edited by Raymond J. Healy and J. Francis McComas.

Between 1948 and 1954, Derleth edited nine science fiction anthologies, from *Strange Ports of Call,* to *Portals of Tomorrow.*[8] These were generally well-chosen anthologies, with stories emphasising the human element over the scientific. The stories tended to dwell on the effects of future developments rather than on the developments themselves. Most volumes contained reprints by well-known as well as lesser-known authors. Some volumes contained original work, and occasionally stories by Derleth himself, under a pseudonym.

As well as simply presenting a collection of stories, several of the anthologies were edited with objectives in mind. *Beyond Time and Space* (1950) was intended to show the development of science fiction, from Plato to Ray Bradbury. *The Outer Reaches* (1951) gives the opportunity for a group of writers to select their favourite among their own stories, and to explain their choice. *Portals of Tomorrow* (1954) was intended to be the first in a series of 'Best of the Year' anthologies – a concept that was briefly used by E.F. Bleiler and T.E. Dikty in 1949 and only really developed by Judith Merril and others from 1956 onwards, to the present.

Derleth's qualities as an anthologist were not always appreciated by those more heavily involved in science fiction than Derleth was himself. Damon Knight, in his collection of criticism and reviews *In Search of Wonder* uses the contents of the all-original *Time to Come* (1954) to question Derleth's judgement when it came to selecting stories that made sense as modern science fiction. It underlined Derleth's apparent general lack of concern with, and understanding of science, except its use in passing, to make or illuminate some aspect of a human character or situation.[9]

***

August Derleth's best work, whether fiction, nonfiction, or poetry, is concerned with people and their surroundings, their interrelationship, and Derleth's observations of these. His Sac Prairie Saga work, which chronicles in detail the history of his part of Wisconsin and its people, is the greatest example of this. In his best work Derleth explores people's motivations, and reactions to forces, whether self-caused, or beyond their control.

Derleth's science fiction also does this, although on a far less exalted level. His concern is to illuminate something of the oddball people he perceived as needing to have their stories told. In the Tex Harrigan stories and his other science fiction, Derleth uses the framework provided by the genre, together with his natural humour and occasionally rather laboured satire, to achieve this same result.

One of Derleth's literary mentors, H.P. Lovecraft, wrote of Derleth's lack of feeling for the awesome and chill vastness of the universe.[10] Derleth was not affected by this perception in the way that Lovecraft was, and many of the best writers of science fiction have been and are. (This accounts for the fact that Derleth's own 'Lovecraftian' fiction is so weak in comparison with Lovecraft's). Derleth related everything solidly to this world, and preferably his own small corner of it, and the sort of people that he knew. Derleth's use of the idea of the microcosm reflecting the macrocosm is of relevance here, as in his regional work. The passing of time, and change, aided and abetted by science and scientific development, was abhorrent to Derleth. Since science fiction very often deals with these issues, by avoiding them Derleth's work could never be of more than minor importance. And in any case, in fiction the uncanny and macabre was his first love.

In his poem 'The Planetary Arc-Light' Derleth connects the mundane world of Sac Prairie with the boundless outside world, which is that of science fiction:

The important thing was that he noticed it out there.
What he called it did not count. Perhaps somewhere
far outside, somebody pointed Earth to say,
'I see they've put a new streetlight out there.'[11]

Derleth associates the two objects, the planet Venus and the streetlight, and all but leaves it at that. For Derleth, when it came down to it, the inner world of the human mind and its situations and challenges was more fascinating and important than the outer world of space and time. In his science fiction this shows.

Bibliography
Wilson, Alison M. *August Derleth: a bibliography* contains synopses of all Derleth's science fiction stories and anthologies. The anthologies themselves have appeared in both the US and UK, in a variety of hardcover and paperback editions. Derleth's *100 Books by August Derleth* (1962) contains full details of the anthologies.

The science fiction anthologies are:
   S*trange Ports of Call* 1948
   The Other Side of the Moon 1949
   Beyond Time and Space 1950

Far Boundaries 1951
The Outer Reaches 1951
Beachheads in Space 1952
Worlds of Tomorrow 1953
Time to Come 1954
Portals of Tomorrow 1954

Notes

1. Warner, *All Our Yesterdays*, Chicago 1969, p.15
2. 'The Colour Out of Space' was published in *Amazing Stories* Sept. 1927; 'At the Mountains of Madness' was serialised in *Astounding Stories* February- March 1936; 'The Shadow Out of Time' appeared in the June 1936 *Astounding Stories*.
3. See my *The Horrors Out of Wisconsin: August Derleth's Cthulhu Mythos Fiction*, Haddenham, England, 1986
4. From the dustjacket
5. See Irwin Strauss, *Index to the SF Magazines, 1951-1965*, and Mike Ashley, *The History of the Science Fiction Magazine 1946-1955*
6. As in 'McIlvaine's Star', 'An Eye For History', and 'The Island Out of Space'
7. For example, Smith's *Out of Space and Time* (1942) and Wandrei's *The Eye and the Finger* (1944)
8. See the Bibliography for a list of the science fiction anthologies
9. Knight, *In Search of Wonder*, Chicago 1967, pp.129-130
10. For example in *Selected Letters III*, p.196
11. *Collected Poems* (1967), p.205

Story-Telling Wonder-Questing, Mortal Me: The Transformation of 'The Pale Brown Thing' into *Our Lady of Darkness*

In this essay I wish to take one of Fritz Leiber's best and yet most neglected stories, and, like Cinderella, take it to the ball – for the story has been left behind (although by only the one sister, and not an ugly one at all). One of Fritz Leiber's finest and best-known novels is *Our Lady of Darkness*. But that book did not appear out of nowhere. There was an earlier version: 'The Pale Brown Thing'. So it is my intention in this essay to take a closer look at the earlier and eclipsed story, and to explore how it became an all-time classic horror novel – how 'The Pale Brown Thing' went to the ball.

'The Pale Brown Thing' appeared as a two-part serial in the January and February 1977 issues of *The Magazine of Fantasy and Science Fiction* (*F&SF*). Later the same year, *Our Lady of Darkness* was published in hardcover, to be followed by other hardcover and paperback editions on both sides of the Atlantic. Bruce Byfield, in his so-far definitive study of Fritz Leiber's works *Witches of the Mind*, rightly devotes a fair amount of space to *Our Lady of Darkness*. Byfield describes the process by which the later book was expanded from the earlier novella as having been by the 'addition of secondary narratives.'[1] A little further on, he also tantalisingly quotes Leiber himself as saying that the two stories should really be regarded as one: '...the two texts should be regarded as the same story told at different times. If Franz's story is longer in *Our Lady of Darkness*, the reason is that he recalls more the second time he tells it.'[2]

'The Pale Brown Thing' was the latest then published of what turned out to be a succession of stories by Fritz Leiber which concerned aging, somewhat lonely men coming to terms with their place in the wider universe through an experience in their own apparently highly circumscribed and ordinary world, and which along with them is transformed in the process. These stories include 'The Death of Princes', 'Catch That Zeppelin!', 'The Button Molder', and 'Horrible Imaginings.' The central character undergoes an experience, an encounter with the Other or the Outside after which nothing is quite the same again, and which enriches (even as it can terrify or suffuse with awe) the remaining time before his death.

It was another Leiber – Justin, Fritz Leiber's son – who wrote in his fascinating essay/memoir 'Fritz Leiber and Eyes' that as his father's art 'progressed in his growth in self knowledge' he also 'came to employ richer and more complicated forms, came to use himself and his artistic self-image in his art, came to play the mirror tricks of high art.'[3]

'The Pale Brown Thing' was a prime example of this, in which Leiber used his tricks to produce high art out of his life.

***

Fritz Leiber employed more than mere complication in his rich transformation of 'The Pale Brown Thing' into *Our Lady of Darkness*. Several full 'secondary narratives' were added, usually in the form of extended anecdotes by existing characters, and the interactions between the characters, all adding depth to the story. But the original story was also expanded by simply adding to descriptions, dialogue, thoughts, and so on – a few words here and there. The informality and immediacy – and therefore impact – of the narrative was already enhanced by Leiber's characteristic habit of making his characters 'think out loud' and of displaying their thought-processes and additional thoughts in the form of bracketed phrases and individual words.

The additions cover a wide range. Many of them concern the story's San Francisco setting, and the history and topography of the city. Leiber further develops it into a character in its own right, rather than as simply the background for the story. Thus San Francisco takes on the stature of Arthur Machen's London and Wales, and H.P. Lovecraft's New England, in the verisimilitude of the setting, as well as the menace that it passively harbours or actively encourages.

In 'Fritz Leiber and Eyes' Justin Leiber refers to his father as 'a great student (professor?) of cities.'[4] By the time that he was writing 'The Pale Brown Thing' he possessed a pair of binoculars, and made great use of them. In the stories binoculars enhance the vision of the city and the surrounding world. (Leiber himself also used binoculars for his hobby of roof-top astronomy, which play a major part in that great late story 'The Button Molder'.) We are shown that 'Outward vision is inward vision.'[5] Looking outwards into the city and the sky makes links with things that come to affect the inner being.

> There is the dark, eternally silent, unknown universe; there are the friend-enemy minds shouting and whispering their tales and always seeking the three miracles -- that minds should really touch, or that the silent universe should speak, tell minds a story, or (perhaps the same thing) that there should be a story that works that is all hard facts, all reality, with no illusions and no fantasy; and lastly, there is lonely, story-telling wonder-questing, mortal me.[6]

In one of the most eerie and unsettling passages in 'The Pale Brown Thing' (left unchanged in *Our Lady of Darkness*) Franz Westen first sees, while using his binoculars, what he is up against, what has awakened. Looking at something, or someone, magnified, isn't necessarily a one-way process. Can it not also mean that the eyes are stared back into, and can become the means of entry into the mind? Mixing can occur. The outward vision is linked with the inward vision, and vice versa. Not only is self-knowledge gained and increased, but something from outside can get to know someone as well.

Thus in *Our Lady of Darkness* Fritz Leiber fleshes out the character of his narrator, Franz Westen. His almost symbiotic relationship with the city is developed, and Westen's inner state is further explored. Leiber mixes his art with reality in an even headier cocktail that it had been in 'The Pale Brown Thing.' He had already been using his fiction as forms of therapy and catharsis, writing a lot because he had a lot to say about the death of his wife, his battles with alcohol, and now living alone in a great city, and coming to terms with age, loss, and death.

On a more obviously mundane level, we find out more about Westen's daily habits, and the web of friendships that form much of his world within the small world of his apartment building, as well as the city outside it. Westen has also acquired a regular writing job – that of novelising episodes of *Weird Underground*, an occult and fantastic TV series. Leiber mentions this aspect of Westen's life so many times that it is tempting to read more into it than simply the business of making Franz Westen into a still more credible character. (In his real life Leiber had also published a novelisation, *Tarzan and the Valley of Gold*, in 1966). Several times Westen contrasts the sort of scenario that he had to use from *Weird Underground* with the strange events that are happening in his own life.

Westen's friendships are explored in greater detail, especially those with Cal, and the rather Fafhrd and Gray Mouser-like Gunnar and Saul. Two extended episodes in *Our Lady of Darkness* (Chapters Four, Nine, and Ten, plus connecting passages) explore the complex relationships between Gunnar and Saul, the two men and Cal, and all three with Franz.

If 'The Pale Brown Thing' is the protagonist Franz Westen telling the story for the first time, then the longer version, *Our Lady of Darkness*, is the story as told again later, expanded and amplified, with the addition of much 'secondary' matter of all kinds. 'The Pale Brown Thing' and *Our Lady of Darkness* are simply best regarded as being two versions of the same story. And it is the best way to regard the two versions as recollections of one main sequence of events, told at two different times. (Not unlike how the three Synoptic Gospels recount one basic story, in three ways from three viewpoints, for different audiences.) But the additions are not secondary in the sense of being second-rate or less important. They are secondary only in the sense that they are recollected and told later rather than sooner.

Events recalled first are not always what can turn out to be the most important, and later additions can have the effect of achieving a better balance, and of adding depth and understanding to the earlier version of the narrative. The later version may well represent, possibly, the 'preferred' version, in the sense that the addition of later memories and impressions contribute to, and complete, what it is that needs to be recalled and put across.

***

'The Pale Brown Thing' is a viable and complete story in its own right, and worth knowing in addition to its longer version in *Our Lady of Darkness*. I have no idea whether or not Leiber did actually write 'The Pale Brown Thing' first and then literally expanded it for subsequent book publication. I am inclined to think that he did, as the additions can be seen to so obviously work in that way.

Although the remarks already quoted from Justin Leiber's essay 'Fritz Leiber and Eyes' were clearly made in the context of the novel *The Big Time* – and the Change War stories in general – I think that they are appropriate for much else that Fritz Leiber wrote.

> Any dream may realise that it has a dreamer, but then the dreamer becomes a part of the dream, and the dream acquires another level of structure. But the dream that this sort of dreamer dreams is itself a still greater dream and so must have still another dreamer, and so on. High art plays endlessly on this paradox and its analogs. Like Eddison's *Worm*, it is always swallowing its own tale/tail.[7]

In my view both 'The Pale Brown Thing' and *Our Lady of Darkness* were certainly the highly structured dreams of a master. And the essay is itself a piece of work that swallows its own tale/tail, with its interpenetrating layers of exploration and meaning.

As has been mentioned, Fritz Leiber's fiction grew more personal, and sometimes even positively confessional, as he grew older, and the quantity of his work began to decline. But the quality certainly did not. 'The Pale Brown Thing' and *Our Lady of Darkness* are two of Leiber's most personal stories. The narrator of both accounts of the story, Franz Westen, is a lightly-fictionalised version of Leiber himself. The San Francisco settings are taken from life, and there are many references to real people, both living and dead, some of whom Leiber knew personally and were friends. Leiber clearly enjoyed himself when he invented names for these characters. Some of this circle makes their appearances in the stories (but Leiber drew from the living ones).

At the beginning of his essay, Justin Leiber made the point that:

> When I talk with philosophers, linguists, and psychologists, I am often struck by the way in which not only arguments but whole phrases of their recent writings appear in their conversation. They are, or become, what they write.
>
> This can be disappointing unless I remind myself that people who don't write usually have much less to say, and they generally don't change their patter much from year to year.[8]

Fritz Leiber wrote much, and did have much to say. He became what he wrote, and wrote what he became. And both were high art.

The additions to 'The Pale Brown Thing'
I have listed the additions to 'The Pale Brown Thing', and how they dovetail into *Our Lady of Darkness*. It can be seen that, like a

carefully built structure, 'The Pale Brown Thing' has been partially dismantled, as it were, and new sections of greater or shorter length skilfully inserted, leaving a new and integral whole. Both versions exist on their own terms, and the continued existence of the two versions is to be preferred. They both leave the presumably now complete body of Fritz Leiber's work enriched.

Page numbers referred to first are those for *Our Lady of Darkness*, following the UK Millington edition (which is identical to the 1978 Fontana paperback edition). Page numbers in brackets refer to the magazine serialisation of 'The Pale Brown Thing'. This version has no chapter divisions.

p.5	[Entire quotation from De Quincey]
p.7	l.7-14 (p.6): The waxing ... Mount Diablo.
	l.19-24: An observer below ... for months.
p.9	l.6-24 (p.7): The TV tower ... another matter.
pp.9/10:	l.24-28/1-7: Faint dismal ... to their jobs.
p.11	l.13-34 (p.8): [There is a more elaborate description of the Sutro Tower]
p.14	l.4-6 (p.9): A sudden ... freakish gust.
	l.20-29 (p.10): [No mention of *Weird Underground*.]
	l.30-34: But this ... a trifle,
p.15	l.3ff: [Considerably expanded]
pp.15/16	l.5-27/1-8: In the hall ... knocked at 407.
pp.16/17	l.23-35/1-25: I came down ... *The Flute*.
p.17/18	l.26-35/1-6: Franz told Cal ... down easily
p.19	l.30-31 (p.11): What sort ... he do?
pp.19/20	l.32-36/1-2: There's absolutely ... Egypt.
p.21	l.1-2 (p.12): [No mention of de Camp and Squires]
p.23	l.10-15 (p.14): But as ... ahead!
pp.23/27	[Chapter Four added]
p.29	l.18-20 (p.15): and humorously ... those jinn.
	l.22-25: He had added … mailed it.
p.30	l.34-35 (p.16): Beyond ... breathing.
p.33	l.6-9 (p.17): from the faintly ... beyond them.

	l.17-21: He chucklingly ... tourists.
p.34	l.16-17 (p.18): [No mention of *Weird Underground*.]
p.35	1-17-20 (p.19): Grace Cathedral ... Cathedral Hill.
p.37	l.28-31 (p.20): But what ... more sense.
p.38	l.18: Really, he couldn't get home too soon.
	l.19-20 (p.21): The far side ... central city.
p.39	l.1-6: He thought ... things alone.
	l.19-22: The neighbourhood ... his pocket.
pp.40/41	l.31-35/1-2 (p.22): Had he thrown ... helpful scavenger.
	l.20-23: Remembering this ... their words.
pp.41/42	He was a tall man, ashen blonde, a fine-down amiable Viking.
	[Deleted at this point in *Our Lady of Darkness* and used in the completely new Chapter Four]
pp.45/46	l.36/1-4 (p.25): Saul's eyes ... Mrs Luque.
	l.16-17: The nearest ... the Potrero.
pp.46/47	l.24-28/1-2: and at Twin Peaks ... laughter.
p.48	l.9 (p.26): and the name ... had one.
	l.17-32: Gun and Saul ... their orders.
p.49	l.17-18 (p.27): They are both ... have power.
	l.20-21: Music? ... learn that.
	l.24: [No mention of *Weird Underground*.]
	l.25: Bonita protested, No!
	l.26: ...and the more serious junk,
pp.49/50	l.35-36/1-5: Saul said ... Her mother
pp.51	l.7-end p.65/p.66 l.1-2 (p.28): Bela Szlawik/ Fernando ... rating
p.66	l.6-13: From time ... come early.
p.67	l.17 (p.29): The green dwarf and the spider.
	l.18-25: Passing a shaft ... dead asleep
	l.27-36: For San Francisco ... Aldebaran.
p.70	l.13-17 (p.30): Franz picked up ... journal.
p.72	l.6-7 (p.31): that twentieth-century puritanic Poe from Providence,

l.11-13: (And hadn't Lovecraft ... by correspondence.

p.74   l.19-27 (p.33): Mostly not ... steaming coffee.
p.75   l.10-14: Oscar Wilde's ... their titles
pp.75/76 l.26-end/1-3 (p.34): Scanning ... drug-widened
          awareness.
p.77   l.14-17: But White ... Robert Ingersoll!
p.78   l.11-22 (p.35): It was she ... unexpected sides.
          l.30-34: You know ... was wondering.
p.80   l.13-20 (p.36): with a symphony ... paper snow.
p.81   l.28-32 (p.37): the latter ... elder brother.
p.82   l.19-23: though that last ... hotels too.
pp.82/83 l.35-36/1-2: Then he tramped ... believing that.
p.83   l.12-14 (p.38): thinking somewhat ... compulsive life!
p.85   l.24-27 (p.39): and then stroll ... suggested.
p.86   l.3-4: who was kneading ... blonde hair.
          l.10-12: Nothing at all ... charming.
          l.25-27 (p.40): And there ... as lingam.
p.87   l.8-13: He perversely ... for that matter.
          l.21-23: making itself ... smog over it.
          l.24: and north in Marin County
          l.27-33: He found himself ... of the Bay.
p.88   l.8-12 (p.41): It was funny ... mind did.
          l.16-19: And the pale blue ... punch-card.
          l.25-31: Why, he'd been ... gilded cross.
p.92   l.15-21 (p.43): Approaching Beaver Street ... the city.
          l.28-30: Cal had said ... gold trim.
p.94   l.10-12 (p.44): Or something ... some novelty?
          l.15-21: And he turned ... now behind him. l.24-29
          (p.45) Franz recalled ... with him.
p.97   l.9-11 (p.46): This pear wine ... sun-kissed slopes.
p.98   l.30-36 (p.47): I went ... and yesterday.
p.99   l.1-8: But even ... Donaldus so!
p.100   l.5 (p.48): ...and Cal.
          l.14-19: It helped too ... filigree on it
p.101   l.7-12: Which is odd ... never sure.

pp.103/104   l.18-36/1-11 (p.50): Rapidly travelling ... upon the
              scene.
p.104   l.28-36/p.105/p.106, l.1-4: Mention of Lovecraft ...
              culture and art.
p.107   l.8-end/p.108/p.109/p.110, l.1 (p.51): Of course ...
              Donaldus continued,
p.110   l.16-21: you know ... Gabriel Jogand...p.111 l.9-12:
              Unfortunately ... very obvious.
p.112   l.5-11 (p.52): Say, Franz ... But I digress.
              l.33-36/p.113, 1.1-16: Big buildings ... father, perhaps?
p.113   l.31-36/p.114/p.115, 1.1-25 (p.53): Though there is ...
              atmosphere at least.
p.116   l.12-23: Jack London ... at a distance.
p.117   l.1-10: Byers' eyebrows ... At any rate,
p.118   l.1-8 (p.54): And there's ... Tigress after them.
              l.14-23: Ricker ... got cold feet.
              l.24-36/p.119, l.1-4: Franz interposed ... he insisted.
p.119   l.15-16: She died ... very tragic.
p.121   l.12-15 (p.55): And now ... picture him as a
p.125   l.22: TdC [End of Pt.1 of serialization]
p.128   l.33-35 (p.117): And it makes ... foreign ones.
p.131   l.18-27 (p.119): Just the four ... to his story.
p.134   l.23-33 (p.120): Also, he went ... Corona Heights!
p.136   l.1-2 (p.121): or to the Queen ... outside.
pp.141/142   l.30-36/1-2 (p.126): So many of ... on him. And
p.146   l.26 (p.129): judging from here.
pp.146/147   l.34-36/1-10: One young couple ... by greybeards.
p.147   l.16-25: And then ... the concert hall,
p.150   l.20-22: (p.131) It was important ... but didn't
p.151   l.15-17: A half-dozen ... another Lady.
p.152   l.26-28 (p.132): He noted ... that either.
p.157   l.10-12 (p.136): Franz found himself ... fine tremor.
p.160   l.12-13 (p.138): Spider ... groaning commands.
p.161   l.23-30 (p.139): What else had ... Veiled Lady?
p.167   l.28-31 (p.143): [Questions made into statements.]

p.168	l.9-11: Then he pointed ... en muralla [deleting part of 'The Pale Brown Thing' paragraph] l.23-25: as if headed ... boxer would.
p.169	l.12 (p.144): *Weird Underground* – it was ironic.
p.172	l.24-34 (p.146): And speaking ... and pall me.
p.175	l.3-5 (p.148): Perhaps it would ... against magic.
p.176	l.15-16 (p.149): But perhaps ... for the next
p.179	l.5-6 (p.150): All her movements ... and beautiful.
p.181	l.7-13 (p.152): He realised that ... Our Lady of Darkness. l.18-22: He thought in ... Corona Heights.
p.186	l.19-25 (p.155): Gun kept some ... affair.)
pp.187/188	l.34-36/1-5 (p.156): Gunnar's Ingrid ... a grimmer period: l.20-23: *The Hound of the Baskervilles* ... into that.
pp.188/189	l.34-36/1: The pillar flew ... inches deep.
p.189	l.10-29 (p.157): Once, in a ... he lit a cigarette.

Notes

1. *Witches of the Mind* p.63
2. *Witches of the Mind* p.63 ('An Hour with Fritz Leiber')
3. Reprinted in *Fantasy Commentator* Vol. XI, Nos. 1 & 2 (Summer 2004) p.93
4. *Fantasy Commentator* p.84
5. *Fantasy Commentator* p.84
6. *The Leiber Chronicles* p.524
7. *Fantasy Commentator* p.90
8. *Fantasy Commentator* p.81

The Edge of Shadows:
A Look at the Shades Series
by Robert Hood

1 Introduction

Robert Hood published the four novels that make up the Shades series in successive months during 2001. The individual books are: *Shadow Dance*, *Night Beast*, *Ancient Light*, and *Black Sun Rising*. Despite their appearing as separate novels, the Shades series can also be regarded as one episodic novel in four volumes.

The series was planned as a whole. Hood has stated that his publisher required outlines, and so Hood had to do more planning and thinking ahead than might have otherwise been the case.[1] For some authors, this approach to writing and plotting might have imposed limitations on the development of the characters and the story. However, in the case of Shades at least, this approach of overall planning and writing the series all at once as a unity paid a dividend in terms of the cumulative effect of the books. Although each novel is narrated in the first person by one of the four main characters, the fact that each possesses a different (and distinctive) narrative voice helps to keep the overall narrative fresh and vivid, while the continuity is maintained by the presence of the other recurring characters and the settings, which weave the whole larger picture together. Hints and ideas earlier in the series are developed and sometimes explained later, and the main characters and others assume greater or lesser roles at different times, coming to the fore and receding into the background again, as part of a greater design. Mysteries are created, cleared up, and occasionally allowed to remain, over the course of all four books as well as in the individual parts of the series. Thus, while the story forges ahead, a sense of continuity and suspense is also sustained. There is always something to look forward to, keeping the reader hooked. (No doubt getting the reader to buy each new book in the series also had something to do with it. The first three novels also contained, at the end, the first chapter of the next in the series.)

Hood explains and describes the Shades as follows:

> There are creatures abroad, like ghosts, but less ethereal – teenagers who have been taken out of their time and place by forces they can barely imagine.
>
> Removed to another dimension, known to those who fear it as the Dark Realm, these creatures have powers ordinary humans merely dream about – but they also have limitations.
>
> Being only partially of this world and mostly of the Shadow Realm, they function better in the absence of light. Strong sunlight and even artificial light cause them to fade and they are forced to wear sunglasses to protect their eyes. Over-exposure to full daylight will send them back to the Shadow Realm. Forever.
>
> Uncertain about their place in this world, the Shades soon learn that there is conspiracy afoot and they are inexorably forced to confront the evil that would turn the living world into a barren darkness, a horrifying extension of the Shadow world.
>
> To overcome the Darkness, the Shades turn to each other, some unwillingly, and are forced to make alliances with ordinary humans around them. In their fight against the Shadow world, the Shades will confront their own fears and learn the answer to the most terrifying question of all: who are they?[2]

Shades was conceived and marketed as a series of Young Adult (YA) novels, but Hood intended Shades to be 'adult-friendly' as well.[3] But as they were definitely not intended for children, Hood had the freedom to explore the sensitive issues and sometimes violent situations that he does.

The concept of the Shades works as a metaphor, but Hood doesn't overdo this aspect of the series. 'The teenage years are a time of change and alienation. The Shades could provide a wonderful metaphor for the feelings of displacement and discontent that often characterise teenagers, I thought. Caught between childhood and adulthood feels a lot like being caught between one world and another, not knowing who you are, but sensing your difference. Where do you fit? Why does everything feel like a threat? I was suddenly very keen to explore this metaphor.'[4]

Although it can cost the reader some effort to immediately get to grips with the deeper aspects of what the characters are going through, this is well worth doing, and doesn't detract from the action. The Shades series is a dramatic and frightening story – no more and no less.

2 A New Mythology

The Shades series grew out of Robert Hood's 'desire to create a supernatural or SF series based on a "new" mythology' with 'a new type of ghost'.[5] Hood certainly succeeded in that aim. Despite its often gothic atmosphere, and its use of the trappings of supernatural horror, with evocations of various mythologies, Shades is not supernatural. It is, however, certainly horror. Hood's new mythology is really a science-fictional one. The supernatural occurrences are actually part of the natural order, but manifestations of hitherto unknown and unexplained parts of it. The series has a thoroughly scientific rationale, a speculative one involving theories of other universes and dimensions, travel in and between them, and the omnipresent dark matter. (Another unorthodox YA author, Philip Pullman, whose *His Dark Materials* trilogy [1995-2000] also appealed to adults, also made use of some of the fascinating proposals concerning dark matter. Hood's use of dark matter is markedly different to Pullman's.)

Hood's use of the terminology of the supernatural and mythology is consistent with his intention to create something new. Hood gives new meanings to well-used words and notions, as well as inventing special terminology and definitions of his own. For example, there is the vitally important Shadowedge – 'a vast, thin, and perhaps infinite space connecting all shadows everywhere throughout the world and even the universe'.[6] Hood worked with existing definitions of some of the most important ideas, then expanding on them and weaving them into the action of the story. There is a rich multi-layered usage for some words. For instance, 'shade' itself:

> In the Shades books, 'Shades' is the name given to teenagers who have been taken to the Shadow Realm (Tenebra) at the moment of death, but have now returned to our world...
>
> Basically, 'shade' is defined as 'partial or comparative darkness; absence of complete illumination' (OED), just as the Shades characters are partial forms of what they once were. 'Shade' is also the basis of the word 'shadow'. As a shadow is an image cast by a body that is standing against the light, so the Shades are like an image of themselves formed out of Tenebran dark matter and cast back into our world.
>
> The word 'shade' also has a related meaning that refers to protection or covering. For example, we place a shade over a veranda or a lamp to 'shade' us from the glare. I like this meaning in reference to the Shades, as they have a protective function: they help to protect ordinary humans from the Shadow creatures. They stand between humans and Tenebra, in some

small way covering them against the darkness.

'The shades' in Roman mythology was a term referring to the darkness of the nether world, or Hades, the land of the dead. As a result, the word 'shade' can refer to a ghost, 'the visible but impalpable form of a dead person, a disembodied spirit' (OED). This is an important meaning in reference to the Shades.

And then there's the modern meaning of 'shades', as in 'sunglasses', which the Shades have to wear all the time because they are so sensitive to light.[7]

The Shades series also makes use of some of the more intriguing, controversial, and obscure aspects of history, including modern-day versions of the Knights Templar and the notorious seventeenth century Witchfinder General of England, Matthew Hopkins.

3 Characters and Characteristics
The Shades series is strongly character driven, with characters that are also themselves highly driven. The Shades know that they are different, and are trying to explore and discover more about their difference – what it means and how they can live in the normal world that, due to no fault of their own, isn't designed for them and would almost certainly reject them if it knew the truth about them. And when they are threatened with destruction, along with the world, they take on responsibilities that are often way beyond their (physical) years.

On his website, Robert Hood provides sketches of his four main characters. Nathan Maple:

Looks Like
Dark red-brown hair, cut short at the back and sides, longer on top. Has the shadowy fuzziness of an insipient beard. Slim, with a wiry strength. Just above average height.

Is Like
> Never excelled at school. Easily distracted. Not a big talker. Impatient, especially with planning & rationalisation. Evasive about emotional matters.

Into
> Techno-funk – Prodigy, Korn, Limp Bizkit.[8]

There is a sense that the characters existed before the story opens, and that they continue in their lives afterwards.

The books are highly readable. It is as if the story had been written at the high speed that it can be read at, with the setting and characters having dictated to the author, rather than the other way round. It is clear that the characters mean something to the author – which means that they can also mean something to the reader. This is not easy to achieve, especially in YA fiction.

The action moves forward forcefully with short, punchy sentences and paragraphs. The style fits the fast and breathless action that the plot demands. Resolutions are often swift, and over before the reader quite realises it. However, there is time for reflection when necessary, for catching up on what's going on, with plenty of banter and lighter moments as well. Much of the story is mediated through interior monologues, which allows Hood to give insights into the different characters, as they think through what is happening, and what to do next. The interior moments are also often when reflection occurs.

Right at the beginning, the reader is thrown in at the deep end. From the opening lines of the first book in the series, the reader starts out in no better position than the main character, sixteen year-old Nathan Maple. Everyone has to learn for themselves and piece things together, and get orientated – at speed. Nathan starts out as an anonymous teenage boy pitched into a life-threatening enigma. And although characters and personalities are soon established, things don't change much after that. Nathan finds out that he is a Shade, and he and the other people he is involved with, Shade and human, are always on the edge of an abyss from then on until the last page of the last book of the series is turned.

Nathan, Cassandra, Mel, and Shine, Hood's four main characters, are portrayed as individuals with their own lives, experiences, appearances, mannerisms, and outlooks. None of them are normal in the sense of being ordinary. And yet they are ordinary as well. Before Nathan, Cassandra, and Shine became extraordinary Shades, they had a range of experiences that, while not all pleasant, were not necessarily unusual. Mel's home life and many of her attitudes are not conventional, but, again, they are far from unusual. They are all recognizable types who, even if the reader doesn't know anyone exactly like them, can believe in, and engage with.

The Shades series doesn't avoid family and relationship issues. The friendship between Nathan and Mel sometimes seems about to become a relationship, and sometimes not. Mel's family life, being brought up by an aunt and uncle, is far from ideal, and portrayed as such. But there are no simple good and bad sides to be taken. There is often friction between the main characters. The books contain a fair amount of violence and death, but this is never excessive or gratuitous. It is in keeping with the slowly unfolding over-arching apocalyptic horror theme of the series. Nowhere and no-one is entirely safe: the Shades' town is ravaged by apparently supernatural forces beyond anyone's control. There is no real security, even in well-known and familiar settings and landscapes. In the same way, there are no conventional happy endings, for either the main characters or anyone else involved with them.

This avoidance of the easy solution is a notable feature of the Shades series, and serves to increase the realistic aspect of the series, for both YA and adult readers. It rings true. It is reminiscent of the fiction of Alan Garner, who as well as writing fiction clearly intended for children, also wrote genre-crossing novels that function for both young adult and adult readers, and address issues of alienation, loneliness, and family and relationship friction and breakdown.[9]

Hood's contention that 'evoking horror in the bright sunlight is a very effective way of doing horror' is something that he lives up to throughout Shades.[10] The modern, sunlit towns of the New South Wales coast of Australia do not at first glance make a promising setting for the science fictional gothic horror that breaks out there in Shades. The towns of Albion Bay and Nimjala are based on the real places where Hood lives, or that he knows. The city of Sydney, although never mentioned by name, is never far away. The contrast between a mundane, normal setting and horrific events taking place there is an effective device that has been used successfully many times before. With a cosmic and earth-shattering scenario working itself out in a variety of mundane Australian settings and the sort of situations known to most teenagers and adults, in Shades this is no exception. Parts of *Black Sun Rising* are set in Cairo, and this touch of the exotic, along with the Australian setting also employed, also works effectively.

4 The Plot and Nathan Maple

As has already been described, Shades starts with Nathan Maple on a steep learning-curve trying to stay alive as he figures out where he is and what he has become. Nathan is not only enigmatic because of his entrance back into the world as we know it, but because it starts to become clear from early on in the series that there is something even more special about him than we can yet know. Nathan has a special place in the series, as an enigma holding things together even when he's not there, or when his role seems unimportant. Nathan is unique in the series as he has not only undergone the change into a Shade – he still has further changes to undergo, which become less obscure as the series progresses.

The basic theme of Shades is that there exists another universe, a dark shadow universe called Tenebra, which consists of dark shadow matter. Tenebra is inhabited by beings who wish to break through to this world of light. Hints of Tenebra have appeared in mythology and in humans' fear of the dark, and the two universes can connect wherever there are shadows in this world.

A short synopsis cannot do justice to the complex mixture of concepts and character that is the Shades series.

Nathan Maple is thrown into the beginning of the story as a new Shade – someone taken into Tenebra at the moment of death, and who returns to this world apparently unchanged in appearance, except they have something of the shadow world in them, and physically stay at the age they died. They are unable to tolerate strong light, especially sunlight, which makes them fade away. Shades are not ghosts, but neither are they fully human and corporeal. They constantly live a shadow life, on the borderline between darkness and light. In the Shades series Tenebra starts its final invasion of our world of light, and the Shades have to choose which side they are on, as they – and Nathan in particular – can make all the difference.

It is apparent from the beginning of *Shadow Dance* that Nathan is special, if not unique. Returning to his home town of Nimjala apparently from the dead, he soon shadow-hops into the Shadowedge, where he encounters a monster he thinks of as 'Gatorhead' and survives. Nathan's parents then disappear, and he is the only person who can rescue them. All these events are connected. Nathan had become part of the plan for Tenebra to break through into the world of light (our universe) but had somehow got away from Acheron before he could be fully transformed. For the time being, the shadow realm is prevented from breaking through, but Nathan is disowned by his father, and resigns himself to the lonely shadow-life of a Shade.

The second novel, *Night Beast*, is narrated by Cassandra, who appeared briefly early on in *Shadow Dance*. She has been a Shade since the nineteenth century, so her experiences certainly and completely belie her late teenage appearance. The normally unfazed Cassandra feels threatened by a man she hasn't seen before, while at the same time she meets Alan, who asks her out. Then there is an outbreak of apparent mass insanity in which people believe that their shadows are trying to kill them. The sky darkens unnaturally and the town is struck by powerful storms. The Shades know that these events are caused by Tenebra. Amidst the chaos, death, and destruction, Cassandra is kidnapped by the man who had been stalking her, who is a Templar, dedicated to the destruction of the Shades as demons. Rescued by Alan, who is a renegade Templar, Cassandra goes through a gateway into the shadow world where the Night Beast is forming itself from parts of the humans killed by their infected shadows and in the storms. Cassandra remembers the monstrous shadow beast that she had imagined as a child, and which had always somehow remained dormant. Only Cassandra can destroy the new Night Beast, because it is still linked to her. She turns her childhood memories of terror on the beast, destroying it. The threat from

Tenebra is blocked again, but not ended.

Ancient Light is different in that it is narrated by Melissa, a friend of Nathan, who is not a Shade. She had been away from Nimjala when the destructive events of *Night Beast* occurred, but the house where she lives with an uncle and aunt was damaged, so they are staying in a hotel. Cassandra visits Mel there, and asks her to watch out for a Shade known as Isis, whose boyfriend had been killed in the storms. Mel dreams that she must seek 'Ancient Light' – the only way to save her from a peril she doesn't yet know about. Mel catches glimpses of a figure outside her window. Later, Cassandra has no recollection of visiting Mel. Then a boy that Mel knows slightly is gruesomely murdered, and a strange girl is seen near the scene. More teenage boys are murdered, with the girl being spotted in the vicinity.

On the internet, Mel finds her browser directed to sites called 'The Wisdom of Baphomet' and 'Paranormal Shadowland'. She also researches into the Egyptian goddess Isis, and the Templars. A 'special agent from the government' turns up wanting to see Mel. It soon becomes clear that Isis has become mentally disturbed following the death of her boyfriend, and is possessed, killing boys in order to get body parts to reconstruct the body of her brother and husband Osiris, who according to ancient Egyptian myth was killed and dismembered by Set (also known as Sutekh). The special agent reveals himself as Clement Hopkins, a descendant of the real Witchfinder General Matthew Hopkins (c1620-47) who wants to fight the Tenebra creatures. Isis is now controlling dark matter, bringing Tenebra to this world, as she is under the control of a Savant, Boges, who is using her Osiris fantasies to materialise Tenebra. The only way to destroy Isis and Osiris is to use 'Ancient Light' – the light of the stars, hundreds and thousands of years old when it reaches Earth. After killing Isis, Hopkins reveals that he has a medieval device, the Luxxa, which he uses to focus starlight onto Osiris and kill him. Hopkins was helped by Acheron, who wanted Boges to fail.

Shine has found himself in Egypt at the beginning of *Black Sun Rising*. He has no memory of how he got there. All he knows is that it's too dangerous to shadow-hop back to Australia again. Attacked in a Cairo café, he is helped by Awad, the son of the owner. Awad has recognised that Shine is a Shade, because he is one himself. One difference is that Awad's family are supportive of him, and he doesn't have to be a loner, as Shine has had to be. Awad communicates best by 'mind-talking' – telepathy. All Shades have the gift, but Shine has never used his before. Awad and Shine, together with Awad's brother Mokhtar and their friend Ibrahim, are attacked by Shade-hunting vigilantes and escape to the City of The Dead, a huge cemetery on the outskirts of Cairo. Shine hears Nathan's voice, warning about the end of the world. Shine and Awad are almost dragged to Tenebra, as Nathan's parents had been. Acheron, who is Sutekh to Egyptian Shades, inspires an outbreak of bloody violence in Cairo. Shine phones Cassandra from Cairo railway station. Larvae start to appear, and Nathan and Cassandra shadow-hop to Cairo to help fight against them. Shine fights Nathan, as he has been brainwashed by shadow matter without his knowledge. They go to the tomb in the Valley of the Kings that Shine first appeared in. A Black Sun rises in the west, but falters and breaks up. But it will rise higher every day…

Shine shadow-hops back to Albion Bay and Mel tells him that five days have passed. Nimjala was damaged by a flood at the same time as the events in Egypt. Hopkins reappears, and promises not to kill Shine. Shine is swallowed up in a river of darkness and taken back to Egypt, where he rejoins Nathan, Cassandra, and Awad. But all of this is an illusion. Shine's body is still in the river and he lets Cassandra and Awad enter his mind, while their bodies, along with Nathan, are embedded  in the wall of the tomb. Acheron is active again. Shine has a vision of the Templars at work in a room with computers, trying to break through to the shadow world. But Tenebra breaks through into ours and overwhelms the Templars. Shine had actually escaped this, shadow-hopping to Egypt, losing his memory of what had happened. Alan now reappears, a 'mongrel' who is necessary for Acheron to complete Tenebra's breaking through. The Black Sun rises for the last time. Nathan becomes a creature of light and attacks the Larvae that are forming into Acheron's body. Shine destroys him and disappears into light. In Nimjala Nathan, Mel, and Cassandra start to resume their lives. They cannot see Shine, who walks away, a loner again.

5 The Greatest Unknown

The greatest exponent of gothic science fiction often camouflaged as supernatural horror was H.P. Lovecraft. When he came to write his survey of the horror field, 'Supernatural Horror in Literature', he began with the resounding statement 'The oldest and strongest emotion of mankind is fear, and the oldest and strongest kind of fear is fear of the unknown.'[11] Perhaps the greatest unknown is darkness: that which is hidden, perhaps is hidden, perhaps is waiting in places that cannot be seen, but which are there.

The Shades series makes use of these universal emotions, and adds something to the experience. The ending of Shades is not happy and obviously conclusive, but it is believable. It leaves Nathan and Cassandra as shades, still in the world they knew, still at the mercy of strong light. Mel is still with them, a 'sadness still clouding her features, but finding a place for happiness too.' And as for Shine, the narrator of the final novel, he realises that 'My life had always been a series of adjustments to alienation; ahead of me lay the ultimate alienation. I would beat it.'[12]

The Shades and their allies have saved the world, saved the humanity that they are alienated from, but still end up separate and different. That can't be changed – only understood and accepted. Although the possibility is left open for a sequel or even another series, it is preferable to leave the Shades in their arrested adolescence and young adulthood, even as they continue to grow older, and into adulthood and even past a normal human life-span, with all the experiences that go with it. They can't grow into adulthood as the young adult reader can. The Shades series can be taken into adulthood and enjoyed again in adulthood. There are always levels of meaning and engagement to be discovered. There is always darkness to be overcome, at least for now...

Bibliography

All published by Hodder Headline Australia in 2001

Shades 01: Shadow Dance 168pp
Shades 02: Night Beast 154pp
Shades 03: Ancient Light 162pp
Shades 04: Black Sun Rising 161pp

Notes

1. Author's website: www.roberthood.net/shades/ origins.htm#series. 'Thoughts on Writing Shades'
2. Author's website: www.roberthood.net/shades/chronos.htm. 'Chronicles'
3. Author's website: www.roberthood.net/shades/index2.htm. Review of *Shadow Dance* by Chuck McKenzie
4. Author's website: www.roberthood.net/shades/origins. htm#series. 'Thoughts on the Series'
5. Author's website: www.roberthood.net/shades/origins. htm#series. 'Thoughts on the Series'
6. Author's website www.roberthood.net/shades/origins2. htm#edge. 'The Shadowedge'
7. Author's website: www.roberthood.net/shades/origins2. htm#shades. 'Terminology'
8. *Shadow Dance* p.51; Author's website: www.roberthood.net/ shades/books/a_nathan.htm. 'Nathan'
9. For example *The Owl Service* (1967) and *Red Shift* (1973)
10. Robert Hood interviewed by Kyla Ward: www.tabula-rasa.info/AusHorror/RobertHood.html
11. *The Annotated Supernatural Horror in Literature*, edited by ST Joshi, Hippocampus Press 2000, p.21
12. *Black Sun Rising*, p.161

The Ninefold Kingdom and Others:
Four Fictional Visions of the Political Future

This essay was born in coincidence. It was by pure chance that I first read, very close to each other, two of the four novels that I intend to survey here: *The Lord of the Sea* (1901) by M.P. Shiel, and *Hadrian VII* (1904) by Frederick Rolfe ('Baron Corvo'). Each contains a range of related themes, and when this came up in a discussion it was suggested that I should also read R.H. Benson's near-contemporary *The Dawn of All* (1911). While reading it I also recalled themes in a fourth and much later novel, the most recently published of all: *In the Wet* by Nevil Shute (1953).

In this survey I don't intend to make any claims or connections between these four novels except for the theme in each book, which is either a major or minor one, of a transformation of the existing world order, and a consequent reshuffling of political boundaries and power-blocs and alliances.

I intend to draw no connections or parallels between the authors. On a personal note, from what I know about them, two were fanatics, and would have been men that I would've crossed the road (if not an entire city) to avoid. I suspect that M.P. Shiel would've been a 'character' – perhaps, on occasion, rather like the bore at the pub bar that will never shut up. I suspect that only Nevil Shute was anything like 'normal'! And I doubt whether I would have agreed with the politics of any of them. I think that it is worth pointing out that I do not intend to automatically equate the political and other views of each author with those expressed by characters in his book, whether or not this is warranted.

And yet none of this is strictly relevant to the range of fascinating works that each man produced, and, especially, the particular vision of the future that is a concern in each novel surveyed here.

***

Matthew Phipps Shiel (1865-1947) produced many novels and short stories, all in a fantastic and convoluted style that can often be hypnotic. However, to many readers, he is all but unreadable. In the earlier part of the twentieth century, Shiel wrote several novels using the then-fashionable themes of a war in the near future that would somehow involve the very survival (or not) of western civilisation.

Such novels as *The Yellow Danger*, *This Knot of Life*, and *This Above All* would now be criticised for their racist, anti-Jewish, and other objectionable content. *The Lord of the Sea* would also not be immune from these criticisms. However, objectionable as are many of the views (of the characters) expressed, the novel also contains a wealth of fascinating ideas, and a genuine if rather skewed vision of the politics of the world in Shiel's near future.

After a series of particularly vicious pogroms, the Jews of Europe are systematically expelled, and flee to England, where they soon take over much of the country's land from the financially distressed nobility.

Framed for murder by the new Jewish owner of the estate upon which he worked, the yeoman Richard Hogarth escapes from prison. Before he was jailed, an asteroid made of diamond had landed on the estate, and Hogarth discovers and uses the diamond to finance the reinvention of himself as the 'Lord of the Sea'. Just as empires and their rulers were lords of the land, Hogarth creates a world-wide network of gigantic floating fortresses, and proceeds to rule his new domain, and the only area of the world not already claimed by right of possession by any other country – the Sea.[1]

For many reasons *The Lord of the Sea* must have created a sensation in its time. The United Kingdom was the world's most powerful nation, yet it largely depended on its rule of the sea in order to survive and grow. The freedom of the sea was vital to allow the unhindered importing of many of the country's needs, and the export of its manufactured goods. The Royal Navy was seen as the ultimate way of ensuring that this hegemony over the sea was maintained, and the accurate term 'gunboat diplomacy' surely dates from this era before World War I.

Even the slightest possibility that a fleet of invincible metal islands, real Dreadnoughts in the age of the naval race between the United Kingdom and the new German Empire, could be realised, must have provided a real *frisson* to many readers, if not their governing classes!

After Hogarth's seizure of the Sea, he invites the maritime and trading nations of the world to enter into treaties with him.

Of course they refuse, and are blockaded.

Even after treaties are eventually signed, the world economic scene is transformed by the effects of the Sea's taxation of any ships using it, entering its 'territory'. An Act of Union between the British Empire and the Sea is passed, and Hogarth becomes Regent.

But Albion is ever 'perfidious' and the Sea's forts are sunk or deliberately scuttled by agents placed in them over a long time previously.

This is no place to explore the other themes of *The Lord of the Sea* – for example Shiel's religious and racial views, which he was far from unique in holding. And, to be charitable, it is really only Shiel's fizzing and coruscating style that can even begin to make up for a plot that frequently verges on the incoherent, and still be able to take the reader with it. Nevertheless, the reader can be carried along, and into a unique product of a unique imagination and personality, one which, whatever its faults in execution, never fails in audacity and in provocation.

***

Religion – in his case, Roman Catholicism – was the world-view assumed as only natural by Frederick Rolfe (1860-1913). He liked to appear in print as 'Fr. Rolfe' – as if he was 'Father' Rolfe, and had attained his ambition of ordination. A.J.A. Symons' utterly absorbing biography *The Quest for Corvo* (1934) reveals Rolfe to be a thoroughly unpleasant man with an amazing gift for all-consuming self-pity and the alienation of everyone who wished to help him. Claiming that the title of Baron Corvo had been legitimately bestowed upon him, Rolfe was an immensely talented writer whose life-story often read like a novel (as does, in many respects, Symons' biography).

Out of his deeply-held Catholic faith, and his deeply flawed and unfulfilled life, Rolfe produced *Hadrian VII*, a sustained *tour-de-force* of the power of brooding injustice, and of those injustices being made right in just about the most bizarre yet useful way possible.

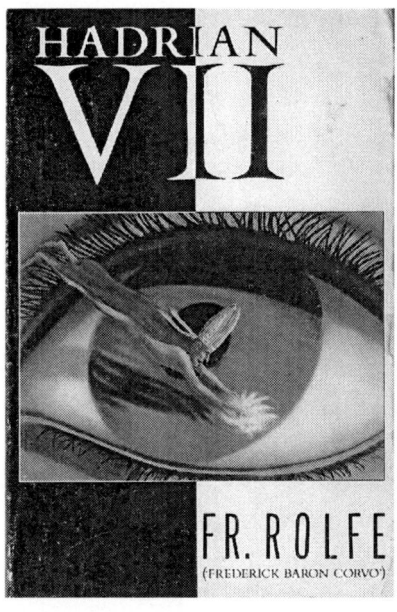

George Arthur Rose, a failed would-be Catholic priest, is rehabilitated and ordained. At the conclave that shortly follows after the death of the Pope, Rose is elected. The chaos he causes at the Vatican by his attempts to practice his brand of true Christianity is as nothing when compared to the plans that unfold for the world-wide enhancement of the Papacy under the new English Pontiff Hadrian VII. He becomes the Supreme Arbitrator, and declares that the 'anarchy' of countries such as France and Russia means that they cannot rule themselves and should submit to rule by the 'Ruler of the World'.[2]

The Pope quickly restructures the political world order. Nations that had survived in 'undiminished energy' were allowed to remain as they were. The lucky few were England, America, Japan, Germany, and Italy.

The Scandinavian monarchies and other European countries such as Greece, Switzerland, and San Marino were to be allowed to survive as sovereign states. Poland was to be resurrected, and Hungary and Bohemia to be detached from

Austria-Hungary.

Europe was to be restored to a new Roman Empire under a Northern Emperor (the King of Prussia) and a Southern Emperor (the King of Italy). The borders of Germany would be allowed to stretch from the English Channel to the Urals, and the Northern Emperor William would federate countries and nominate ruling dynasties as he saw fit. The Southern Emperor Victor Emmanuel would preside over the Mediterranean countries and much of the Balkans.

The United States of America would include all the countries of North, Central, and South America (except Canada).

The Japanese Empire 'was authorised to annex Siberia'.

Everywhere else, including Africa and Asia (except Siberia) was 'to be added to the dominions of the King of England, Ireland, Wales, and Scotland.' And since 'the title Emperor being antipathetic to the English Race (on account of its primary significance 'War-Lord')' he would be called 'The Ninefold King'.[3]

This breathtaking reconstruction happens with the minimum of fuss. As shall be seen below with R.H. Benson's *The Dawn of All*, the acceptance of world-wide Roman Catholic hegemony was seen as the culmination of a new twentieth-century growth of common sense on the part of those who had previously rejected its claims, like naughty children.

At the height of his power, Hadrian VII is assassinated. The novel ends: 'Pray for the repose of his soul. He was so tired.'[4] Hardly surprising!

***

In *The Dawn of All* R.H. Benson (1871-1914) gives us a dying lapsed Catholic priest who finds himself in the body of

Monsignor Masterman, Secretary to the Cardinal Archbishop of Westminster in an England once more firmly and apparently happily restored to Rome. It is 1973, and divorce and fornication have been made illegal. Benefit of Clergy has been restored, and Church courts are able to convict for heresy and hand convicted 'criminals to the secular arm.' The establishment of Roman Catholicism as the State Religion is just around the corner.

Pretending that he has merely lost his memory, 'Masterman', and so the reader, is treated to lectures on how the world of 1973 came to be from that of Benson's time. Masterman is then taken on a tour of parts of Europe, with light duties and retreats, in order to reacclimatise him to the present, just as another series of upheavals connected with the further growth of the Roman Catholic Church is about to begin.

Benson's vision is altogether more sinister than Rolfe's, the product of a true fanatic (and another convert from the Church of England). Shiel's future is simply outrageous fun (despite the political and racial views of the characters, whether or not they are those of the author). Rolfe's is the intriguing outworking of a man obsessed by Catholicism, and in a love-hate relationship with it, as it denied and condemned him for what he was, as well as offering the only true release and forgiveness, and showing what he could be.

R.H. Benson's story is that of someone who feels that, in effect, the Inquisition was reasonable in order to save people from their errors by killing them. The logic is remorseless; the supposed common-sense of it all is oppressive. It is the Ultramontanist's wet dream. And yet, it is to Benson's credit that Masterman comes to be deeply disturbed, if not repulsed, by much of the Church's involvement in the political future that he has been catapulted into.

Through Masterman's eyes, the reader is shown how late twentieth-century Roman Catholicism dominates in a variety of ways. During a visit to the French Court at Versailles, we see the Church as a social power, organising all society on a social guild-like basis, presumably on the same corporate impulses that led at various times to authoritarian or paternalistic Catholic regimes such as those of Portugal, Spain, Austria, and Eire.[5]

Catholicism and Science are reconciled, and symbolised by the tremendous medical and religious facilities of Lourdes. Ireland has been turned into a gigantic contemplative monastery and mental hospital.[6]

The 'intoxicating nightmare of democratic government' has been all but replaced by an effective Papal rule over the world, with isolated Socialists, Protestants, Jews, and a few other troublemaking groups surviving and being barely tolerated.[7]

The reception of the Emperor of Germany into the Roman Catholic Church threatens to set off a chain of events that could endanger this new world order, even as it seems to be moving towards the further strengthening of the Church's power. Shortly after the Kaiser's conversion, the Church is finally re-established in England, and there are moves 'between China, Japan, the Persian Empire, and Russia as to the formal recognition of the Pope as Arbitrator of the East.' All this really is only the beginning of the 'last conflict.'[8]

The United States offers Massachusetts as a refuge for the Socialists, who no longer have any place in England or Germany, and Masterman visits the new 'Socialist State.' Although he admits of the State's decency and cleanliness, he sees none of the 'hidden fire' of a Christian atmosphere. But there is enough hidden fire for him when he is suddenly called back to a Rome deep in crisis. The remaining Socialists of Berlin have seized the city and threaten to execute the Kaiser.[9]

The Paris Commune and Siege of 1871 was surely in Benson's mind. The Archbishop of Paris was murdered, and the government's eventual response to the brutalities of the Commune was itself brutal in the extreme. Catholic envoys are martyred, and tremendous force is threatened unless the revolutionaries unconditionally submit to the Pope, who travels to Berlin in person in order to demand it.

Witnessing the final apotheosis of the Church some months later in London, Masterman allows himself to speculate (and hope) that 'Europe itself at last dwelt again with one mind in her house' and that the liberties granted by the Pope after the Berlin revolutionaries' surrender would show that the Church can reconcile power with love.[10] And as he sees this dream become reality…

***

In the Wet by Nevil Shute (1899-1960) offers a sustained vision of a future and transformed British Commonwealth that is coolly rational and secular by comparison to those discussed above, even though it does owe a great deal to Shute's admiration for the concept of British constitutional monarchy and the evocative power of what was often regarded as the new 'Elizabethan Age'.

Shute's novels sometimes read like historical novels today, for all that they are fast-moving adventures, with the resolution of tense edge of the seat situations often depending on human bravery, decency, and the intimate and practical knowledge of engineering and aviation that Shute possessed. And yet there is also a vein of mysticism and sense that there is 'more' to the world than meets the eye, and that this 'more' is to be encountered in life-threatening or enhancing situations, and by ordinary people, as much as by clergy or people committed to a religion in a formal religious setting.[11]

If the novels by Shiel, Rolfe, and Benson discussed above could be said to encapsulate the worst of organised religions  and their adherents, then *In the Wet* could be said to contain the unfashionable virtues of the best of 'Church of England' sensibility – an unwillingness to be the cause of fuss, coupled with an unshakeable conviction that tolerance and compromise are both worth something.

Isolated in a remote Queensland village during the rainy season, Hargreaves, the local vicar, ministers to Stevie, who has a deserved reputation for being a drunkard and general trouble-maker. But when Stevie falls seriously ill and is dying, he starts to tell the vicar his 'beautiful dreams.'

In his 'delusions' Stevie is David Anderson, a Royal Australian Air Force pilot who is seconded to perform special duties with the Queen's Flight. Seamlessly, Shute dovetails the background setting of a hot and dank village with David Anderson's future 'dream life'. For over forty years since World War II, Britain has had an almost unbroken succession of Labour governments, presiding over an impoverished and austere country. Under one of Clement Attlee and Aneurin Bevan's successors a constitutional crisis is looming, as the government considers further economies by abolishing the Queen's Flight, thus curtailing the Monarch's freedom of movement throughout the Commonwealth. The Australian and Canadian governments offer to pay for the Queen's Flight themselves, and the Queen has accepted.[12]

One of Shute's English characters describes the Queen's dilemma of ruling a country which is Royalist at heart, but which also prefers to elect Socialist governments. The Commonwealth Dominions have elected largely Right Wing governments over the same time, and monarchy has had an easier time in those countries.[13]

Connected with all of this is electoral reform. The Dominions, of which the Queen is also Head of State, now have a multiple vote system, where extra votes are awarded on the basis of a minimum earned income, completing higher education, service in the armed forces, service with a recognised church, and so on.[14] The British government is suspicious that the Queen and Dominions want to introduce the system to Britain, while the Dominions think that the abolition of the Queen's Flight is part of a plan to strip the monarchy of its remaining power, prestige, and ability to hold the non-Socialist Commonwealth together.

As ever, Shute tells a gripping story, with plenty of the engineering and aviation detail that he knew so well, and that adds to the book's verisimilitude. The political and electoral discussions never become lectures and take over the action – they form part of the background and the reason for the story's events happening in the first place.

Eventually the Queen and immediate Royal Family leave England in the aeroplanes of the Commonwealth-funded Queen's Flight, and, with them safely out of the country, the scene is set for a restructuring of the Commonwealth. And

David Anderson, the pilot at the centre of things – starts to complain about suffering from dreams of being seriously ill, and of a 'mad priest'…

A Governor-General is to be appointed for England (sic), and electoral reform is on the cards at last. The monarch is to officially spend a regular amount of time in each of her Dominions. Thus the Commonwealth, and all of the good things that it stands for, stands its best chance for preservation.

Nevil Shute explicitly brings out this theme in an 'Author's Note' at the end of the novel:

> Since personal strains and tensions must inevitable affect the future of the Commonwealth, it seems to me that fiction is the most suitable medium in which to make this forecast. Fiction deals with people and their difficulties and, more than that, nobody takes a novelist too seriously. The puppets born of his imagination walk their little stage for our amusement, and if we find that their creator is impertinent his errors of taste do not sway the world.[15]

Not a bad way to sum up all four of the works surveyed here. All four writers undoubtedly wrote from their political, religious, and racial viewpoints, and were also men of their times. All were writing what amounted to Utopias. The reader who likes to speculate about the future (or read what is, and effectively always was, alternate-world science fiction) is given plenty to think about. Political vision is one thing. Whether any of the visions as described here would have been better than the world that we have actually ended up with, is a personal decision, that persistent and wistful 'what if…' and 'if only…' that never goes away.

Notes

Page references are to the following editions:

R.H. Benson, *The Dawn of All* Hutchinson, n.d.
Frederick Rolfe, *Hadrian VII* Wordsworth Classics 1993
M.P. Shiel, *The Lord of the Sea* Souvenir Press 1981
Nevil Shute, *In the Wet* Pan Books1978

1.   M.P.Shiel, *The Lord of the Sea* pp.144f
2.   Frederick Rolfe, *Hadrian VII* pp.325ff
3.   Frederick Rolfe, *Hadrian VII* pp.326ff
4.   Frederick Rolfe, *Hadrian VII* p.368
5.   R.H. Benson, *The Dawn of All* pp.66ff
6.   R.H. Benson, *The Dawn of All* pp.126, 192
7.   R.H. Benson, *The Dawn of All* p.137
8.   R.H. Benson, *The Dawn of All* p.244
9.   R.H. Benson, *The Dawn of All* pp.245ff
10.   R.H. Benson, *The Dawn of All* pp.309ff
11.   Nevil Shute, *In the Wet* pp.280f
12.   Nevil Shute, *In the Wet* p.66
13.   Nevil Shute, *In the Wet* pp.100ff
14.   Nevil Shute, *In the Wet* pp.86ff
15.   Nevil Shute, *In the Wet* p.283

Two Deaths

The American writer August Derleth (1909-71) is not generally regarded as having been a writer of ghost stories, and rightly so. The record of his huge involvement with the whole of the field of the fantastic, which included pioneering work as a publisher and editor, as well as a considerable number of macabre and science fiction stories, contains very little work that can be categorised as 'ghostly' fiction.[1]

Derleth's first collection of macabre fiction, *Someone in the Dark* (1941), contains a preface entitled 'When the Night and the House are Still', in which he claims that he has never taken the time to write a first-rate ghost story.[2] This is probably not false modesty: Derleth's working habits, and the need to produce large amounts of fiction and other writing in order to pay the bills, would make the production of first-rate work unlikely.

Derleth did attempt several stories in the tradition of classic English ghost-story writer M.R. James, which are collected in *Someone in the Dark*. He adhered to the Jamesian dictum that the circumstances of a good ghost story ought to be familiar, and that the majority of its characters, and their conversation 'should be such as you might meet and hear any day.'[3] Unfortunately, Derleth's Jamesian stories never quite come off, due to his different circumstances and world-view: the great pitfall of writers of pastiche. As in his fiction based on the work of H.P. Lovecraft, Derleth reduces ambiguous and morally open situations and occurrences to a simple conflict between good and bad. Virtue is rewarded, and evil punished.

However, when Derleth wrote Derlethian ghost stories they were far better, and bear comparison with the output of the best 'classic' ghost story writers. Derleth's fantastic fiction has been published in several collections of uneven quality, which usually contain a wide range of macabre fiction, from ghost stories and vampire fiction to stories of alien invasion.[4]

In my view, Derleth's best ghost stories appear in a single collection, ironically published under a pseudonym. This is the 1963 collection *Mr George and Other Odd Persons,* as by Stephen Grendon.[5] As the book's introduction makes clear, the stories were all originally written in the mid-1940s, under circumstances which would not make for the production of quality work: 'it was often late at night – never earlier than nine o'clock, and on, frequently, to two o'clock in the morning – before I could begin the daily story.'[6]

Mr George contains seventeen stories covering a wide range of the macabre. Most are variations on the theme of supernatural revenge for wrongs done. Stories such as 'The Wind in the Lilacs' and 'Miss Esperson' are similar to Derleth's best regional Sac Prairie fiction. 'Mara' is a benevolent ghost, and in this story Derleth could be exploring autobiographical themes. However, in this article I wish to examine two other stories from *Mr George.* These are the title story, often regarded as Derleth's best ghost story, and which is placed first in the collection. The other is the final story, 'Mrs Manifold', a piece of 'delightful cold grue' and a story of supernatural revenge that leaves a smile on the reader's face.[7]

***

The opening situation of the main character of 'Mr George' is a routine one. Priscilla is a five year-old who has been left in the care of unscrupulous relatives after the deaths of her mother, and her companion or lover, the Mr George of the title. The relatives – Laban, Virginia, and Adelaide – are prevented, by the very fact of Priscilla's existence, from inheriting the property and fortune that now belong to the young girl. Her life is therefore in the balance. Derleth writes of the situation as it would be experienced by the child herself, an innocent abroad in a world in which adults are conspiring against her. Other adults are sympathetic, but can do nothing. Priscilla's only help can come from Mr George himself, who has 'gone away', but later begins to intervene to help Priscilla when she needs him:

> Just short of him [Laban] something stopped her, something like an invisible hand pressing her back. Something tall and dark took shadowy shape beside Laban where he knelt, waiting for her, something that reached down and tore the sustaining book from beneath the trunk-lid, something that pushed the trunk-lid down with weighty impact upon Laban Leckett's neck.[8]

In 'Mr George' the boundary between fantasy and reality, life and death, is blurred, as the child walks unknowingly between them, menaced by her human relatives and helped by her ghostly friend. The 'voice' which tells Priscilla how to avoid the murderous situations made by her relatives is natural and good to her, despite the fact that it spells death to the evil adults, and is not comprehended by the good ones.

'Mr George' is a satisfying story of supernatural revenge, with the ghost being malevolent to those who deserve to be on the receiving end. What is under threat is not simply an innocent girl's life, but all that it stands for: simplicity, truth, affirmation of life, freedom from adult conventions. Derleth pits these virtues against the corresponding vices of hypocrisy and lying, 'no-saying', and 'provincial' dullness and a loss of child-like wonder at the world: 'they [the relatives] are selfish, greedy, lazy, and evil people, who, behind their old-fashioned respectability, are capable of absolutely anything...'[9]

Writing about, and pillorying the values of, these sort of people (as Derleth saw them) formed a major theme throughout his writing career: in his mainstream fiction, poetry, autobiography, and volumes of published journals. 'Mr George' is one further example of Derleth putting across his preferred values, and the priorities of morality that he held as important. In this instance he chose to put his views across by means of a ghost story published in a pulp magazine, rather than in a hardcover novel from his major New York publisher. Perhaps the menace that Derleth felt resulted from the threat to his positive values makes the externalisation of the conflict in the terms of a ghost story an appropriate use of the form. Certainly 'Mr George' rings true in ways that much of Derleth's more 'Jamesian' fiction does not. Derleth put his heart into 'Mr George', and gives a quietly horrific portrait of what people who live by his negative values can do. What is more unfortunate is that victims are not usually so ambiguously lucky as Priscilla was.

***

'Mrs Manifold' is a much more straightforward story of revenge from beyond the grave. What makes it memorable is its gruesome humour and the feeling that Derleth simply wanted to let his hair down and give himself and his readers a good laugh. The only one with no cause for laughter is Mrs Manifold herself.

Robinson, the story's narrator, takes a job as a clerk in a sailors' hotel run by the reclusive Mrs Manifold. She seems on edge, and asks to be informed of the appearance of certain of her guests, as if she were looking for someone. It turns out that there had been a Mr Manifold, but his wife had returned to

London alone. No one knows what happened to her husband, or where he is now. A visiting sailor tells the story of Mr Manifold's disappearance, along with a cask of Madeira wine, from the 'fancy house' that Mrs Manifold had run in Singapore. Eventually a stranger comes to stay, bringing with him an overpowering smell of wine, causes Mrs Manifold to change:

> There was a greater furtiveness about her: there was less sly humour, almost nothing of humour at all; there was unmistakable grimness, a kind of terrible bravado; and there was above everything else something about her that made her far more horrible than she had ever seemed to me – something that made me think of death and fear of death, of violence...[10]

The reader is right. The strange sailor with the smell of wine is Mr Manifold, returned at last to take revenge on his murderous wife. And *was* there a connection between Mrs Manifold's death by strangulation, the bones scattered around her room, and an empty barrel once containing Madeira wine, washed up by the Thames, and with a few human bones left inside?

It would not do to give the closing lines of the story, but they are unforgettable: an example of laconic black humour that is far removed from the eerie menace and innocence of 'Mr George'.

***

I hope that this brief examination of two of his best stories will help to put August Derleth into his proper place in the field of the fantastic, as a skilled story-writer in his own right, and not just as an editor, or imitator of other people's work, whether of H.P. Lovecraft or M.R. James. All Derleth's collections are worth seeking out, and *Mr George and Other Odd Persons* especially so. There are many treats in store – lovers of Madeira not excluded!

Notes

Mr George and Other Odd Persons was first published by Arkham House. A United Kingdom paperback edition appeared from Tandem in 1965, confusingly re-titled *When Graveyards Yawn*.

1. For example, Derleth's contributions to *Weird Tales* alone take up a two-column listing in Sheldon Jaffery and Fred Cook's *The Collector's Index to Weird Tales*. For a consideration of Derleth's contributions to science fiction, see my 'Somebody Pointed Earth' in James Roberts, ed., *Return to Derleth*, Vol. 2 (1995) and included in this book.
2. *Someone in the Dark* (Jove ed.), p.7
3. *Someone in the Dark* (Jove ed.), p.8
4. Derleth's collections within the fantastic field are: *Someone in the Dark* (1941); *Something Near* (1945); *Not Long for This World* (1948); *The Mask of Cthulhu* (1958); *Lonesome Places* (1962); *The Trail of Cthulhu* (1962); *Mr George and Other Odd Persons* (1963); *Colonel Markesan and Less Pleasant People* (1966); *The Watchers Out of Time and Others* (1974); *Harrigan's File* (1975); *Dwellers in Darkness* (1976)
5. 'Stephen Grendon' is a character used by Derleth in many autobiographical stories and novels. Thus there was little chance of *Mr George's* true authorship not being known. Also, a photo of Derleth appeared on the dustjacket of the Arkham House edition!
6. *Mr George and Other Odd Persons* p.vii
7. *Mr George and Other Odd Persons* p.vii
8. *Mr George and Other Odd Persons* p.16
9. *Mr George and Other Odd Persons* p.22
10. *Mr George and Other Odd Persons* pp.236-237

Yours Truly, Daniel Morley: An Examination of Robert Bloch's Novel *The Scarf*

Introduction

The Scarf was Robert Bloch's first novel. It was published in 1947, when Bloch was 30. This essay will consider *The Scarf* as a novel about crime and the criminal, involving the psychological but not the supernatural. However, *The Scarf* certainly is a novel of horror, involving at the very least mental illness and the emotions of terror and revulsion. I also intend to place *The Scarf* in the context of Robert Bloch's literary career and with other relevant works by him, as well as place it in context alongside similar American crime and psychological novels from the period.

The text of *The Scarf* used for this essay is that of the 1972 paperback edition from New English Library, which was the novel's first publication in the United Kingdom. Page numbers therefore refer to this edition. Bloch had made a few revisions to the 1947 text (mainly the ending) for a new American paperback edition in 1966.[1] The UK edition reprinted this text, which has now, in effect, become the author's preferred text. Even so, *The Scarf* retained its 1940's feel and mood, worthy of a novel from that time by any of the better practitioners of the 'hard-boiled' school of crime fiction writing.

The Bloch Bargain

When *The Scarf* appeared in 1947 Robert Bloch was a recognised writer of horror fiction, and somewhat less well-known as a science fiction writer, although his often offbeat contributions to that field had sometimes been noteworthy. Bloch had started out in the mid 1930s as a teenage author whose work was strongly influenced by H.P. Lovecraft. Unlike some of the other young (and not so young) writers whom Lovecraft encouraged, Bloch quickly started to sell fiction regularly. He did not restrict himself to a purely Lovecraftian style or outlook for long. By the late 1930s he was writing stories, developing his own style and voice, while still on occasion displaying an effective fidelity to his first great literary influence.

Bloch's development as a writer included a growing interest in psychology, and the psychological side of horror fiction, often combining the psychological with the macabre and supernatural. Bloch shifted his focus of horror away from that which H.P. Lovecraft had emphasised: horror of the non-human unknown, from outside, where revelation follows upon revelation, and known certainties are overturned and the opposite shown to be the reality. Instead, he moved towards exploring the horror of the human and known, the psychological, but where all can still be overturned in death. Bloch later recalled: 'By the mid 1940s, I had pretty well mined the vein of ordinary supernatural themes until it had become varicose. I realised, as a result of what went on during the Second World War and of reading the more widely disseminated work in psychology, that the real horror is not in the shadows, but in that little twisted world inside our own skulls. And that I determined to explore.'[2]

The publication of a full-length novel might seemed to have been quite a departure for Bloch, the author of numerous short stories in *Weird Tales*, *Amazing Stories*, *Fantastic Adventures*, and other magazines. Highly regarded though his stories were, a novel seemed to be a great leap from the sort of fiction in which a situation is created and resolved within a short length and then put aside by the reader as the page is turned for the next story. But Bloch made his handling of a longer work appear effortless. *The Scarf* was an apparently straightforward and even plain novel. Its short, punchy sentences and paragraphs, its filmic dialogue and sketched-in moody settings, masked what was in fact a complex,

challenging, sometimes phantasmagorical, and un-settling book. For Robert Bloch, as well as his readers, *The Scarf* was very different to anything that had gone before.

But perhaps it was not such a drastic departure after all. Just four years earlier, Bloch had published a notable short story, 'Yours Truly, Jack the Ripper' (*Weird Tales* July 1943). In some ways this work of pulp fiction art was a forerunner of *The Scarf*. The story is told in the first person, and set firmly in the present, in drab and squalid streets and bars in Chicago. Bloch allowed the Victorian serial killer to survive and prosper into the 1940s by apparently supernatural means, although a psychological explanation was also possible. Bloch immediately makes the story different when the reader is told that the Ripper has become the prey rather than just the predator. Jack's pursuer also had a connection with the mean streets of the East End of London in 1888, and has been driven to hunt him down by the desire for revenge, being convinced that he was still alive, and keeping alive through further murders. Bloch used a thoroughly contemporary background to explore and work through the motivations of his characters, and to entertain and pull the reader up short at the same time. In the conclusion, the Lovecraftian legacy of 'everything you know is wrong' is also employed, in a similar way to how he would soon to do in *The Scarf*, and without invoking the supernatural or other unknown outside factor.

At first glance the protagonist of *The Scarf*, Daniel Morley, does not seem promising material for a serial killer. Like Robert Bloch himself, young Morley was a bookish, somewhat isolated child who had to learn fast. Eventually, in order to secure a regular income and develop his writing, Morley secures a job writing radio continuity and advertising. Similarly, Bloch wrote copy for an advertising agency for over a decade. Bloch later explained the arrangement: 'I put my work on the right-hand side of my typewriter, and the layouts and notes for advertising copy on the left-hand side. And when I exhausted what was on the left-hand side, I would put my material in the typewriter.'[3] This was with the blessing of his employer, and 'Yours Truly, Jack the Ripper' and *The Scarf* were among the stories written during this time.

The environment into which Robert Bloch was born was a thoroughly ordinary one, as was his family and upbringing. This is reflected in the settings that he used for *The Scarf*. The large and busy cities of Minneapolis, Chicago, New York, and Hollywood were the backgrounds for the novel, and they were not treated in any sort of exotic or special way. The city streets with their bars, cheap restaurants, and run-down rooming houses where Daniel Morley lives and breathes – and does his killing – are thoroughly recognizable. But Bloch found that he was able to delve into the darker and decidedly abnormal side of families and relationships. He had learned well from H.P. Lovecraft to use ordinary settings and apparently outwardly normal characters in order to provide the contrast with their inner reality and the events, with their dreadful consequences, that he wanted to write about.

Opening the Black Notebook

The narrator and protagonist of *The Scarf* is Daniel Morley. He grew up as a sensitive and studious boy. When he was eighteen his teacher, Miss Frazer, who was twenty years his senior, and had been encouraging his literary ambitions, fell in love with him. Just before Daniel was due to leave for college, she invited him to her home and gave him a maroon scarf as a present. She attempted to seduce him, and got him drunk. When he had passed out, she tied his hands with the scarf and turned on the gas, so that they would die together. Morley woke up in time and escaped by jumping through a window, injuring himself. Miss Frazer was dead. When he was released from hospital, he ran away, and from then on 'hated women, books, everything.' But he held on to the scarf.[4]

The opening of the novel is an extract from Morley's Black Notebook in which he summarises his experience with Miss Frazer and the effect it had on him. These entries recur throughout *The Scarf*. The Black Notebook serves Morley as a place to write down his thoughts, to think out loud in writing. The Black Notebook works as a memory storage space for what Morley doesn't always want to consciously remember all of the time, but which he doesn't want to lose completely. Morley uses the Black Notebook as a refuge and a resource. He doesn't entirely forget what goes into it, but isn't constantly reminded either.

Morley is embarking on his autobiography: the recollection of what has happened to him so far. What Morley is going to tell – the narrative of *The Scarf* that lies just ahead – has ended with him in prison or a mental institution. The scarf itself is present from the beginning: Morley is gazing at it as he speaks, or writes in the Black Notebook. He has come to the realisation that the scarf is a fetish for him: an object that has overwhelming and sexual significance, and from which he cannot bear to be separated. So Morley is abnormally obsessed with the scarf, and is doubly dependent upon it as he uses it to strangle his victims. In effect he needs the scarf, both mentally and physically, in order to achieve the feeling of power and sexual gratification that only committing murder gives him.

But the power Morley exercises when he kills obscures the fact that he has to keep on running away. For as long as he commits murder after murder, he is on the run. The first escape from Miss Frazer has become never-ending, as he has to escape from woman after woman as time goes on by. And he always carries his fetish, the scarf, in his pocket. Dan Morley begins a life of moving from city to city and drifting from one dead-end job to another. He is unable to make friends, and build steady relationships with women. At some point he becomes a serial killer of women, always strangling them with the scarf that Miss Frazer had given him. Morley's hatred of them leads to him from murder to murder, apparently as casually as changing rooms in a cheap lodging house.

Eventually Morley is living in Minneapolis, trying to make a start as a writer. He has grown tired of his current girlfriend, Rena, and plans to get away and move to Chicago. To keep her quiet Morley tells her that the story he is writing is actually about her. Rena continually bothers him about it, and he strangles her with the scarf, and escapes to Chicago. Morley is aware of a connection between his writing and the sort of people around him, especially the type of women he knows. He realises that he killed Rena with such effortlessness because to him she was not a real person. She had become a mere character. 'You get her down on paper, where she can't hurt you any more... She's on paper, where she belongs. Where you can control her.'[5]

Once in a new city Morley changes his self-identity slightly but significantly, calling himself by his full first name once more. He decides that he doesn't find committing murder to be frightening.[6] In a Black Notebook entry Morley reveals some more of the origins of his hatred of women. First there is his mother. When he was nine years old she had punished him when she found out about an episode of childish sex play with one of the girls from his neighbourhood. At night his mother tied his hands to the bed. On one occasion he escapes and glimpses his parents having sex. So his parents were as 'filthy' as his mother had accused him of being. Later, he is in love with Lucille, a girl at his school. Morley declares himself the best way he knows, and writes her a poem. But she laughs and rejects it, and shows it to her friends, humiliating him completely.

Morley wonders if everyone wants to kill someone sometime, or whether it is only him. He thinks that perhaps he is just more honest in actually admitting that he would like to kill. Or maybe he is the abnormal one, after all. He'd like to 'come out' and show everyone what he is – and his method is to use the scarf.[7] The scarf is a weapon, but it was something that was first used against him, when Miss Frazer had tied his hands with it. Morley's other memory of being physically unable to exercise control, when his mother tied his hands, emphasises the fetish aspect of the scarf for him. He is fascinated by it, and uses it, although the scarf, or something similar, has also been used against him. Morley controls the scarf, but at the same time he is under its power. Luckily for him, he is adaptable.

In Chicago, Morley becomes a cab driver so he can have time to write. He meets the freelance model Hazel Hurley, who is attracted to him as a contrast to her current boyfriend, but especially because he told her that he is a writer. Morley wants to become Hazel's lover as soon as he can, so flatters her. But he has no illusions. He is aware that 'you don't fall in love with what you feed on.'[8] Through Hazel's contacts Morley gets a job writing radio continuity. He doesn't make any friends except for Lou King, his immediate superior. Morley confides in Lou about his writing plans. Writing seems to offer Morley some sort of release, and a way of using his flawed experiences with women, although there is more to his fiction than a thinly-disguised autobiography. Because he is only able to write about what he knows, he isn't able to create fiction derived from his imagination or insights into the lives of others.

Morley starts to write a novel about a woman like Hazel. Lou King helps him to get a literary agent, and he makes good progress with his writing. Morley makes the error yet again of telling his girlfriend that his writing is about her. Now Hazel constantly bothers him about it, and won't ever leave him alone. Phil Teffner, Morley's agent, likes Morley's novel, entitled *Queen of Hearts*. As before Morley soon wants to run away again and escape from his relationship and job. He confides in Lou King about leaving, and tells him that he is going to New York. Instead he rents a new room so that he can have peace while he continues to work on the book, and to avoid Hazel. She discovers where he is living, and finds out about his plan. Morley calms her down by telling her that going to New York was going to be their honeymoon. They go out on the town to celebrate, and while waiting for a train home he tries to strangle Hazel with the scarf, but she falls under a train instead. It will look like suicide.

Running away again, Morley falls asleep on the train to New York and dreams about Miss Frazer and Rena and having his hands tied by the scarf. Waking up, he decides that he has learned that he will have to stop killing. In New York, Morley is hailed as a new writer on the brink of success. Morley meets his agent, and his editor Patricia Collins, who guides him through the revisions that the publisher wants him to make on his novel. Kleeman, the chief editor, is demanding: "'You know Kleeman,' answered the girl. "I'd hate to think of what would have happened if King James had come to him with the Bible.""[9] To begin with Morley is almost overwhelmed by the publisher's criticisms of *Queen of Hearts*, but he sees that they are right. Pat reassures him, makes it clear that she believes in him and his work, and encourages him to start on the revisions, because despite Morley's doubts of himself and his novel, he will improve it. Morley is soon strongly attracted to Pat, who is a very different woman compared with the type he normally goes for. Now he feels he has a future. There will be no more running away. Then an entry in the Black Notebook describes surreal dreams within dreams. Reality and dream seem indistinguishable, and Morley wonders whether or not he has ever woken up.[10]

Pat Collins starts to change Morley's image and appearance in advance of the publication of his novel. He enters literary polite and not so polite society and meets Constance Ruppert, who makes him uncomfortable when she says that she's sure she knows him from Chicago. Morley also meets Constance's ex-husband Jeff Ruppert, who is a successful psychoanalyst. He is usually on the defensive by these two new acquaintances. There is always the feeling that they see into him, through him, and will find out the truth, or somehow cause him to betray himself. Constance tells Morley that she associates him with the colour red, an intimation of his maroon scarf.[11] Ruppert thinks that Morley is a 'fake,' and running away from something.[12] Morley is also dismayed to find out that Pat is engaged to Ruppert.[13] What seems to be a possible genuine love relationship for Morley is over before it could begin, and he has lost Pat to a man who he dislikes and who might be the only one able to penetrate his secret and bring him down.

In a Black Notebook entry, Morley writes about how words have become stronger than actions, because of literacy. People learn to worship words. Words are magic formulae which are needed to get through life. Words define until people are words themselves. But 'deep down inside, there's a "you" who doesn't need words, can't use them.'[14] The words can't be used, and there can be no communication. Nevertheless, Morley knows that Truth is a word. And that 'big word' is – murder. Murder means nothing because it is a word. 'Murder isn't a word. Murder is a deed'.[15]

Constance starts to pursue Morley, but he isn't interested, because of his continuing feelings for Pat Collins, despite her engagement to Ruppert. *Queen of Hearts* is published, and becomes an immediate bestseller. Now he has a future. There will be no more running away. Jeff Ruppert thinks that Morley writes about women objectively, like a trained observer.[16] When Morley tells Ruppert that he lives off women, Ruppert says that Morley hates them. He responds that he isn't Jack the

Ripper (see the references above to Bloch's story 'Yours Truly, Jack the Ripper'). Ruppert and his former wife both try to advise Morley. Ruppert tells him that Constance might try to kill him, while she says that Ruppert tried to drive her insane. Constance knows that Morley wants Pat, and when she insults her, Morley hits her. Ruppert says that Constance is a 'nympholept' – a nymphomaniac. She is definitely a maniac, with her sexual over-activity possibly also contributed to by a glandular disorder. Ruppert confides that for Constance, their marriage symbolised the excuse for the abandonment of all repression. The unstable Constance projected all her guilt on to her husband.[17]

Lou King unexpectedly pays Morley a visit, and mentions Hazel's suicide, then says that he knows that Morley 'killed' Hazel. He means that she committed suicide because of the book Morley was writing. King has told Constance about his views. Morley tells Constance she helps him to forget, and she asks him to marry her. She says if they are married she will keep quiet about Morley's past, because she knows he really did murder Hazel.

When Morley comes down with flu, Constance says he should start wearing a scarf. Morley dreams of killing Constance. Leaving him at home ill in bed, Constance goes to inspect a possible house for them. Morley drives there, strangles Constance, and sets fire to the house – apparently the perfect crime, as he has an alibi, being unable to go out. Jeff Ruppert thinks Morley killed Constance: he questions details about the whereabouts of the car, and why no-one answered the phone when Morley was supposed to be at home ill. Morley tries to convince him that Constance's death was suicide.

Morley starts work on *Lucky Lady*, his second novel. Jeff

Ruppert and Pat Collins leave for Hollywood. Then *Queen of Hearts* is sold to a Hollywood studio. In a Black Notebook entry Morley thinks about past serial killers – Spring-Heeled Jack, and Jack the Ripper. Morley wonders why he is a killer, but doesn't know the answer. Morley thinks he's smart – he won't need the 'crutch' of the Black Notebook any longer. This is the last entry in it.[18] Morley takes the opportunity to get away again, and leave for Hollywood.

On the plane journey to Hollywood Morley meets the film director Lloyd Ainsworth who drunkenly reminiscences about his past career.[19] In Hollywood, Morley still carries the scarf about, even when he meets Pat. In a bar he sees a man in a green sports jacket, who seems to vanish. Morley tells Pat that Ruppert won't love her when they're married. He sees the man in the green sports jacket again, and attacks him, but no-one else has seen him, and there's no evidence of their struggle. Morley now openly wears the scarf all the time.

Morley meets Duke Kling, a photographer who has read an advance copy of *Lucky Lady*. Morley feels strange, as when he saw the man in the green sports jacket. Kling tells him that he should write a book about true murders. He takes Morley home to look at his own 'black book' – grisly photos of murder victims. Morley is revolted by the book, but Kling says that Morley really likes it, and that he knows what Morley is. Morley thinks that perhaps Kling is right, that he is someone who enjoys seeing death. But he runs away.

Then Morley's work on the screenplay of *Queen of Hearts* starts to go badly. As he is about to lose Pat to Jeff Ruppert, he starts to write a character like her into his film script, but destroys the manuscript after talking to 'the guy in the mirror'. Morley's own reflection – his unconscious -- tricks him into admitting the possibility that he could strangle Pat.[20] Jeff

Ruppert continues to probe at Morley, and tells him he isn't able to claim some money left to him by Constance, because an insurance investigator thinks that she didn't commit suicide after all, but was actually murdered.

Morley runs away again, and eventually picks up Verna, a hostess in a bar. They set out to drive to Tijuana, across the border in Mexico. Morley tries to strangle her with his scarf, but she escapes, and takes the scarf with her. He returns to Hollywood. Pat breaks with Ruppert, who reveals that he made up the story about an insurance investigator and the problems with getting the money left to him by Constance. Morley and Pat agree to marry and elope. Morley reads Jeff Ruppert's new book *The Assassin: a Study*. Morley and Pat travel to Mexico by same route as he did with Verna. Although he no longer has the scarf, he believes that when he is with Pat he doesn't need it. On the way to Tijuana, they decide to spend the night in a motel, and Pat accidentally reveals that she has Morley's scarf. Verna had survived and contacted Pat and Ruppert, who decided to see if Verna's story was true.

Morley decides to kill Pat, when Miss Frazer suddenly appears. She had not died, but had retired, and was living nearby. She calls Morley 'Daniel'. The past returns, and he is the adolescent who Miss Frazer attempted to seduce. He wants to hold Miss Frazer. It turns out that the beginning of the story recorded in the Black Notebook was actually the reverse of what had really happened. Morley's twisted version in the Black Notebook was a catharsis, but he has always been living in unreality. That is unchanged, although the truth is revealed. He remains obsessed with Miss Frazer at the end, which is also the beginning. Morley is using the Black Notebook again.

'Psychology Has a Lot of Words'

Robert Bloch's interest in psychology, and the themes that he had explored in *The Scarf*, were probably still in his mind a year after the novel was published. As Fan Guest of Honour at the World Science Fiction Convention at Toronto (Torcon) in 1948, Bloch delivered a speech entitled 'Fantasy and Psychology'. It is recorded that he did an impersonation of Peter Lorre, whose film debut in Fritz Lang's *M* (1931) was a detailed portrayal of a sexually-motivated serial killer.[21] The film is an unflinching depiction of a murderer who cannot simply be dismissed as somehow evil. Bloch would continue to investigate these themes in future novels.

When Bloch wrote *The Scarf*, he produced a book that, while using the outward form of a crime thriller, also explored the life and mentality of a serial killer, with the associated horror being handled in a completely non-supernatural way. The real horror was psychological, and was enhanced by the killer's own matter-of-fact narration of his actions. These sprang from the consequences of his upbringing and the malign influence of the people whose words and actions had turned him towards the bad. There is no attempt by the author to justify any of the characters' actions and their results, whether good or evil. In the case of Daniel Morley, there is no suggestion that murder is to be condoned, or the murderer relieved of responsibility. But even so, there is more to be explored and hopefully understood. Any moral judgements are left to the characters themselves in the context of the novel, and to the reader.

In *The Scarf* Bloch displayed a characteristic honesty in confronting and exploring the dark aspect in an apparently normal character, and so all people – and therefore in himself. For Bloch there was no need for a 'good' character to be the narrator or protagonist. This amoral approach is typical of the best and most challenging crime fiction (as well as the best *film noir* of the time). It is also unlike more traditional crime fiction, in which a good character is pitted against bad criminals. For example, Raymond Chandler's character Philip Marlowe, who, although he is no saint, is clearly on the side of good (honesty, decency, law and order) against evil (corruption, chaotic human values, dishonesty). Later crime novels often followed the line that Bloch did rather than Chandler's, and blurred the distinctions between good and evil, moral and immoral. They were more willing to explore the point of view of the murderer and other often repellent characters. People are rarely to be seen as simply good or bad. Their crimes are made to spring out of a definite context, rather than as if from out of thin air. They are shown as being just slices from the different lives that Morley finds himself moving through. Bloch confirms what is already known: that an artist with a talent need not necessarily be good in a particularly moral sense, but it is still not normal to be a serial killer.

In *The Scarf* there are no portrayals of any especially good characters, except for the two people who Morley genuinely likes, and who genuinely like him. These are Lou King, Morley's employer and mentor in Chicago, and Pat Collins, who helps him to improve his work and whom he comes to love. Even if Morley's responses to King and Collins are mainly because they didn't seem to want to take anything from him, but are at first simply doing their jobs, Morley's two friendships stand out in a novel which is otherwise a chronicle of arid relationships dependent only on transactions and setting conditions.

As a contrast, there is Duke Kling, whose 'black book' of

photographs possibly serves a similar function to Morley's Black Notebook of writing. There is also the surely deliberate similarity between the names Duke Kling and Lou King, which serves to emphasise the difference between the two men. Apart from Morley himself, Kling is probably the most obviously loathsome character in *The Scarf*. Although Kling doesn't apparently kill people, he makes his living from the results of death. Although it is all legitimate, Kling's business photographing victims lets him get thrills out of it as well. He seems to consciously and actively enjoy what he likes: his enthusiasm for death. In Morley, Kling thinks he recognises a fellow connoisseur. But even Morley is repulsed by Kling. But it could be that Morley, too, does recognise Kling as someone who does have some idea of the 'little twisted world' there is inside his head. Kling is very different to Lou King. King is pleasant and helpful at the beginning of Morley's writing career (as Bloch's employer was) while Kling wishes to help in a voyeuristic and sensational way at what will turn out to be near its end.

At one point Morley launches into a tirade against the aims of the psychoanalysis that Jeff Ruppert practises with such success. Morley maintains that 'abnormality pays off.' The artists and writers are known to be crazy, but there is also the 'so-called common herd' that are generally accepted as being fairly adjusted. But Morley, as one of them, says that they are not. But they get along. Morley says that the 'normal' people, who deal with these 'misfits', are unhappy because they have to hide their troubles. If that is normal, then the aims of psychoanalysis, which seeks to make the adjustment, are all wrong. People are maladjusted, because they haven't been prepared for the failure that is the lot for most of them.[22]

The Scarf is a portrayal of several maladjusted people, and of Daniel Morley in particular. These portraits make the meaning of the psychological horror and terror aspects of the novel. There is much evidence that Morley's personality is disordered and his sanity is doubtful – for example, his dreams within dreams, the discussion with his reflection in a mirror, and the apparition of the man in the green sports jacket. Morley knows the truth but lives as if he doesn't. He lives under the illusions he despises in others. The ending is a bleak one: that is challenged, it is not overcome. There is no mention of Morley being on death row, or having to pay for his crimes with his own death. So Morley was not responsible due to his insanity?

The horror that is depicted in *The Scarf* is that people can be born, influenced, coerced, into doing terrible things and continuing the vicious circle. Life without horror is a life with illusions. Bloch is nothing if not honest.

Note on 'Anachronisms' in *The Scarf*

The revisions that Bloch made to the original text of *The Scarf* for its 1966 reprint created several anachronisms, or what would be anachronisms if the contemporary 1947 setting of the novel is still to be regarded as the present. Here are some of the most obvious (at least to this writer) anachronisms in *The Scarf*:

Morley and Hazel dance in a bar to a Bob Dylan song on a jukebox. Dylan was born in 1941 and his first album was not released until 1962.[23] Morley and Pat mention the war in Vietnam. Although it had been a trouble spot since at least 1945, American involvement really began to escalate during the presidency of John F. Kennedy after 1960.[24] The film director Ainsworth laments to Morley that so few people had ever written a good book about Hollywood. He mentions

'Shulberg' as one of the exceptions.[25] Budd Shulberg's popular Hollywood novel *The Disenchanted* was not published until 1950. Morley mentions using a credit card, which were not invented until 1950.[26]

In any case, establishing an exact date for the setting of *The Scarf* is not important. It is enough to know that it is the urban United States of America between the mid 1940s and mid 1960s. Even over forty years after the text of *The Scarf* was last revised by its author, it is a period that still retains enough associations and connections with our present. The settings of *The Scarf* are still recognizable, and navigable by the reader, as much as any novel which has a contemporary setting that has now become the definite past can be. The types of human nature and actions explored in the novel remain more obviously timeless.

Conclusion

The Scarf captures the feel and mood of the time it was originally written. Several high-publicity serial killing 'psychopaths' had attracted publicity in the United States since the mid 1930s. Memories of the atrocities committed during the Second World War by often apparently otherwise normal people were still fresh.[27] These sorts of issues, along with the not uncommon violence and institutional corruption in much of American public life, had naturally also long been reflected in American fiction. Dashiell Hammett's novel *Red Harvest* (1929) still remains an outstanding example of this. The 1930s and 1940s are thus now seen as the golden age of a particular school of crime fiction. By the time *The Scarf* was published, novels and short stories by such writers as Raymond Chandler, James M. Cain, Dashiell Hammett, and Cornell Woolrich were well on the way to achieving recognition as literature and had to be taken seriously. This literature presented an alternative and sometimes almost dreamlike, but nevertheless real, portrait of a nation.

Publication of *The Scarf* marked Bloch's emergence as an author whose work could stand alongside such famous names. In particular *The Scarf* is also in the same class as John Franklin Bardon's intense and deeply disconcerting psychological crime novels *The Deadly Percheron* (1946), *The Last of Philip Banter* (1947) and *Devil Take the Blue-Tail Fly* (1948). Much of the low life and mean streets atmosphere of *The Scarf* feels like the original story treatment behind a Hollywood *film noir* or suspense thriller from that era, with the more sexually fetishist serial killer aspects being reminiscent of a film like *The Spiral Staircase* (1945) and, eventually, the film made in 1960 from what became Robert Bloch's best-known novel, *Psycho*.

Bibliography

Robert Bloch, *The Scarf* editions:
Dial Press 1947
Avon Books 1948 (*The Scarf of Passion*)
Fawcett Gold Medal 1966
New English Library 1972
Robert Bloch, 'Yours Truly, Jack the Ripper'
Randall D. Larson, 'Precursors of *Psycho*: The Early Crime Novels of Robert Bloch'. Originally published in *The Scream Factory* #11 (1993)
Sam Moskowitz, 'Robert Bloch' in *Seekers of Tomorrow*
Douglas Winter, Interview in *Faces of Fear*

Notes

1.   Randall D Larson, 'Precursors of *Psycho*: The Early Crime Novels of Robert Bloch' (http://mgpfeff.home.sprynet.com/

bloch.html). Originally published in *The Scream Factory* #11 (1993)

2. Douglas Winter, Interview with Robert Bloch in *Faces of Fear* p.27

3. Douglas Winter, Interview with Robert Bloch in *Faces of Fear* p.26

4. *The Scarf* p.8

5. *The Scarf* p.15

6. *The Scarf* p.18

7. *The Scarf* p.25-26

8. *The Scarf* p.31

9. *The Scarf* p.56

10. *The Scarf* pp.61-63

11. *The Scarf* p.69

12. *The Scarf* pp.72-73

13. *The Scarf* p.74

14. *The Scarf* p.76

15. *The Scarf* pp.75-77

16. *The Scarf* p.80

17. *The Scarf* p.89

18. *The Scarf* p.113

19. *The Scarf* pp.115-118

20. *The Scarf* pp.135-136

21. Sam Moskowitz, 'Robert Bloch' in *Seekers of Tomorrow* p.336

22. *The Scarf* pp.69-70

23. *The Scarf* p.30

24. *The Scarf* p.72

25. *The Scarf* p.117

26. *The Scarf* p.120

27. Randall D Larson, 'Precursors of *Psycho*: The Early Crime Novels of Robert Bloch'. Originally published in *The Scream Factory* #11 (1993)

The Secret and the Secrets:
A Look at Machen's *Hieroglyphics*

Hieroglyphics is set in a single room, in a single house, in one of Arthur Machen's favourite North London districts, Barnsbury. Although on the surface a work of nonfiction, *Hieroglyphics*, like much of Machen's genuine fictional output, has a microcosmic setting serving as a counterpoint to thoughts and opinions that can embrace considerably wider settings. From the commonplace and ordinary can come precious gems, and the extraordinary becomes a way of life.

Hieroglyphics is presented as one side of a series of conversations with an unnamed friend, presumably Machen himself. Although a work of nonfictional literary theory, *Hieroglyphics* is thus immediately given a quasi-fictional rationale, and does in fact share many of the characteristics of the author's better-known fiction.

Roger Dobson has pointed out similarities with 'The White People'[1]. Both works involve reclusive and obscure literary figures who live in old and mouldering houses in North London. Both *Hieroglyphics* and 'The White People' are enabled to take place in this setting of apartness, and withdrawal from the world, and both are concerned with 'ecstasy' – which can be defined as 'standing apart'.

And into this work of literary theory there also intrudes a hint of the supernatural:

> I recall the presence of that hollow, echoing room, the atmosphere with its subtle suggestion of incense sweetening the

dank odours of the cellar, and the tone of the voice speaking to me, and I believe that once or twice we both saw visions, and some glimpses at least of certain eternal, ineffable Shapes.

And in a letter written to the Boswell-like listener by the Hermit, giving him permission to publish the record of their conversations, he says: "'Remember: keep the secret, and the secrets.'"[2]

Machen's other great connected fictional themes, those of 'sorcery' and 'sanctity', also have their place in *Hieroglyphics*. Each is 'an ecstasy, a withdrawal from the common life'.[3] For Machen this meant true reality. And while his fiction tends to deal with the 'sorcerous' side of reality, the dangerous and destructive side, in *Hieroglyphics* he chooses to encounter the 'sanctified' – the life-enhancing and constructive – in a theory of literature which uses ecstasy as its starting-point and distinguishing feature.

In my essay 'A World of Great Majesty: The Pattern in Arthur Machen's Carpet' (included in this book) I argued that, in his fiction, Machen effectively tried to compensate for what he saw as the weaknesses in contemporary organized religion.[4]

So in *Hieroglyphics* he tried to provide a basis for the re-evaluation and enduring worth of true literature and those who write it. In line with the book's title, Machen wished to say that the craft of the writer should be a hierophantic one – an expounder of sacred mysteries. Authors of true literature are hierophants, and not mere entertainers, and their work is art, and not just entertainment.

And while not condemning entertainment and its purveyors (and so consumers), Machen sets out in *Hieroglyphics* to make it clear that true literature, through the hierophantic author, is often, through symbols, seeing and conveying reality as it is. And authors are therefore to be regarded as 'priests' of ecstasy: being able, through ecstasy, to produce its feeling in the reader:

> ...if we, being wondrous, journey through a wonderful world, if all our joys are from above, from the other world where the Shadowy Companion walks, then no mere making of the likeness of the external shape will be our art, no veracious document will be our truth; but to us, initiated, the Symbol will be offered, and we shall take the Sign and adore, beneath the outward and perhaps unlovely accidents, the very Presence and eternal indwelling of God.[5]

The setting of *Hieroglyphics* in a labyrinthine and large old house is reflected in the structure of the book itself. Machen decides on a theme and asks a question – and then spends the length of a whole book going round in a cyclical argument. The reason for the book is the question: What distinguishes true literature from mere writing, even if interesting writing? The answer, given early on, is ecstasy:

> Yes, for me the answer comes with the one word, Ecstasy. If ecstasy be present, then I say there is fine literature; if it be absent, then, in spite of all the cleverness, all the talents, all the workmanship and observation and dexterity you may show me, then, I think, we have a product (possibly a very interesting one) which is not fine literature.[6]

And then comes the labyrinthine, the wandering of Machen's thought and arguments, much livened by the one-sided conversational, if not lecturing, format of the book.

In the scene-setting opening, Machen's Hermit, when he has recovered from the surprise of finding that his talks have been noted down, suggests as a title 'Boswell in Barnsbury'. And Machen's Boswell-like action in recording their conversations, in what he calls the 'cyclical mode of discoursing' reinforces the sense of wandering, around a large old house, one with many rooms and passages, some neglected, others less so.[7] So Machen hints, in a self-deprecating aside, that the Hermit might be deceived in his search for 'real essential knowledge', and answer to his question.[8]

In *Hieroglyphics*, perhaps the labyrinth – which usually surrounds a centre, a heart, a destination – actually surrounds a void, without allowing it to be fully explored. To Machen, the mystery of literature is only to be approached through cyclical argument, or to be found after a journey, a series of discussions.[9] However, in Machen there is also a creative tension and possible contradiction. It can also seem that the experience of the search for the mystery, for ecstasy, is at least as important as – and certainly no less interesting than – the goal itself. The means are as important as the end, and are certainly more obtainable, than a fleeting and constantly out of reach answer.

Hieroglyphics is as much a book about looking for an answer, as it is about providing an unassailable answer in itself. Just as The London Adventure is a book about not writing a book called *The London Adventure*, rather than the actual book itself, so *Hieroglyphics* is as much a 'hieroglyph' itself, rather than an explanation and revelation.[10] Machen does get around to answering his question, but not in a way that is satisfactory to all. It is as if Machen said, 'I don't really know what ecstasy is, but I recognise it when I see it.' His examples are open to question. The process of examining ecstasy, of sifting writing to discover that which is true and fine literature, and that which does not measure up, is not open to question. It just happens.

The labyrinthine setting of *Hieroglyphics*, and the manner in which Machen expounds his theory, has already been noted. It is also worthwhile to note that the literary works that Machen discusses as fine literature, that is, as possessing and giving ecstasy, also seem to be of a wandering, cyclical, if not labyrinthine, cast. Machen prefers the expansive in fiction. He lists, in particular, Charles Dickens' *The Pickwick Papers*, Cervantes' *Don Quixote*, and the works of Francois Rabelais.

These are among his favourite books, mentioned and praised in other connections.[11] They are, doubtless, fine literature by Machen's standards, and his theory of literature. This is perhaps good luck, although of course Machen would also say that this is a coincidence. These books are generally regarded as classics, and the fact that they contain and produce ecstasy in the reader is enough to explain that.

Machen also decides that some other books, that were also highly regarded by many of Machen's contemporaries in the late nineteenth century, and have attained classic status now, are not fine literature. Machen insists that they may very well be fine books, but works by such authors as Jane Austen, William Makepeace Thackeray, and George Eliot do not have ecstasy present and are not, therefore, fine literature.

So, for example, Machen's Hermit says:

> I claim, then, that here we have the touchstone which will infallibly separate the higher from the lower in literature, which will range the innumerable multitude of books in two great divisions... I will convince you of my belief in my own nostrum by a bold experiment: here is *Pickwick* and here is *Vanity Fair*; the one regarded as a popular "comic" book, the other as a serious masterpiece, showing vast insight into human character; and applying my test, I set Pickwick beside the Odyssey, and Vanity Fair on top of the political pamphlet.[12]

It may be thought that Machen was being misogynistic in his choice of literature not to be awarded the prize of being fine literature. After all, he effectively writes off the works of Austen and Eliot. However, I think that it is more correct to say that Machen simply did not care for the type of fiction that these authors wrote. Along with Thackeray, Machen discusses the reasons for not allowing their works to be considered fine literature.[13] But Machen did consider many of the works of one woman, Mary E. Wilkins, to be fine literature. A New England author little-known today except for her ghost stories, for over thirty years from the late 1880s she was a fairly prolific author.

Machen, in an 'Appendix' spends time showing the Wilkins' work does deserve its place in the canon of fine literature by virtue of its possession of ecstasy:

So this is my plea for Miss Wilkins. I think that she has indicated this condition of 'ecstasis'; she has painted a society, indeed, but a society in which each man stands apart, responsible only for himself and his God. You will note this, if you read her carefully, you will see how this doctrine of awful, individual loneliness prevails so far that it is carried into the necessary and ordinary transactions of social life...[14]

In *Hieroglyphics*, Machen realises that, in setting forth his literary theory, he is open to the charge of being subjective. Machen knows the books that he likes, and therefore calls them true literature. He then fits them into his literary theory of ecstasy, as they contain that which defines and makes fine literature. This is a circular argument. Therefore, for example, out of two of the greatest writers of the nineteenth century, Charles Dickens and George Eliot, only one of them ever wrote fine literature. And the difference may not have been apparent to most readers!

Machen heads off this accusation by saying that taste is what is subjective, and not art. Thus art is there, and has nothing to do with popularity and enjoyment, 'classic' status, and so on. How the book is done, and all that follows from that, is not the point, to Machen:

> You see, I think that the question of liking a book or not liking it has nothing whatever to do with the consideration of fine art. Art is there, if I may say so, just as the Tenth Commandment is there; and if we don't like them, so much the worse for us... But when we leave the utterances of the eternal, universal human ecstasy, which we have agreed to call art, and descend to these lower levels that we are talking of now, it seems to me that the question of liking or not liking counts for a great deal. We must still distinguish...
>
> You see how, here again, we come to the generic difference between fine literature and interesting reading-matter. We read the Odyssey because we are supernatural, because we hear in it the echoes of the eternal song... we read Miss Austen and Thackeray because we like to recognise the faces of our friends aptly reproduced, to see the external face of humanity so deftly mimicked, because we are natural.[15]

Thus Machen avoids the charge of subjectivity. It is the art in a piece of writing that determines whether or not it should be accepted as fine literature. And art, to Machen, is of the 'supernatural' – and speaks to that same quality in humanity. While Machen's staunch adherence to non-Protestant Christianity enables him to claim this high ground of objectivity, it still does require acceptance of, or at least sympathy with, that world-view. As the Hermit says: '...you will realise that to make literature it is necessary to be, at all events subconsciously, Catholic.'[16] This objective base is quite necessary, in that *Hieroglyphics* would otherwise just be an interesting diversion and a labyrinthine shaggy-dog article (which is not, to this reader, intended to be any sort of denigration at all!)

Towards the end of *Hieroglyphics* Machen divides people into two camps: the rationalists and the mystics. He is, of course, on the side of the mystics, and continues to try and prove the objective nature of his literary theory by showing that if rationalism is correct, '...then all literature, all that both sides agree in thinking the finest literature, is simply lunacy, and all the world of the arts must go into the region of mania.'[17]

At the beginning of this section of *Hieroglyphics*, Machen parodies rationalism by giving a series of questions lifted from a rationalist examination paper.[18] And he does precisely that: provides an outrageous and hilarious parody which is great fun to read, but which also necessarily involves the wholesale acceptance of Machen's premises in order to really support and explain his literary theory, and make it credible against all criticism. Machen describes such a version of rationalism that his views can only be proved to be the correct ones. There must be things that are done and enjoyed without being able to give reasons for doing so, and this does have to be admitted by rationalists.[19]

Machen's literary theory as promulgated in *Hieroglyphics* is effectively only correct if all his premises are accepted. If they are not, then *Hieroglyphics* does become merely very interesting, and is seriously flawed as a work of literary theory in the absolute and dogmatic sense that Machen seems to wish it to be understood and accepted. As is the case with the acceptance or rejection of a religion or political stance, it takes more than intellectual argument to convince. Viewpoints accepted on intellectual and logical arguments alone can often he held with a tenacity that is in proportion to the viewpoint's credibility. The heart must be involved, as well as the head.

The two are not in harmony in *Hieroglyphics*, and the Hermit's strong convictions and loquacity are clear symptoms of this (maybe the 'break of some sort' in his early life is relevant!)[20] *Hieroglyphics* provides *a* literary theory, not *the* literary theory, and, as has been seen, too much stands or falls on the necessity of accepting Machen's world-view, and understanding of the nature of humanity and its place in a universe created by God.

For all that, *Hieroglyphics* is a fascinating and lively setting-forth of a theory. Machen's view that it is ecstasy that distinguishes fine literature is a viable and defensible one, and worth arguing for. (As an aside, it would be interesting to see if the same arguments could be deployed, using twentieth century literary examples.) But it is Machen's attempts to give his personal views an absolute and universal basis, which by its nature then has to denigrate other views, that causes problems.

In *Hieroglyphics* Machen makes a valuable and timeless definition of fine literature. But it begs the question as to whether or not such a definition is really needed in the first place, and whether it is worth all the effort that Machen and the 'Hermit' put into it.

But perhaps the joke is with Arthur Machen.

The reader is treated to a series of lectures, if not tirades, and may well come to feel that the Hermit is someone that it would be a good idea not to encounter too often, despite the vehemence and liveliness of his conversation. There is always the nagging possibility that the reader has been taken for a Machenesque ride, and that the Hermit is simply enjoying himself as the long-winded bore at the end of the bar does. (And certainly this reader always emerges from *Hieroglyphics* feeling that he has been the mental equivalent of ten rounds in the ring.)

It is the journey and experience that is the thing, and the labyrinthine quest around the heart of literature is what is eventually left. The reader withdraws from the world in the experience of reading *Hieroglyphics*. The reader thus experiences ecstasy. And whether or not Machen has proved his point becomes a rather secondary consideration.

Bibliography

Dobson, Roger 'The Hermit and the Mystic: Two Who are One' in R.B. Russell, ed., *Machenalia* Vol.1, Tartarus Press 1990

Joshi, S.T. 'Arthur Machen: The Mystery of the Universe' in *The Weird Tale*, University of Texas Press 1990

Sweetser, Wesley D. *Arthur Machen* Twayne Publishers 1964

Valentine, Mark *Arthur Machen* Seren 1995

A selection of contemporary views of *Hieroglyphics* can be found in Machen's *Precious Balms* (1924).

Notes

Pagination: the edition of *Hieroglyphics* referred to is the New Adelphi Library reprint of 1926; that of 'The White People' is in Volume 1 of the Panther paperback edition of *Tales of Horror and the Supernatural* (1975).

1.   Roger Dobson, "The Hermit and the Mystic: the Two Who are One", in R.B. Russell, ed., *Machenalia* Vol. 1, 1990

2.   *Hieroglyphics* pp.8, 10

3.   'The White People' p.65

4.   See 'A World of Great Majesty' in *Avallaunius* 17, 1997 (also reprinted in this collection)

5.   *Hieroglyphics* p.139

6.   *Hieroglyphics* p.18
7.   Attributed by Machen to S.T. Coleridge. See pp 10, 14, and 85f of *Hieroglyphics*
8.   *Hieroglyphics* p.10
9.   *Hieroglyphics* p.86
10. This observation is pointed out by S.T. Joshi in *The Weird Tale*, p.35
11. Rabelais is used in *The Secret Glory*. Cervantes and Dickens are the subject of the essay 'True to Life', reprinted in *The Secret of the Sangraal*. A trawl through the 'Periodicals' section of the Goldstone and Sweetser Bibliography will reveal many pieces whose titles would seem to refer to these works and authors
12. *Hieroglyphics* p.19
13. *Hieroglyphics* p.87
14. *Hieroglyphics* p.159. Wilkins also published under her married name Mary E. Wilkins Freeman. A selection of her stories and a bibliography can be found in Barbara H. Solomon, *Short Fiction of Sarah Orne Jewett and Mary Wilkins Freeman*. I surveyed a selection of Freeman's ghost stories in 'Lavender and Lilac: Ghosts, Visits, and Old Ladies' (*Dark Horizons* 38, 1999) and 'Old England, New England: M.R. James, Mary Wilkins Freeman, and Sarah Orne Jewett' (*Wormwood* 6, 2006). The latter essay is also included in this book
15. *Hieroglyphics* pp.44, 48
16. *Hieroglyphics* p.162. See also Gerald Suster, 'Arthur Machen – Satanist?', in *Faunus* 2, 1998
17. *Hieroglyphics* p.126
18. *Hieroglyphics* p.124. See also Joshi, p.14
19. *Hieroglyphics* p.126
20. *Hieroglyphics* p 5. See also Dobson.

Published by The Alchemy Press

Astrologica: Stories of the Zodiac

Beneath the Ground

Doors to Elsewhere

In the Broken Birdcage of Kathleen Fair (ebook)

Invent-10n

Merry-Go-Round And Other Words

Rumours of the Marvellous

Sailor of the Skies (ebook)

Sex, Lies and Family Ties

Shadows of Light and Dark

Swords Against the Millennium

The Alchemy Press Book of Ancient Wonders

The Alchemy Press Book of Pulp Heroes

The Alchemy Press Book of Pulp Heroes 2

The Alchemy Press Book of Urban Mythic

The Komarovs (ebook)

The Paladin Mandates

Where the Bodies are Buried

www.alchemypress.co.uk

Lightning Source UK Ltd.
Milton Keynes UK
UKOW04f2142090815

256627UK00002B/17/P

9 780957 348974